Praise for Rema

"*Remains in Coyote Bog* opens a window into the authentic experiences of law enforcement. Sergeant Corky Aleckson's upbeat, honest, and competent character gives us assurance that in the dark recesses of a horrible crime, there are good people fighting for justice." ~Colin Nelson, author of *Flash-over, The Amygdala Hijack, The Inca Code, and Ivory Lust*

"*Remains in Coyote Bog* fascinates with a touch of Stephen King offset by doses of Midwest pragmatism. Husom holds in suspension horror, humor, sorrow, and romance through a compelling plot. Like her other Winnebago mysteries, this tale features a strong sense of place—in this case Minnesota's peat bogs, a hot-button topic—and a sharp understanding of police work as merging detailed procedure with a powerful drive for compassion and justice." ~Priscilla Paton, author of Cities Mysteries including 2018 Foreword Indies Finalist *Where Privacy Dies*

"It's a race against time to catch a demented killer preying on society's most weak and vulnerable. *Remains in Coyote Bog* is both heart pounding and heartbreaking—another winner from Minnesota author Christine Husom. I love the world that Christine Husom has created in her Winnebago County mystery series." ~Timya Owen, author and editor, *Dark Side of the Loon* and Twin Cities Sisters in Crime President

"By the time I reached the last third of *Remains in Coyote Bog*, I was holding my breath. Each volume in the series gets more intriguing." ~Rhonda Gilliland, author and editor, Cooked to Death Series.

"Remains in Coyote Bog cements Sergeant Corky Aleckson's position as a first-rate investigator for this small Minnesota county sheriff's department, and it opens the window a bit wider into her developing personal life as well. Christine Husom's attention to procedural and forensic detail is spot-on; her knowledge of small-town life and accurate investigative workings brings authenticity to this latest installment in the Winnebago series. It's a quick and satisfying read." ~Amy Pendino, multiple-award winning author of *The Witness Tree.*

"Remains in Coyote Bog by Christine Husom kept me reading all the way to the end. It's another great book from her Winnebago mystery series. Corky once again leads her team as they investigate the identities of the numerous bodies hauled from the Coyote Bog. Love interest Smoke is also part of the team as they bring the angel of death to justice." ~Barbara Schlichting, author, White House Dollhouse mystery series.

"The latest in Christine Husom's Winnebago County Mystery Thriller series, *Remains in Coyote Bog*, is an excellent police procedural involving Sergeant Corinne "Corky" Aleckson and lover and partner Detective Elton "Smoke" Dawes. The discovery of multiple bodies in a rural roadside bog stuns the small county community, shocking their sense of peace when details of the deaths are revealed. A complex investigation is undertaken, hoping to discover the victims' identities and the ritualistic serial murderer or murderers before death comes again. The intensity ratchets higher and higher in this thriller as Corky and Smoke struggle to find the fiends and keep their own relationship alive." Steve Hoffmeyer, author and arbitrator

Also by Christine Husom

Winnebago County Mystery Series:

Murder in Winnebago County, 2008

Buried in Wolf Lake, 2009

An Altar by the River, 2010

The Noding Field Mystery, 2012

A Death in Lionel's Woods, 2013

Secret in Whitetail Lake, 2015

Firesetter in Blackwood Township, 2017

Snow Globe Shop Mystery Series:

Snow Way Out, 2015

The Iced Princess, 2015

Frosty the Dead Man, 2016

REMAINS IN COYOTE BOG

Eighth in the Winnebago County Mystery Series

Christine Husom

The wRight Press

The wRight Press edition published November, 2019.

Cover photo by Thomas B Dingeman, Pixaby
Cover design by Precision Prints, Buffalo, Minnesota.

The wRight Press
804 Circle Drive
Buffalo, Minnesota, 55313

Printed in the United States of America

ISBN 978-1-948068-08-6

Dedication

To all the people in the medical and healthcare fields, including many of my friends and family members, who are first-rate providers. You are the overwhelming majority and this story is not meant to cast a shadow on your dedicated, selfless service. Instead, it follows a caregiver who lost her way and headed down a path of evil destruction.

Acknowledgments

It takes a team to turn a story into a published book and get it into the hands of readers. My humble thanks to my faithful beta/proofreaders who gave me their time, careful reading, and sound advice: Arlene Asfeld, Judy Bergquist, Terri Bishoff, Cathlene Buchholz, Barbara DeVries, Rhonda Gilliland, Ken Hausladen, Elizabeth Husom, Chad Mead, Timya Owen, and Edie Peterson. And to DJ Schuette at Critical Eye Editing for formatting the manuscript for publication. And to all the great authors who read the manuscript and wrote a review blurb. I greatly appreciate each one of you for sharing your talents and expertise.

Last, but certainly not least, with deep gratitude to my husband and the rest of my family for their patience and understanding when I was stowed away for hours on end, researching and writing.

Thank you all from the bottom of my heart.

1

I'd been awake a while listening to birds sing their pre-dawn calls, alerting stirring creatures the sun was about to rise. Smoke was asleep on his back, his head sunk into the pillow. His lips were parted slightly, allowing deep, rhythmic breaths until one caught midstream. His body tensed and his sky-blue eyes shot open. My own breath stopped in kind until Smoke blinked away whatever had haunted him. He rolled onto his side toward me, reached for my hand, and smiled.

I'd lost track of the times I cherished watching him snooze away, until he startled awake. I gave his hand a gentle pull. "When are you going to let me in, tell me what spooks you like that?"

The pillow swallowed the side of his face, his grin charmingly lopsided. "My darling, Corinne, why would you want to know the bad and the ugly from my long ago, almost forgotten past? I'd rather concentrate on the incredibly good moment we're sharing right here in the present."

As I considered a response, he leaned in closer, gave me a nibble of a kiss, then rolled out of bed. “Sorry, gotta go.” That signaled our dogs, Rex and Queenie, to get up and at ′em. I stretched and pondered what bad and ugly secret Smoke kept hidden. And how I'd get the key to unlock it. He walked through the room with a big yawn. “I'll get the coffee brewing.”

“I shouldn't have kept you up so late.”

My heart skipped a beat at his devilish smirk that deepened his long dimples. “It was well worth any lost minutes of sleep.”

“I—” His ringing phone cut me off. Calls before 6:00 in the morning rarely brought good news.

“Detective Dawes. . . . What? Can you repeat that?” His face was set and solemn. My body tensed. I got out of bed and prayed it wasn't about a loved one. “Tell them I'll get out there a-sap. Sheriff notified?. . . And the M.E.'s office? . . . Thanks.” He shook his head and pushed the end button on his phone.

I gave his arm an impatient shake. “What?”

“You know how the highway guys were starting the project on County Road Thirty-five and County Seven, where it crosses Coyote Bog today?”

I envisioned a horrible accident. “What happened?”

“The crew got an early start, right at daybreak. Went in with an excavator to do some clean out off the side of the road, and lo and behold, came up with a body in the bucket on the second scoopful.”

“What?”

“I need to get a move on.”

He slipped into the bathroom before I could ask another question. And I had a lot of them. Coyote Bog was in the service area I was assigned as a supervising sergeant. I jogged downstairs with the dogs in tow, made Smoke a cup of coffee in the single-cup brewer and poured it in a travel mug. I was spreading peanut butter on bread when Smoke joined me. He slid his gun holster on his belt. With his tall, lean body, he looked his professional best in a gray suit and mauve button shirt. He'd no doubt lose the jacket and roll up his sleeves at the scene.

"I'll drop Rex off at home." His house was along the way.

I handed him breakfast. "How about I put him in Queenie's kennel with her for the day?"

"Thanks. Sure, sounds like a plan. See you out there, Sergeant Corky." He gave me a sweet parting kiss and was off.

I took the steps by twos and got through my morning hygiene lickety split. I pulled my shoulder-length blonde hair into a bun on the top of my head and donned my gear. I took the usual practice draws of my service weapon and jogged down the stairs. The dogs were in the front entry looking out the window. They no doubt wondered why Smoke had broken the routine and left without Rex.

"Okay, it's kennel time. Yes, Rex, that means you, too." He tipped his head to the side like he hadn't heard right but followed Queenie and me into the garage. I opened the kennel door and they scooted in.

I went outside to my squad car, hopped in, and started the ignition. The sheriff's radio came to life with three calls in quick succession. Nearly thirty minutes left on the overnight shift and it sounded like at least two deputies would not be off duty at 7:00. An erratic driver on County Road 6, and a suspect on the run after he committed a witnessed act of vandalism at a retail store.

"Six-oh-eight, Winnebago County," I squeezed in between calls.

"Six-oh-eight?"

"I'm Ten-eight with Unit Twenty-three." On duty.

"You're Ten-eight at six thirty-six. And Sergeant, I'm sending a call report to your screen."

"Copy that. I'll report directly to that scene, if there's nothing else pending."

"No other calls."

"Ten-four."

I sat in the driveway a minute and read the information on the mobile data terminal screen, a fleshed-out version of what Smoke had relayed. The names of the three highway crew members were listed, with the excavator operator's name in caps. The sheriff per office policy, and the medical examiner per Smoke's instructions, were notified and would be en route to Coyote Bog. How long had a body been in the swamp? Centuries? Probably not. My guess: since it was close enough to the road to be scooped up by the excavator, it was buried there sometime after County Road 35 was built. Or it would have been discovered during the original construction.

I imagined a possible scenario of someone riding a bicycle across that area, wiping out, and landing in the swamp. If he got caught in the peat bog under the top few feet of water, he'd have a heck of a time swimming out. If that, or something similar had happened, there would be a missing person's report. Somewhere. Maybe many years before and not necessarily in Winnebago County.

The stretch of road that spanned the wetland was a challenge to maintain. It had a low dip in the middle, flooded over several times most years, and inconvenienced the estimated three thousand daily travelers who were forced to take an alternate route. Winnebago County road crews repaired it every few years, built it up and smoothed it out. It helped for a while, but the road would sink and shift over time, and the uneven surface was a safety hazard. Vehicles crossing the bog rocked back and forth and forced drivers to slow down with both hands gripped on the wheel to maintain control and stay on the road.

After many years of trying different methods to improve the sinking road, mostly by adding more layers of heavy bituminous, an innovative method had been engineered to raise the road by buoying it up with foam blocks as the base. When the county board approved its implementation, the highway engineer gave it top priority, and slated it as the first project of the construction season. The masses who traveled County Road 35 every day—and had to take detours when a heavy rain or winter snow melt made it impassable—looked forward to the upgrade. I was curious how the project would turn out.

The irony of it all: after all the preparation and planning, the operation had come to an abrupt halt on the first day of construction. The highway department had run into all kinds of snags maintaining and improving the hundreds of miles of county roads over the years. Without a doubt, scooping up a body from Coyote would be written in bold letters in their record book.

County Road 7 was just over five miles from my house. I headed west on County Road 35 and was there in as many minutes. A blockade of metal and wood spanned across County 35, at County 7. Two signs, ROAD CLOSED and DETOUR, with arrows pointing both north and south on 7, were attached to the front of it. I parked behind Smoke's vehicle on the road's shoulder. Another squad car sat on the opposite shoulder.

My mind captured a snapshot of the scene, noting a few key details. Smoke stood in the middle of the road with Sergeant Leo Roth, the overnight supervising road sergeant, along with several men from the highway department. Bart, Nick, and Andy were easily identifiable by their fluorescent green vests and yellow hard hats.

The excavator loader, a giant tractor-like piece of equipment, sat near the edge of the road at a forty-five-degree angle from the bog. The excavator's bucket was suspended in the air at what I estimated had been the eye level of the operator. It was too high up for me to get a good view of what it held. A dump truck sat some feet west of it. The intended destination for the spoils collected from the clean out, I surmised.

The call had not gone out over the radio, the reason Roth was the lone deputy on the scene. I made my way around the roadblock and joined the group. Bart was in his late twenties and the youngest of the crew members. His face held a tortured look, one I'd seen on many others who had witnessed something awful, something they'd never be able to completely banish from their minds as long as they lived. Everyone's eyes fell on me as I stepped into their loosely formed circle. We all knew each other.

"Sergeant Aleckson," Smoke said.

I intrinsically knew from his sober expression something was abnormally disturbing about the recovered body from the bog. "Morning, Detective."

The rest of us exchanged short greetings then I zeroed in on Bart. "I understand you were the one operating the excavator?"

He nodded and crossed his arms tightly against his chest. "And I wish I'd been in bed with a bad bug this morning instead."

"That's a good way to describe how I've felt when I witnessed something really bad," I said.

Bart considered my words. "I guess you deputies can relate, for sure."

Smoke took a step toward the machine and lifted his hand for me to follow. "You might want to have a look for yourself."

My muscles tightened as I climbed up and into the excavator's cab. Smoke was close behind me. I peered into the bucket. *Dear Lord.* Discovering a dead body was bad enough, but one in that condition was much worse. No wonder Bart wished he'd been sick.

Smoke's hand brushed mine. "About as disturbing as it gets."

"This one is more recognizable than the burn victim on our last big case, but the significance behind the way she died—however that might have been—is way more alarming. Her skin looks leathery. Reminds me of mummies I've seen in museums."

"That's a fact. Bogs are low in oxygen and highly acidic, conditions that lend themselves to mummification if a person has the misfortune of falling into one. But the chances are slim to none that's what happened here."

Her body had a similar, yet distinctively different, appearance as the bodies we'd recovered on another case. They had spent decades in a car on the bottom of a deep lake. In

Minnesota, lake bottoms remained cold, even in the heat of summer. Those bodies had been preserved by adipocere, often referred to as grave wax. It formed under special conditions: cold, wet, anaerobic. Like in the bog, but without the acidic component.

The victim had a small frame and laid on her back in the excavator's five-foot wide bucket that served, effectively and unnervingly, as an open coffin. Swamp water partially covered the lower areas of her body and surrounded her sides. A dumbbell weight plate with a hole in its middle, rested on her stomach. It was held in place with what looked like plastic-enclosed metal wires tied around her.

The victim's skin had an orange tinge and I wondered if a medical condition had caused it. Chunks of peat clung to her thin, gray hair and floated around her head. Hair strands lay across her face and neck. She wore a translucent gown, its original color likely not the dirty beige it was now. Her arms were crossed on her chest and not bound. A sign she was deceased before she was buried in the bog.

I finally focused my attention on the figure of a black angel burned into her forehead. If not for that, the crosses on each wrist may have been mistaken for tattoos.

"Someone branded her," I said quietly.

"That adds a particularly vicious element," Smoke said.

"What a depraved sicko."

"No doubt about that. When I got the call, Communications noted the angel branding on the forehead. I didn't know what in the hell that meant, whether we were looking at a criminal matter, or if it was a case of accidentally disturbing an old burial ground. In which case, we would've had to call in the Minnesota State Archeologist."

"Yeah."

"It may not be a hundred years old, but it's a burial ground, nonetheless. And the bastard that tied the weight around her meant to keep her down there," he said.

My stomach started to churn. I drew a long, slow breath through my nostrils to calm my insides as I studied the body. "She's certainly well preserved, in an unnatural way. It's hard to tell how old she was, aside from being elderly."

"Appears elderly, but does that mean seventy or a hundred?"

"The docs at the M.E.'s office should be able to figure that out." I found my phone and snapped a photo then whispered to the victim, "We'll find out who you are, and will do everything possible to track down the monster who did this to you."

Smoke nudged me. "You got that right."

We were silent for a time then Smoke said, "If she's been here for decades, that adds to the challenge."

"No question. On the drive out here, I was thinking it must have been since they straightened out the county road, spanned it across Coyote. Or they should have found her then. That was about fifty years ago, right? And they've done maintenance work on it many times since then. But the road keeps sinking."

"Is it any wonder, sitting on top of a bog?" Smoke shook his head. "Back to the time frame. Her gown and the weight secured around her may help narrow that down. We'll find out when the weight was manufactured."

"That's a start. Have you interviewed the highway guys yet?" I said.

"Some general questions when I got here, but mostly I listened to them vent, then took photos of the scene, the body."

"Did the M.E.'s office give you an ETA?"

Smoke glanced at his watch. “Yep, it’ll be about half an hour, give or take.”

I took a last look at the body, lifted from her burial ground by a piece of heavy equipment, and puzzled over how she had met such an ill fate. “Let’s go talk to Highway.”

Smoke was the first one off the excavator, then held out his hand and assisted me to the ground. Sergeant Roth walked over to us and patted the memo pad in his pocket. I seldom worked with him, unless one of his cases ran into overtime. He was around my age, early thirties, nice looking, not big on casual conversation. I appreciated his sharp mind and thoroughness.

“I got statements from each of the witnesses for my report. You need me to stick around, keep the perimeter secure?” Roth said.

“No, we’re covered.” Smoke narrowed his eyes. “Are you gonna be able to catch some sleep, Leo?”

Roth shook his head. “Not unless I catch that bad bug Bart mentioned. Lord, that poor woman. Tough stuff to shut off.”

Smoke put a hand on his back and nodded. “Rest as best you can.”

Roth’s shoulder lifted in what looked like a doubt-filled shrug. “Catch you later.” He walked to his car like he had gained a hundred pounds, barely able to move the extra weight.

2

Vehicles approached on County Road 7 from both the north and south and from the east on County Road 35. Passengers and drivers strained their necks to find out what had happened. Smoke pulled his phone from its holder and called Communications. “Robin, I’m going to need two deputies out here to keep the crowds at bay. After the M.E. gets here, a lotta people won’t care if they’re late for work or not. . . . Okay, good to know. Thanks.”

Smoke disconnected. “Weber’s in the area and Edberg’s about ten minutes out. Neither has any pending calls. Sheriff is reporting here directly from home, a little earlier start on his day than usual.” Sheriff Mike Kenner had been in his position less than a year, appointed after Dennis Twardy left midterm, due to health issues.

Smoke and I hung out at the barricade a few minutes until Deputy Vince Weber arrived. He was a compact bulk of strength, and a good choice to hold back any curious members of the public. He wore a questioning frown. “Mornin′. Our highway crew found what?”

“Go have a look,” Smoke said.

Weber jogged over to the excavator, climbed up into the cab, and spent a minute looking at the body. He returned to the barricade and shook his head. "Ah, geez. What kind of creepola would do that to a little old lady?" His face screwed together, etching deep creases in his forehead and cheeks.

"The same sort of questions we ask ourselves over and over in this job, and never get a very satisfying answer," Smoke said.

"Yeah. So what's the deal with the bog? I thought this was a swamp," he said.

"Bogs are also called peat swamps," I said.

"Yeah?"

"I understand the peat goes down sixty feet deep in this area," Smoke said.

"Had no idea," Weber said.

"I didn't either, until Highway proposed this project. This bog's deeper than a lot of our county lakes. When the glaciers moved through, they carved out basins that filled with water and gave us our lakes. I remember from geography class that if the mineral count in the water was low enough, plants filled in and created bogs."

"Huh. Yeah well, now that I got my science lesson for the day, I feel a little smarter."

Smoke gave Weber a nod. "We'll leave you to it then."

I followed Smoke back to where the highway crew was huddled. We pulled out memo pads to record the information for our reports, required for all deputies at crime scenes. Smoke asked the questions and we each jotted down the names, dates of birth, and addresses of the three men. Then he asked for details of the event.

Bart was the first one who spotted the body in the bucket as it was lifted out of the bog. The other two saw it a minute later. They all attested the bucket went in empty and came out occupied.

"Where, specifically, did you drop the bucket in?" Smoke said.

"I'd say eight feet from the edge of the road, about straight out from where the excavator is sitting now," Bart said.

"So you started the clean out, got one bucketful, and the second load held the victim."

"That's right."

"Would you say the body had been laying in an east to west position, same as the road, or north to south?" Smoke said.

"East to west, with the head to the east."

Smoke wrote that down. "Did any of you take pictures of the deceased with your phones?" When each stated he hadn't, Smoke nodded. "Good deal. Until we figure out what we got going on here, I need you to do your civic duty and keep a lid on the details of this. We'll release a statement about a body being found. But anything beyond that could compromise the investigation."

Andy spoke up, "When I talked to Wendell, he asked questions about the body, and I told him it looked like a woman and that she had a weight tied around her." Wendell Peltz was the Winnebago County Highway Engineer.

"We'll talk to him when he gets here. Word will spread fast, so be prepared. Your co-workers will ask for a complete recap. But like I said, keep any particulars on the down low for now."

They all understood.

Smoke softened his tone when he continued, "You have a right to be upset, and I know for a fact the sheriff will set up a debriefing for you guys, help you deal with this. We do that after we have critical incidents. And believe me, it does work."

I thought of the debriefings I'd had. "The detective's right. It helps a lot."

The muscles in Bart's face tightened and his fists clenched. "I've never had a worse scare in my whole life. For a split second, I didn't know what I was looking at, what it was for sure. I wondered if it was one of those models that stores put clothes on. You know, those mannequins? I was thinking maybe some kids stole it, used it as a prank, something like that. And then when they wanted to get rid of it, they threw it in here. People are always dumping stuff in ditches." He rubbed his hands together like he was warming them.

All sorts of things were tossed in highway and township road right-of-way areas, ditches, and other convenient places. Mattresses topped the list of discarded items with couches at a close second. Littering small things was bad enough but casting large items on others' properties were thorns in the sides of those who had to remove them and pay to properly dispose of them besides.

Bart continued, "After it hit me that it might really be a person, it took me a few seconds to bring the arm of the bucket to a halt. And then when I got a better look and saw it was a human body, I got the hell off the machine, further away from it." His eyebrows squeezed together. "Being that close gave me the heebie-jeebies."

"Pretty shocking, that's a given," Smoke said.

Bart shivered.

Andy, the tallest and roundest of the three took over. "Nick and me were wondering what the heck was going on, but all Bart did was point. He couldn't even talk. So we climbed up and had a look for ourselves. We couldn't believe it. I mean, how could we? None of us stayed up there looking for long, that's for sure. Andy here called nine-one-one."

Andy nodded. "Thank God Sergeant Roth came a few minutes later."

Bart's shiver turned into the shakes and beads of sweat popped out of his pores. He pulled off his hard hat and swiped at the droplets with the sleeve of one arm and then the other. His face paled to an even lighter tone, despite a head start on his summer tan.

"Bart, let's get you over to your truck so you can sit down for a while. Have you got water to get yourself hydrated?" I said.

He shrugged. "Yeah, I guess I should sit down."

Andy put a hand on his shoulder and looked at me. "I'll take him. We got extra bottles of water in our trucks." *Thank you, Andy.*

"You know, it's a good idea for all of you to go chill out in your vehicles for the time being. We'll figure out the next steps when your boss gets here," Smoke said.

They followed Smoke's directive, but before they'd reached the blockade, the highway engineer's sedan pulled up and parked a short distance away. Wendell Peltz and the highway supervisor, Ron Sutton, climbed out. They stopped by their men and talked for a minute. Their facial expressions switched from disbelief to solemnity. Peltz gave Bart's shoulder a firm squeeze then he sent the crew on their way.

When Peltz and Sutton joined us, they didn't bother with greetings. Peltz's skin was pulled tight against his facial bones, and his jaw was locked. He'd left his gregarious disposition at the office. Sidekick Sutton wore a worried frown. They were a tense team, for sure. With valid reason, if there ever was one.

Peltz shook his head. “Bart dug a body out of Coyote Bog? Unbelievable.”

“That it is. I know your men gave you the skinny, but we need you to keep the details quiet for the time being. If you want to have a look in the bucket, see what your guys saw, I don’t have a problem with that,” Smoke said.

Peltz and Sutton looked at each other and weighed their options.

“I guess I should look. Maybe it’ll help me understand better.” Sutton’s words didn’t sound convincing, but Peltz nodded and they climbed up for a quick view. Back on the ground, they appeared far worse for the wear.

“I can barely comprehend what I saw was real. What do we need to do?” Peltz said.

Smoke’s eyebrows rose slightly. “Aside from putting your project on hold for the time being, nothing. I’m thinking we’ll need your equipment and a crew member or two to do some more digging around the site. See if we can uncover any evidence to help in the investigation. We’ll get some direction from the sheriff and medical examiner first.”

“They’ll be here shortly,” I added.

“Man, a simple clean out of the area off the road led to this. Why?” Sutton said.

“I’ve been in this business long enough to realize when bizarre things happen, it’s not happenstance,” Smoke said.

Sutton worked his foot into gravel. Peltz watched him a moment then nodded at Smoke. “You could be right.”

I’d thought the same thing over the years. Like when a dog found a woman’s dismembered leg on a swim in a small lake. Or when the sheriff’s recreational vehicle and underwater recovery sergeant decided to test the new side view sonar technology in one of the county lakes and discovered an old car—occupied—on the bottom. That opened an unsolved case of a couple who'd gone missing decades before. We had many cases, not all of that magnitude, but important to solve, nonetheless.

Oftentimes, when we were in the throes of an investigation, we caught what was termed a "lucky break." Methodical detective work was crucial, but many times the right thing happened at the right time that led to the right path. We couldn't pass those incidents off as luck.

"Winnebago County, Seven-oh-three," Communications Officer Robin called over the radio.

"Seven-oh-three," Deputy Bob Edberg responded.

"We have report of two students fighting in the Oak Lea High School parking lot. No known weapons involved."

"Seven-oh-three copies. ETA four minutes."

Weber would fly solo at his post until Edberg cleared, or they recruited another deputy.

Sheriff Mike Kenner pulled up to the blockade and parked next to Peltz's car. He got out and gave Weber a light punch on the bicep as he passed. Kenner had served as chief deputy under Sheriff Twardy for years and was the county board's top candidate when Twardy retired. The vote was unanimous. A natural and effective leader, Kenner had stepped into the role as the county's top law enforcement officer with relative ease. Even so, after ten months on the job his brown hair had started to gray, a sign that considerable stress had taken its toll.

Kenner was genial by nature and took a minute to see how everyone was doing before he climbed aboard the excavator for a gander at the victim's body. One of the random things that popped into my head at crime scenes and death scenes was that victims had no choice who viewed their bodies, in whatever state they were in. Or what tests and procedures their remains might be put through in the course of the investigations. Even though they were beyond caring about anything in the physical world, I still felt compassion for the people they had been, and for any loved ones they left behind.

For a long time, one of my continued prayers was that none of my loved ones would disappear or suffer a tragic death.

Kenner shook his head on the walk back to us. "That's about as bad as it gets." He looked at Peltz. "How are your men doing?"

Peltz shook his head. "We haven't had much chance to talk. Bart, the guy who was running the excavator, seems to be having the most trouble."

"Understandable. Man, it's one of those times when the M.E. can't get here fast enough—for you folks, especially," Kenner said.

"Sheriff, the highway workers are in two trucks over there." I lifted my hand in their direction. "Like Wendell indicated, Bart is especially struggling. We told the crew to wait there until we got direction from their boss. But you and the M.E. will have the final say."

He nodded. "Sure."

"Sheriff, my suggestion is we do some more excavating, check to see if there's any kind of evidence in the area where the body was found," Smoke said.

"I agree, and that's my directive. But no more digging for Bart," Kenner said.

"That's a given," Smoke said.

"All our road crew guys are trained to operate the equipment. I'll talk to them; see if one of them is willing. If not, I'll pull in someone from one of the outlying shops," Peltz said.

And if the willing worker had known what he'd be getting himself into, he might have taken a pass after all.

3

Mama and Rufus

"**M**ama, it's bad."

Mama looked at her son. She'd named him Rufus, the same name Simon of Cyrene gave to his son. Simon had carried Jesus' cross. Mama struggled with the cross she had been given to bear, and thankfully had Rufus to help her carry out her mission.

Mama admired how he'd grown into a giant of a man. What Rufus lacked in brains, he made up for in brute strength. It made the burden lighter for both of them, and the mechanics of what they had to accomplish went much smoother. Mama couldn't have completed the tasks alone, so she willed herself to be patient with Rufus when he said things that didn't make much sense or did foolish things. She reminded herself time and again it wasn't his fault he was on the slow side.

"What is it, Son?" she asked.

"They dug one of ′em out."

"What are you talking about?"

"The road guys, they dug one of ′em out with that big machine. I saw him," he answered.

"Rufus, you aren't making sense." The tempo of Mama's heart beats picked up speed. She didn't know what to think and couldn't fully comprehend the ramifications. One of the people they'd sent off on the spiritual journey had not made it to Heaven.

4

Both Sheriff Kenner and Wendell Peltz were on phone calls but ended them post haste when the Midwest Medical Examiner's van arrived. Dr. Bridey Patrick, a woman I admired for her professional skills and no-nonsense manner, got out of the passenger side. I didn't know the man with her. He climbed out of the driver's seat, opened the back door, and pulled a black case from the seat.

The two were like Mutt and Jeff, size-wise. Patrick was short and thick-set, whereas her gaunt-looking companion stood two heads taller than her. They walked over to us, Patrick with noted purpose in each step ready for the challenge ahead. With his long legs, the man took one step for Patrick's two. Her intense brown eyes briefly scanned over each of us, paused for a nanosecond on Smoke, and then settled on the sheriff.

"Morning, Doc," Kenner said.

"Sheriff, this is Roy Swanson, the new death investigator for this area. He started last week."

"Just retired as a Carver County deputy." Swanson smiled and a dozen lines on each side of his face deepened. He reminded me of the fictional character, Skeletor, popular years ago.

"Welcome aboard. I don't believe I've made your acquaintance," Kenner said.

With Swanson's distinctive looks, I would have remembered if I'd ever met him.

After Kenner shook hands with Swanson, the rest of us exchanged a few acknowledging words.

Patrick nodded then pointed at the excavator. "Let's take care of the decedent."

I'd been on several death scenes with the medical examiner, and when she honed in on a victim's body, time stood still. If a breeze stirred in the air, it calmed to a mere breath. At least that's what it felt like to me.

Patrick captured all of us with the complete attention and encompassing focus she showed deceased victims. Nothing in the world was more important to her at the moment. A good thing since her office was responsible to determine the cause and manner of death of those in her jurisdiction. Her first encounter with a deceased who died under suspicious, or questionable, circumstances started that process.

Patrick waved at Peltz and Sutton. "If you could bring the bucket down to ground level."

It took Peltz a second to respond. "Oh, sure." But he didn't move.

"I can do that." Sutton climbed aboard the excavator and fired up the engine. With some manipulation of the handles, he backed the machine from the shoulder into the westbound lane of the road then slowly lowered the bucket until it rested on the asphalt.

I'd had a good look at the body earlier, but being next to it, up close and personal on ground level, momentarily took my breath away. Wendell Peltz gasped behind me. Sutton turned off the machine and got out.

Smoke eased his way from the shoulder where he watched the progress and joined the highway men. "Gentlemen, Doc Patrick will do an initial check of the body, so we'll need you to leave this area. Go ahead and wait on the other side of the blockade, if you want to hang around. Or we can give you a call when we finish up. The same goes for your workers."

"We'll stay, and check in with our guys," Peltz said. He and Sutton headed to their crew's vehicles.

The sheriff got another phone call, walked some distance away, and returned a minute later with a frown. "I need to take care of something. You have things under control here. But if you need me, I'm a phone call away."

"See you, Sheriff," Smoke said for the group.

Dr. Patrick paused a moment while she took in the overall view of the body. "My, my," she uttered. She walked up to the bucket and then around it, carefully studying the details of the victim's appearance. "I'll be curious to learn how long she was in the bog. A month, a year, ten years?" she said, mostly to herself.

It was about impossible to tell at first pass how long the person had been dead. Especially if no artifacts, or clothing specific to an era, were found. Thankfully, scientific technology and testing continually improved and provided more accurate information to assist with that.

I was drawn back to the body, amazed it was not marred, at least from what I could see. Getting scooped out of the bog by a piece of heavy equipment could easily have done great damage. Maybe the underside was. The peat blanket around her had likely offered some protection. I couldn't hazard a guess at her age, within ten years, that is. Her face was relatively unlined and thin, and her hands revealed she was elderly. Her fingernails were thick and had dark, lengthwise ridges, a fairly common condition among seniors. Like Smoke had questioned earlier, was she seventy or one hundred when she died?

If she had suffered a violent death, it wasn't captured in her facial expression since muscles relax after death. Her mouth and eyes were shut, and her lips formed a half-smile. Either she'd had a natural upturn or the person that branded religious symbols into her forehead and wrists had manipulated her lips to present a peaceful countenance.

My arm hairs stood on end. Had the victim been maltreated by someone she trusted? Had she known her fate, but didn't have the ability to escape or fend him off?

Dr. Patrick's voice roused me back to the business at hand. "Roy, let's get some photos."

Swanson went over to the black case he'd set on the roadway and knelt down beside it. He unlatched the locks then opened it, revealing dozens of see-through pockets with a treasure trove of items for any given death scene. I saw a variety of evidence bags, gloves, shears, marking tents, measuring tapes, a compass, and much, much more. Swanson removed a camera then rose and made his way to the body where he snapped pictures from different angles.

"We know she didn't die in the bucket of this excavator nor was she intentionally placed there, but we'll take samples of the water and whatever particles are in it. She has organic matter clinging to her, of course, and the lab will analyze it. We'll find out if there is other material present not consistent with what we find in this peat bog. The decedent was in the bog for an undetermined period of time and the chances of finding anything remarkable is remote, but not impossible," Patrick said.

"I'm thinking slim to none," Smoke said.

Patrick raised her eyebrows and nodded. Swanson collected samples, put them in glass containers, marked them, and secured them in the case.

"We'll do some more digging here, look for evidence, see if we can find any possessions that might help identify the body or give us clues," Smoke said.

"Good." Patrick nodded then turned in Swanson's direction. "Roy, you can get the gurney."

"Doc, if you have a few sets of impervious suits for us we'll help you lift her out of the bucket," Smoke said.

"Of course. Roy?"

"Sure thing." He put the camera back in the case then started toward the van.

"I'll help." I fell in with him and picked up my pace.

Weber did his best to keep traffic moving, but a large number of vehicles had pulled onto the shoulder. The occupants milled around and watched the action, waiting for more. As people gathered closer, Weber called out that they needed to stay back.

The medical examiner's van on a scene attracted decidedly more attention than our squad cars. People wanted to know who died, and how. Deputy Amanda Zubinski drove up and pulled in beside Weber's car as Swanson and I approached the barricade. "Well, Vince, it looks like your partner has arrived," I said.

"Yeah, and a good thing, too. All the folks trying to close in are makin′ me kinda claustrophobic."

His comment, given the wide-open space, brought a smile to my face. When Zubinski got out of her car, I nodded from Weber to her. "Vince is glad you're here."

She lifted her hand and pointed backward with her thumb. "You are drawing quite the crowd."

"You know what they say about timing. We have a built-in audience with the hundreds of morning commuters that take this route. The good news is, this stretch of Thirty-five was already closed and the barricades were all nicely in place before the discovery," I said.

"Yeah well, somebody's gotta look on the bright side, I guess." Weber switched his attention to Swanson. "New guy in town?"

"Yep, Roy Swanson. Deputy from Carver who retired and now is a death investigator. Roy, Vince Weber and Amanda Zubinski," I said.

Swanson nodded. "Good to meet you."

"Likewise," Weber said.

"Yeah. And good luck with your new career," Zubinski said.

"Huh. Maybe that's what I'll be when I grow up," Weber said.

"You think that will ever happen?" she retorted.

We headed to the van to take care of our assignment. Swanson opened the back door, pulled suits and a body bag out of a side compartment, handed them to me, and then rolled the gurney out onto the ground. I could almost visualize antennae sprouting from the heads of our audience members.

We got back to the team by the excavator and I handed the suit-filled bags to Smoke. "Maybe we should pull Weber in for this," I said.

"Sounds like a plan. First off have them attach crime scene tape to the barricade, alert folks that not only is the road closed, they're officially ordered to stay out," he said.

"I'm on it and will be back with Vince."

I retrieved crime scene tape from my squad car's trunk and we had it stretched and attached to the barricade in minutes. "Mandy, holler if you need help," I said.

"Ten-four."

Weber and I reported for body-removal duty. Dr. Patrick, Roy Swanson, and Smoke had donned protective jumpsuits. He handed over suits. A small one for me and an extra-large one for Weber. Swanson gave each of us a pair of goggles and two pairs of gloves. We were ready to go. Members of a team prepared for a far from typical operation.

All of us—and I was certain that included Swanson—had helped move and remove bodies from unlikely places and under strange circumstances over the years. I wished some of the more gruesome removals I'd been on would magically disappear from my memory bank, banished forever into the stratosphere.

Per Dr. Patrick's instructions, Swanson rolled the gurney over to the south side of the bucket then picked up the body bag. He and Patrick stretched it open on the gurney to accommodate the remains.

Smoke cleared his throat. "Doc, if I can make a suggestion? You and Corky position yourselves to help make the initial lift, then you can go around to guide the victim onto the gurney. Vince, you slide your arms under the shoulders. Corky, the upper ribs. I'll get the middle and lower back. Roy, how about you take the upper legs, and Doc the lower legs."

Patrick nodded. "That should work well."

We all moved into position.

The strong, dank smell of swamp from the peat-filled water in the bucket both escaped from, and clung to, the body. I held my breath against the olfactory assault for as long as possible. Then I took in a shallow mouth breath before holding it again.

"I shoulda grabbed some mentholatum," Weber said. I made a closed-mouth sound in response.

We got our arms and hands into the appointed places then Smoke said, "On the count of three. One, two, lift."

The victim was small in stature. Coupled with the dehydration process, her body had little weight. We lifted her with relative ease then let some of the water drain off her body. "Okay, let's move. One, two, go," Smoke said.

The men had it under control, but I slid around to the opposite side and back into position to keep support on the victim's body balanced. Dr. Patrick did the same. After a few short steps, we set the body on the gurney. Patrick was the only one who didn't take a step back. She put her hands on the body and conducted a brief tactile exam. I knew the skin and tissue felt a lot like dried clay.

"We'll take the decedent back to the office and start the initial tests. The autopsy should provide answers to most of our questions." Patrick started to zip up the bag and Swanson stepped in to help her complete the task. I closed my eyes as they neared the face. I'd had trouble with that final closure since I watched it done to my grandmother.

Although vaguely aware the group of onlookers had grown, I was surprised at the crowd that stood on the shoulders of the road. Zubinski had done a good job keeping them at bay.

"Roy, there's a trash bag in the case to dispose of the jumpsuits," Dr. Patrick said.

I was relieved to strip off the suit and gloves and stuff them in the bag. The doctor sealed the bag of waste then passed around a bottle of antiseptic cleaner. We took turns squirting it on our hands and rubbing it in.

Smoke and Roy Swanson wheeled the gurney to the van. I opened the back door and they rolled it inside. Weber followed with the black case. When everything was secured, Patrick and Swanson left on their journey with the unidentified remains.

5

Mama and Rufus

They sat in their older Dodge Caravan on the right shoulder of County Road 7 south of County Road 35 and watched.

Mama's heart pounded faster and harder with each passing minute. She was caught in a nightmare. A black van with the words "Midwest Medical Examiner" on the door meant that Rufus was right after all. They had found a body in the bog. She could only hope and pray it wasn't one of theirs.

She tried to think of something besides what the officials were doing by Coyote so she counted the sheriff's cars and matched them with the number of people in uniform. She'd seen three of them. Two were inside the fenced area and the other was standing guard on the outside of it. Other people were there, too. A detective with the medical examiners? Two men had been inside and now were sitting in a car this side of the fence. Why? Trying to figure it all out left her dizzy and discouraged. Her breaths quickened, audible in the small space.

"Mama?"

"Hush now, Son. Mama needs to think."

When Rufus's head dropped, she reached over and patted his arm. He had always been a sensitive boy, eager to please. She had to stay mindful of that. Making sure he felt needed and appreciated was important. She needed him at least as much as he needed her.

"I'm sorry, Son. I have to believe that everything will turn out just fine."

But she didn't believe that at all.

6

Smoke phoned Communications. "Hey. Mason and Carlson on Major Crimes this week? . . . We're ready for them at our location. Thanks." He disconnected. "They're at the office and will be out here shortly."

"They will be thorough," I said.

"No doubt." Smoke signaled for the highway engineers and road crew to gather near the barricade with us. The group emanated a sense of teammanship, of camaraderie. They were involved in a traumatic incident and needed to stick together. Bart's skin color was back to normal, and his muscles were more relaxed. Thankfully. The medical examiner had assumed custody of his unearthly find so that worry was over.

"Wendell, your crew was doing some clean out of the swampy area in preparation for the construction project?" Smoke said.

"That's correct. But they'd barely started."

"Then it looks like the clean out going forward will serve a dual purpose. We need to look for articles that may have belonged to the victim," Smoke said.

"I see what you mean. At least we've got one thing on our side this spring—the water levels are low, not like the last two years," Peltz said.

"Yeah, that helps all the way around. If I remember right this road was under water about this time last year," Smoke said.

"Yes, it was," Sutton said.

"I can run the machine," Andy offered.

"If you're sure," Smoke said.

He lifted his chin. "Yeah, I mean we were all pretty freaked out before, but I'm okay now."

"You good with that, Wendell? If not, we can call in someone else."

"No, we're good." Peltz turned to Bart. "If you need to take a personal day, I'd encourage you to do that."

"No, I think I'll feel better if I keep working," Bart said.

"All right. Nick?"

He nodded. "I'll stay. I'll drive the dump truck."

"Vince and Mandy, the observing crowds have dwindled but it'd be good if one of you can hang out for a while," Smoke said.

Weber raised his hand. "That'd be me. Mandy's gotta do an interview when she clears from here."

"I'll let Communications know." I pulled out my phone and made the call. "It's Corky. Assign calls in Weber's area to another deputy until he clears from here. . . . Thanks." I hung up and looked at Weber. "You're here, unless things get too crazy."

His eyebrows lifted. "Crazier than here?"

"You got a point," I said.

Smoke clapped his hands together. “No time like the present to figure out our strategy. The crime scene team will join us shortly. We’ll dig through the collected peat and search for any evidence—”

Before Smoke finished, a Ford minivan pulled up near the barricade and parked. I recognized the vehicle. “Someone tipped off our trusty *Oak Lea Daily News* reporter,” I said.

Paul Moore got out of his vehicle with a pen in his right hand, its natural place. I’d never seen him without it. A digital camera hung from a strap around his neck.

“Let’s go talk to him, Sergeant,” Smoke said.

We met him before he reached the barricade. “Greetings, Detective, Sergeant. I understand some sort of tragic accident happened here this morning. But no calls came across the sheriff’s scanner, not that I heard anyway.”

“You are one for two. No accident here this morning. However, a body was recovered from Coyote Bog. And you’re right, it didn’t go over the radio.” Smoke said.

Moore drew in his chin and glanced over at the Winnebago County Highway vehicles. “They were supposed to be starting that big project here this week and you’re saying they found a body in the bog there?”

“Paul, at this point I’m not at liberty to say how it was found, or who found it. The sheriff’s more than likely preparing a statement as we speak, but we haven’t gotten the official word from him yet. Check with the office in an hour or two and you’ll have your story.”

“So it wasn’t an employee, one of the highway crew?”

“No, it was not,” Smoke said.

"Well I guess that'll have to do for now. Thanks." Paul turned, walked to his car, then lifted his camera to his eye and snapped shots of the scene.

Zubinski lifted her hand in a wave as she got into her squad car and I followed Smoke to the dump truck where Wendell Peltz and company stood.

Peltz pointed at the truck. "The first load of brush is in there."

"Yeah, we'll have a look. Where were you planning to haul this?" Smoke said.

"To an old depleted gravel pit that's taking fill."

"In the meantime, can we dump the contents on the road?" Smoke pointed. "Maybe over there in the eastbound lane, down a ways? That should give us enough room to do the excavation work on the north side."

"That's fine," Peltz said.

The Winnebago County Mobile Crime Unit rolled in around the barricade and stopped. Todd Mason poked his head out the driver's side window. "Where do you want us?"

Smoke indicated the spot. "Over there. We'll set up a work area a little farther west."

When the mobile crime unit was situated, Deputies Todd Mason and Brian Carlson got out. Smoke, Weber, and I walked over to fill them in. Smoke pulled out his phone, found the photos of the body in the bucket, and handed it over. Carlson held up the phone so they could both have a look.

"Wowser, wowser, that is unreal," Mason said.

"Unsettling," Carlson said.

"Way more graphic in person," I said.

"Man, now that is a prime example of what I'd call the uncanny valley in living color. And those tattoos, do you think that's some kind of cult thing?" Mason said.

"We think she was branded . . . with an iron," Smoke said.

Carlson handed the phone back like it was too hot to hang onto. "Say what?"

"What. Todd, you hit the nail on the head with that uncanny valley remark," Weber said.

"The M.E. will determine what happened with the branding, whether it was pre-or post-mortem," Smoke said.

Carlson's shoulders bounced up and down a couple times.

Mason grunted.

"Let's focus on the task ahead. The dump truck has got spoils from the swamp. We'll have them empty it there." Smoke waved at the spot. "We'll rake through the piles, see if we find anything. And then get more buckets from the area the body was found in. I know it's a long shot, but we're looking for anything that can help identify the victim. Or even an artifact that would narrow down the time frame, help us figure out how long she was in the bog, give an idea of where to start with missing persons' reports."

"What kind of artifact?" Weber said.

"Like the latest, greatest electronic device, or an old transistor radio from the sixties or seventies," Smoke said.

Weber raised his eyebrows. "Transistor?"

"Portable, long before iPods and iPhones."

"Huh, yeah I heard of 'em."

"Let's get to the job at hand," Smoke said.

Nick waited for the go ahead. When Smoke gave it, he jumped in the dump truck and drove to the appointed place. "Stand clear!" He activated the hydraulic lift and the front end of the bed rose. When the top was at a forty-five-degree angle, the tailgate lifted and the mucky contents from the bog poured onto the ground. I spotted peat, vegetation with roots, an old work boot, an aluminum soda can, a few beer bottles.

"This might be a bigger job than I'd anticipated," Smoke said.

"We can deal with this kind of stuff, but here's hoping they don't find a couch down there," I said.

"Wouldn't surprise me." He walked over to Nick's window. "You can drive the truck back to the other side."

Mason and Carlson stood by with rakes that looked like the garden variety. They wore impervious suits and high rubber boots, prepared to wade through the muck and mire. Mason moved to the north side and Carlson to the south. They raked from the outer edges and moved in until they met in the middle. All objects were taken to an area about six feet away.

I pulled on a pair of protective gloves. Smoke did the same and said, "It should be relatively easy to figure out what we need to toss."

The crime scene team raked the items our way and the three of us had a closer look. Weber and I picked out the articles of trash and disposed of them in a garbage bag. A soggy, modern-looking magazine, random pieces of papers, a child's mitten, and a cigar butt added to the collection. But nothing that might lend a clue to the identity of the bog body.

We finished with the load, took off our soiled gloves, and headed across the road to the highway crew. "We need another three or four bucket loads," Smoke told Andy.

"I'm on it. Bart, it's straight out from here, right?" Andy said.

Bart lifted his elbow and dropped his arm with his fingers pointed at the area. “Yep. I’d go about twelve feet.”

The crew had switched to an excavator with a longer arm. It didn’t hold as much weight as one with a shorter arm. The shorter the arm the bigger the bucket and the heavier the lift.

Andy climbed aboard and started the operation. The rest of us stayed a safe distance away when he went in for a scoop. When it lifted, water ran out and over the top. Sticks and plant life were stuck in the front claws. He swung the arm over and deposited the load in the dump truck. The next dig was two feet closer to the road.

But the third load was a different story. Andy halted the arm mid-swing and yelled, “Damn.” He stopped the engine and jumped down. I saw a lower leg and foot hanging over the top of the bucket and moved against Smoke for support.

“Geez, Louise,” Weber said. He was the only one who spoke. The rest of us stood like mute statues for a drawn-out moment. Finally Smoke climbed into the cab of the excavator. He pulled out his phone, snapped some photos, and dialed a number.

“Sheriff, it’s Dawes. You’re gonna want to come back out here. . . . What? . . . The chief deputy? Okay.” He pushed the end button and returned to the ground. “Sheriff’s tied up with a juvenile case so he’s sending Chief Deputy Randolph.”

The highway guys gathered around Andy. They all appeared shell-shocked. Their world was imploding.

Smoke eyed them for a minute. “Wendell, I don’t know the scope of what we got here so you and your men can take off. Suffice it to say, the road construction project may be halted for longer than anticipated.”

Peltz addressed his crew. “You go on ahead, guys. We’ll see you back at the ranch.” They dragged themselves away much like Sergeant Roth had earlier.

“I can help if you need more excavating, or whatever you need,” Sutton said.

“Appreciate that, Ron. Right now I’m at a bit of a loss. I know what we need to do, but I’m not sure how that will work. It may take some time to get our ducks in a row,” Smoke said.

I suspected Smoke was being deliberately vague. Wetland conservation laws were specific and strict, and he weighed his options. Ask for permission or take his chances with forgiveness? If it was the latter then the fewer people in the know, the better.

Smoke continued, “In any case, it’ll take some time for the medical examiner to get back out here. No sense making you hang around. But before you go, I’ll take you up on your offer and ask you to bring the bucket down to ground level. And then dump the truck so we can go through the spoils.”

“Sure.” Even though he had volunteered his services Sutton was slow to climb on board. Reluctance had set in. One major jolt to the system was bad enough; a second one a short time later was life-altering.

The simple ditch clean-out project had turned into an exhumation of scary-looking bodies. Sutton had been tasked to finish jobs his men had abandoned. Twice. He slowly lowered the excavator’s arm until the bucket rested on the pavement, shut off the machine, and got down. He nodded as he got into the dump truck, drove it to where Smoke had indicated, and released the contents.

“Ron, you might as well leave the truck where it is for now,” Smoke said.

Back on the ground, Sutton took out a handkerchief and wiped it over his face and neck a bunch of times. "I guess it's kind of hitting me all the sudden."

Smoke reached over and gave his damp back a pat. "You're not alone feeling like that. You can't prepare yourself for something like this. I told your guys that the sheriff will arrange a debriefing session. It's vital after a critical incident."

Sutton shrugged and looked at the ground.

"I've been through a number of them myself over the years," Smoke assured him.

"It sounds like a smart thing to me," Peltz said.

"Yep. Oh, and Wendell, I meant to ask, you got a permit to do the clean out, right?" Smoke said.

Peltz frowned slightly. "Of course, permits for all the different aspects of the project."

"I didn't doubt it but needed to confirm. Thanks."

Wendell Peltz nodded then he and Ron Sutton were on their way. Smoke, Weber, Mason, Carlson, and I walked over to body in the bucket. It hadn't been scooped up as neatly as the first one. It was nearly face down, like it was stuck at half-turn. Either the bucket had prevented it from turning completely or it had landed that way in the bog. The head, neck, left shoulder and arm, and part of the chest were buried in the peat. The right arm and hand were exposed. My eyes were drawn to the telling mark on the wrist. A cross had been branded into it.

"Dear Lord in Heaven," I said.

Weber made the sign of the cross on his forehead and chest, the first time I'd seen him do that in all our years working cases together. "We already got one on her way to the M.E.'s office. And now we got another one here. Whaddaya wanna bet the evil creep buried more of ′em down there?" he said.

"That's why we need to drain the swamp," Smoke said.

"Literally," I added. "Permission or forgiveness?"

Smoke shot me a "you know me too well" look. "Let's settle for a combination of the two. A normal request would mean completing the required paperwork, jumping through a series of hoops, and waiting for God knows how long for an answer. We got exigent circumstances here, so I'll have our command staff advise the various agencies what we're gonna need to do."

"Definitely exigent," Carlson said.

"Definitely," Mason added.

While we studied the body Smoke said, "Change of subject, but something you should know. You heard that call go out earlier, the fight in the school parking lot Edberg got called to?"

"Sure," I said.

"It was Kenner's kid."

"Jaxson?" Carlson said.

"Jaxson," Smoke confirmed.

"That explains why he was distracted after that phone call," I said.

"Yeah, I thought he was actin′ a little weird. I mean we got this really big deal goin′ on and it kinda struck me when he left so sudden like," Weber said.

"That's why," Smoke said. The sheriff's challenges with his middle child had escalated over the last few months and were taking their toll on his family.

Chief Deputy Randolph pulled up to the barricade and parked. "Randolph's day just got a whole lot more complicated," Smoke said.

7

Chief Deputy Clayton Randolph's eyebrows squeezed together. "Troops. Sheriff got tied up, so I'm here in his stead."

Smoke pointed. "Our second victim."

Randolph shook his head back and forth. "A frightful sight. Doesn't look real, like it's a leathered mummy, or a statue. Like with the kids in the lake a couple years back. Well, not exactly. But similar, in that they didn't go through a normal decomposition process, either."

"Preserved in the bottom of a lake versus preserved in a bog. Medical experts can spell out the exact processes," Smoke said.

Randolph walked around the bucket, his eyes on the body. "With help from the medical examiner, it'll be up to us to identify them and figure out who in the hell put them in there."

"And when they did it. We may want to get a hand from the state archeologist. The unknowns are piling up. As far as the sheriff's office is concerned, this officially became a crime scene," Smoke looked at his watch, "just over two hours ago when the first body was recovered."

Randolph nodded. "Before I left the office I checked in with Wendell Peltz, wondering how his men are doing. He and Sutton had just cleared from here."

"Yeah, we thought it'd be good for them to take off before we got any deeper in this." Smoke paused a second. "We're thinking there could very well be more bodies down there. Our collective opinion here."

Randolph's eyebrows lifted. "You mean like a family group?"

Smoke's jaw moved back and forth. "I wouldn't hazard a guess about that one. The first body was female, elderly. This one appears to be male, but until the M.E. gets here and we get the body out of there . . . who knows? When all is said and done, will it turn out he's related to the first victim? Time and tests will tell."

Weber nodded toward Smoke. "The detective here says we gotta 'drain the swamp.'"

Randolph took a deep breath. "You have a plan?"

"We need to dig a deeper hole a little west of here, let the water in this area drain into it. We'll let the agencies that have control over the water and wetland areas in on the plan. The Minnesota Board of Water and Soil Resources—along with the local office—Winnebago County Soil and Water. The Department of Natural Resources, maybe the Army Corps of Engineers," Smoke said.

"I'll take care of the calls," Randolph said.

"Start with BWSR."

"Right. We have the equipment and manpower to do the job. Unless you think we should call in an independent company."

Smoke shook his head. “Our guys can do it. But the local soil and water should be here. They’re the wetland and drainage experts and hopefully will be amenable to the whole process.”

“Getting the water guys on board is good, all the way around.” Randolph’s eyes fell on Coyote Bog and the body in the excavator’s bucket. “When do you expect the M.E.’s return?”

“With minimal traffic it’s fifty minutes, so hopefully in the next thirty. To say it’s nerve-racking for us to have that body stuck in there is an understatement. We all want to get him out. But without a gurney, we’ll have to wait for them,” Smoke said.

“I’ll have Dina round up the phone numbers of the water agencies, get that ball rolling.” Randolph pulled a memo pad from his back pocket and headed toward his vehicle.

“Let’s get back to the raking project. Cross your fingers that something turns up,” Smoke said.

And so it would.

Randolph came back looking like he had returned from battle. “BWSR said they’d talk to the DNR and the Army Corps. Said we’d have to wait for them to get here.”

“Did they say how long that would take?” Smoke said.

“They hoped by this afternoon.”

“What a load of crap. Did you tell them that?”

“Not in so many words,” Randolph said.

“Clayton, I know Thomas over at Winnebago County Soil and Water pretty well. He should be brought in on this,” Smoke said.

“Wouldn’t surprise me if he wasn’t the first call BSWR made after we hung up,” Randolph said.

"Probably right. If need be, we'll write a search warrant, get a judge to sign it. I'll give Thomas a jingle when we're done with this pile."

"That works." Randolph watched as we sifted through the bog spoils. Mason and Carlson raked. Smoke, Weber, and I sorted the discovered objects. "You got quite the operation here. Could take some time," he said.

Smoke nodded. "Depending on how much area we cover and how dense the peat is. This batch of peat has what they refer to as medium density, I believe. Porous enough that some of the water content released when it was removed and more releases when we rake it, as you can see. That helps when we're looking for objects. But doesn't necessarily make it an easy operation."

"I guess I don't know much about peat," Randolph said.

"The more the plant material decomposes, the denser it gets. My guess is that the deeper you get in this bog, the denser it'll be because there's nothing down there to disturb it," Smoke said.

"The detective here is a regular walking encyclopedia," Weber said.

"I've noticed that over the years," Randolph said.

"Hardly an encyclopedia, but I've been around a while and picked up some things along the way."

"And it sticks in your brain, and that's what counts," Weber said.

Smoke did carry a wealth of information and coupled with his experience, was a valuable resource to the department. And to me. On any number of levels.

We spent the next ten minutes raking and picking out trash. Then Mason pulled his rake back and I spotted something caught in the tine. "Todd, hold on. Lift up your rake."

Everyone stopped mid-task to watch as he raised it higher. A chain and pendant dangled from the tine. Smoke leaned over, slid it free with his gloved fingers then held it up. "What have we here? Vince, mind grabbing some water and a cloth from the van?"

Weber left for the moment and returned with the items. "Corky, snap a before and after photo, will you?" Smoke held it in front of me. I pulled off my gloves, released my phone from its case, and took a picture.

"Go ahead and pour some water on it," Smoke said. When Weber did that, the debris clinging to it washed away and revealed the details of a crucifix cross on a silver chain. The chain was long, around twenty-four inches, and had thick links. The cross was an inch high and a half-inch wide, by my estimates, with the figure of Christ intricately fabricated on the front.

"Looks like a man's pendant," I said.

"A Catholic man's," Mason added.

"But could've been worn by a woman," Smoke said.

"Huh. Well you think there's a chance it belonged to one of 'em?" Weber nodded toward the excavator and the swamp on the other side of it.

"I'll go with there's a fair chance since it was recovered from the same area where the bodies were found," Smoke said.

"I can picture it wrapped around the fingers of one of the victims. You know how they do that sometimes when they're in their coffins for memorial services?" Carlson said.

"You might be right. The clasp is intact, so it wasn't around anyone's neck." Smoke turned the necklace over and held it up for me to read. "What does it say?"

I turned my head for a better view. "Sterling silver."

"That's it? Not where it was made?" Mason said.

"Nope, so it wasn't China," I said.

"Good point. It looks to me like a unique design, but we'll do a search, see what we can find out." Smoke smiled. "We may have located something that belonged to one of the victims."

My heart sped up as it did when a thread of hope presented itself on a case.

"I don't suppose there's any chance we'd find a partial print on that?" Carlson said.

"No, they don't last long in regular water and it'd be an even shorter time in a bog." Smoke handed the necklace to Weber who opened the cloth to receive it. "You can bag it up."

While Weber was in the mobile crime unit, the rest of us continued our search. But we found nothing else of import in the load.

Winnebago County Soil and Water District Manager Thomas Bauer arrived on the scene seconds after Smoke pulled out his phone to call him. Randolph, Smoke, and I met him halfway. The other three cleaned the tools. Bauer held his hands up. "Hey, I come in peace."

"Yeah?" Smoke said.

"The regional manager at BWSR said you had a situation out here, that you want to divert some water," Bauer said.

"We've got a damn crime scene. Two bodies. So far. There might be more. The Winnebago County Highway Engineer got the permits they needed to fix this road and I'd argue that our need to temporarily divert the water that's sitting on top of the bog would be covered by those permits," Smoke said.

Bauer reached his hand around his shoulder and used it to stretch the back of his neck. "I don't have the final say about that."

The medical examiner's van made its timely appearance. "Speaking of final, Thomas, they're here to pick up the remains of the poor soul whose body was very crudely recovered from Coyote Bog. Same as with the first body they found. If there is another one in the bog, I'd like the removal to be done more respectfully, if possible," Smoke said.

Bauer looked at the chief deputy. "They didn't say that a body was still here."

Randolph shrugged. "No reason to share that fact."

"Oh, okay. I suppose."

Smoke waved the M.E.'s van around the barricade to get closer to the body. And hidden from public view.

"If you have any doubts that our request is valid, one look at the victim in the bucket of that excavator should sway you," Smoke told Bauer. Its leg was visible from where we stood.

Bauer had a quick look, nodded, and dipped his head to the side like he was convinced. But he needed to persuade the powers that be.

Smoke walked to a spot eight feet from the excavator and held up his hand. The M.E.'s van parked there. Roy Swanson was accompanied by Dr. Calvin Helsing on this run. Swanson got out of the driver's seat, set his eyes on the most recently recovered body, and cleared his lungs of a noisy cough.

We'd met Dr. Helsing for the first time a few years back when Winnebago County switched from the Hennepin County Medical Examiner to the Midwest Medical Examiner. Helsing was with Dr. Patrick on that first call. He was an attractive American Indian, and nearly as tall as Swanson. In our first few encounters, he'd sent me vibes he wanted to ask me out, but never had. Perhaps he sensed the way I felt about Smoke.

We exchanged minimal greetings. "Doctor Patrick had already started a scheduled autopsy when we got the call," Helsing explained.

"There's no way I'll ever forget my first day on the job," Swanson said, mostly to himself, as he retrieved the black case from the van.

Thomas Bauer stayed with us as we'd migrated to the excavator and no one paid much attention. When Weber, Mason, and Carlson joined us, we grouped together like a small mob.

That's when Smoke noticed Bauer was still among us. "Thomas, you'll need you to move to the other side of the barricade. Sorry."

He seemed disappointed Smoke expelled him, but at least he hadn't been banned from watching altogether. Helsing was ready with his camera and moved in with the ease of one practiced in receiving and examining bodies, no matter the condition. We maintained silence until he'd finished then Smoke said, "Mason and Carlson are already outfitted in impervious suits, ready to assist with lifting the body out of there. We got more suits in our mobile unit if you need more help."

"Four of us should be good," Helsing said.

"I'll grab more gloves," Mason said.

While he was gone, Swanson pulled the gurney out of the van and rolled it into position. A body bag rested on top and Helsing helped him spread it out.

Mason returned and handed a small stack of gloves to Smoke. In case. Then Helsing directed the four of them into position. "Let's turn him so we'll have better leverage lifting the decedent out." They managed that. When the face of the deceased male rose out of the sludge, I let go of an involuntary sucking noise. I'd suspected there would be an angel branded into his forehead, but it got me all the same.

On the count of three, the four men lifted the body from the bucket, walked a few steps, allowed water and some peat to drain off, and set him on the gurney. One arm was across his chest and the other was at his side. He wore a hospital gown and pants and it appeared he was elderly when he died. The branded markings were like those on the first victim. Scanning the faces of the witnesses, I noticed everyone was affected. The victim had either endured great cruelty in life or had been stamped with religious symbols after death.

"It's way worse seeing this in person," Carlson said.

"Man," Mason said.

"Doctor Helsing, I'm hoping the state agencies will agree to let us drain the water in this area, so we'll have better access when we search for more bodies," Smoke said.

Swanson nodded. "Could be more."

"The symbols on the two makes you wonder," Helsing said.

"It might turn out it was just the two of them. If this was some sort of ritual burial from a hundred years ago, we'd never be able to track down whoever did it. But I suspect because of when this road was built and what the victims are wearing, it happened in more recent years," Smoke said.

"In any case, these remains were not left here legally, by any stretch of the imagination," Randolph said.

After the medical examiner's van drove away, Smoke invited Bauer back into the taped-off area. We walked west on the road and checked out the topography.

"Where would you recommend we dig? Seeing how water runs downhill," Smoke pointed at an area about a hundred feet from where the bodies were found, "that lower area seems to be the natural spot."

Bauer's eyebrows shot up and his eyes widened. "Hey, I told you I'm not the one who can make the call. If I was, believe me, I'd say go ahead."

"Thomas, your agency is the local authority, so I think you can call it. I live on a small lake. I have wetlands on my property. You know damn well I'm a good steward of our natural resources. Preserving our wetlands is important, but people are way more important. This swampy bog will still be here after our investigation is over," Smoke said.

"I understand," Bauer said. But his hands were tied.

His phone rang. "Thomas Bauer. . . . Sure. I'm at the site with the sheriff's investigators. . . . See you when you get here." After he disconnected, he told Smoke, "Corey Frank from the regional office will be here shortly."

"I haven't met him. How long's he been there?" Smoke said.

"Started in March."

"A newbie. That's just great," Smoke said.

8

Mama and Rufus

Rufus bent over the telescope that sat on a table in front of his bedroom window. His mother had given it to him for Christmas years back, and he spent most clear evenings looking at the night sky. Mama told him someday he'd be in Heaven, a beautiful place beyond the stars. It hurt his head trying to imagine what that meant, how that was possible. He didn't understand how it worked when he helped his mother send people on their heavenly journey. It really bothered him that they left their bodies behind and he had to bury them in the bog.

Rufus turned the scope to look at what the sheriff's people were doing. His mother had asked him, "Rufus, did you bury one of our patients too close to the road?" His face heated up in shame. "I don't think so," he'd said in self-defense. But he knew that wasn't the whole truth.

When he was getting ready to heave that one lady into the bog, Rufus had stepped on a rock on the shoulder of the road and was thrown off balance. She hadn't ended up as far away from the road as the others had. The ones he sent down the slide. She was small and light as a feather, but he should have used the slide. That got people at least eight feet out, about as far as he could toss the light ones. If he didn't slip. He learned his lesson after that and used the sliding device, no matter how light people were.

Rufus peered through his telescope but couldn't get a good view of what was happening at Coyote Bog. His mother's words kept running through his mind. "They must never discover our secret mission, Son."

He had been a bad boy. Rufus had done a terrible thing, and wondered what his mother would do to punish him. He didn't want her to send him on his heavenly journey. It scared him to think of going so far away.

9

It was clear that Corey Frank, wetland specialist from Minnesota Board of Water and Soil Resources, felt he'd be in over his head if he approved the request at Coyote Bog. "I get it, but the DNR and maybe the Army Corps will want to weigh in on it."

Smoke's face reddened from the neck up, but he kept the tone of his voice at a civil level. "Corey, I can understand your reluctance and I'm willing to cut you some slack, you being new and all. But the day is getting away from us, and if those agencies drag their feet much longer, we're not going to wait. Permission or not."

"We've got one of our captains writing a search warrant for a district judge to sign, authorizing us to search for more bodies," Randolph said.

Corey's features relaxed, and his frown smoothed. "Then it will be out of our hands."

"Our highway guys will be here right after lunch to start digging, if the search warrant is here by then," Smoke said.

By 1:20 p.m., Chief Deputy Randolph had the signed warrant in hand. Thomas Bauer from Winnebago County Soil and Water, backed by Corey Frank from BWSR, had convinced both the Minnesota Department of Natural Resources and the Army Corps of Engineers that the operation was a go, with or without their approval. A district judge's authority trumped theirs. As did a criminal investigation.

Ron Sutton had the excavator in position, ready to dig as soon as he got the signal. Smoke, Weber, Mason, Carlson, Wendell Peltz, and I were on the sidelines, geared up, as ready as we'd ever be.

Or maybe not.

We took a collective pause and I used it to study the wetland. A stunted willow tree grew out of the bog about seven feet from the road and fifteen or so feet west of where the bodies had been. I'd wondered from time to time where the willow's roots had traveled to find the right environment to support its life. A few tamaracks stood on a higher area further north and a variety of herbaceous plants poked through much of the surface.

"Let's make it happen," Smoke called to Sutton.

Sutton was in the excavator and started it in a flash. Each bucketful of vegetation he removed from the designated area shifted the surface water into the expanding basin. It reminded me that when were kids, my brother and I spent hours creating little rivers between mud puddles in our gravel driveway. We enjoyed watching the water run from one to the next. Sometimes we had a network of them flowing, like a river with tributaries.

I loved the sound of running water in creeks and slow-moving rivers. It soothed me. If the circumstances had been different, and the digging machine wasn't disturbing the peace, I may have appreciated the gentle tumbling of the flowing water.

I walked over to where Smoke and Randolph stood with the two men from the water agencies, directly across from where the two bodies had been recovered.

"Surface water's going down. It's about a foot lower," Smoke said.

"More vegetation is visible already," I said.

"Another foot and a half to two feet should about do it, make it easier to use the ground penetrating radar," Smoke said.

Mason, Carlson, and Weber were all trained to use GPR, as part of their possible duties in the Major Crimes Unit. Deputies rotated through the unit and served a week at a time. Winnebago had four teams of two. Some weeks were fairly routine with a number of smaller cases. Other weeks, all hell broke loose with a big case like the one we were sitting on at Coyote Bog.

"So it works on bogs?" I asked about GPR.

"Yes. As a matter of fact, they've used the technology to study bogs around the world to profile them, check out their compositions, that sort of thing," Smoke said.

I grinned. "I guess you are a walking encyclopedia."

He gave me a sly smile back. "I happened to catch an article on it a while back."

Randolph's phone buzzed. He walked away to answer it then filled us in when he returned. "Warner's on his way with the swamp boat in tow." Sergeant Tim Warner was the head of the Winnebago County Sheriff's Recreational Vehicle and Underwater Recovery Division.

"You have a swamp boat?" Frank said.

"Shallow water boat, yes. It's about one grade up from a duck boat and the best way to access this area. It's come in mighty handy over the years on different cases, in all kinds of situations. The boat can hold six guys at least. We won't use the motor, and that'll cut down on the disturbance." Smoke directed his comment at the water agencies guys.

"As much as possible," Randolph chimed in.

"Right. We're hoping there aren't any more bodies down there," Smoke said.

We'd all celebrate if that were the case.

While we waited for Warner, Smoke and I discussed a game plan, mapping out the area.

"Because of where the bodies were located, my guess is they were somehow brought in from the road. The water-covered area of the bog isn't all that big. A few acres, maybe. It would've been nearly impossible for them to bring the bodies in via the wetland to the north, unless they had specialized equipment. And I don't know what that would be." Smoke pointed. "You can see as the elevation increases how it gradually changes from swamp to marshland, then to a type-one wetland on the higher ground where they could grow meadow hay in drier years. Probably most years."

"We have lots of types of wetlands. And I agree, it'd be tough to access this area from anywhere but the road. You'd sink if you tried to walk across the marshland. And it's on someone's private property," Randolph said.

"Speaking of which, we need to have a talk with the homeowners who live in the vicinity." I pointed at the house on the hill that overlooked Coyote. "Especially them."

Tim Warner drove in with the boat loaded on its trailer. He got out of the SUV and nodded at Mason, Carlson, and Weber. "Hey, it's good to see three members of my dive team on site."

"Ya gotta be kiddin′ me. Ain't no way I'm diving, or droppin′ this body of mine into that stuff," Weber said.

Warner pushed his sunglasses to the top of his head and smiled. "Perish the thought, Vince."

I nudged Weber. "He knows what button to push, huh?"

He shrugged. "I guess I'm getting a little punchy by now."

"It seems like we've been here forever. Maybe part of that is wondering what's in store," I said.

"That's a big part of it. Nothing like a major creep element goin′ on to set a guy on edge," Weber said.

Yep, no question about that.

Warner, Weber, Carlson, and Mason put on life preserver vests then Smoke and Randolph held onto the boat's rope while the four of them climbed aboard and got situated. Warner set the ground penetrating radar control unit on a wooden shelf on the inside edge of the boat. The antenna looked like a wand with a flat, round end. Much like the ones on metal detectors. On GPR walking units, it was located on the bottom, between the wheels. The sheriff's twenty-one-foot whaler boat was equipped with side scan sonar that worked well in lakes. But the system's transducer was pulled through the water close to the bottom and wouldn't work in a bog.

Both the whaler and the shallow boat had hydraulic winches for the recovery of bodies, and other objects. Divers often faced a hazardous job, and removing heavier objects from the bottoms of lakes, rivers, and other bodies of water, made it more so. The hook on the end of the winch's line could either be attached directly to the object if that was doable, or to a mesh body bag for the more dreaded recovery operations.

Warner turned on the radar unit and passed the antenna wand to Weber. Mason and Carlson each grabbed an oar and Smoke and Randolph gave the boat a push into the water. Weber positioned the wand with the round receiver a couple of feet above the water.

"When an electrical pulse is produced by the control unit, the antenna picks it up, amplifies it, and transmits it into the ground at a particular frequency," Smoke explained to the group.

Warner watched the radar unit's screen and a couple of minutes later said, "We got something. It looks like it's about four feet down."

Mason and Carlson lifted the oars out of the water. Weber glanced from the antenna to the screen. "Ah, geez."

"What do you need?" Smoke called out.

"We'll try the long nets, see if we can get on either end or on the sides, bring it to the surface, and guide it in," Warner said.

Weber held the antenna in place to provide guidance to Mason and Carlson as they grabbed onto long-handled nets. Warner gave them directions, this way and that, until both of them said, "Got it."

I braced myself as they worked together and lifted whatever it was out of the deep. The water agencies guys moved in beside me when the body surfaced, its head and shoulder area captured by Mason's net, and the legs and lower body secured in Carlson's. Thomas Bauer surprised me when he grabbed my elbow.

When I flinched, he let go. "Dear God in Heaven, I don't believe it," he said.

Others muttered words I couldn't decipher. Randolph pulled out his phone, called the medical examiner's office and told them we had recovered another body from the bog.

Weber pulled the antenna wand into the boat then he and Warner picked up the oars for the short row back to the road.

"We'll make this as smooth as we can, but let us know if you're losing your grip," Warner told Mason and Carlson.

"We could use another set of hands for this part of the operation," Carlson said.

"Next trip," Mason said.

"Next trip," Weber muttered.

The crime scene team had brought over a backboard from the mobile unit. In case. We all had impervious suits on. In case. As the boat, with its riders guiding in their precious cargo approached, Smoke picked up the board. I helped him slide it down the decline from the shoulder of the road to the water's edge. The body was coming in feet first.

"It's a little awkward, but we don't want to lose him by trying to turn him," Warner said.

"No. We'll make it work," Smoke said.

Smoke and I each took a side and Randolph took the end. When the boat came as close as possible, Carlson and Mason moved together to the bow of the boat and placed the body part way onto the backboard. Smoke and I pushed it further up.

"Let's get the straps on," Smoke said. Randolph held the lower legs in place while Smoke and I attached the straps.

"When you get up in the morning, you never know what you might be called to do that day," Randolph said.

When the body was secured, Mason jumped out of the boat to help. We carried the body-laden board up the hill. “Let’s set it in the shade of the dump truck,” Smoke said.

We silently took in the details of our third victim. Another male. Elderly. Bald on top, thin white hair on the sides. Clad in the same type of pajamas as the second victim. Branded like the other two. With a crucifix pendant wrapped around the fingers of his hand. *Dear Lord.*

“How many are down there, do you think?” Randolph said. He knew we couldn’t answer. It was a question for those who’d buried them.

Ten, twenty, none? “I’d be happy with no more,” I said.

“Well, yeah. I’ll grab the other backboard,” Carlson said. In case.

The recovery crew resumed their operation, and it didn’t take long before they discovered another body, several feet from where the last one had been. They followed the same removal process, but switched up their positions on the team, giving Warner and Weber a turn with the long-handled nets. We were ready with the second backboard when they brought it in.

The fourth victim was also male, with the same appalling brandings. It seemed that what was happening could not possibly be real; that we were trapped in an alternate reality. Elderly people branded with religious symbols and left in a bog. For what possible reason? We set the backboard down next to the first one.

It was a relief to see the medical examiner’s office van pull in. Behind it was a transport vehicle, equipped to handle multiple bodies. In case. Dr. Bridey Patrick had returned to the scene. Along with Dr. Calvin Helsing and Roy Swanson. Smoke directed them to where the recovered bodies lay.

Dr. Patrick knelt between the backboards. "This bog is turning out to be a mass burial site. A crime scene growing in scope by the hour." She studied one body and turned to the other.

"Any clues yet as to how long they've been down there?" Smoke said.

"One thing that's consistent on all of them: their sleepwear is composed of polyester materials. That narrows the time frame to the last sixty years."

"I noticed the polyester, too. That's something, I guess," Smoke said.

"We may bring in the expertise of a forensic anthropologist. We'll know more when we autopsy and run tests," Patrick said.

Helsing and Swanson rolled gurneys over. We helped them open the body bags and transfer the bodies onto the gurneys. We loaded one into the van, and the other into the transport vehicle.

"Tim, Todd, Brian, Vince, any of you guys need a break? Corky and I can take someone's place, bring in more reinforcements, if need be," Smoke said.

"Nah. And if we find any more, we kinda got a system goin′ here," Weber said.

The others said they were okay, too.

"You can change your minds. You've already proved that you're heroes," Smoke said.

"Rock stars," I said.

After hours searching the acres of the wetland, we recovered three more bodies. All told, three females and four males were recovered. Seven branded bog bodies.

10

Mama and Rufus

"**M**ama, I think they got all of ′em." Rufus dropped his head and closed his eyes.

"Son, how could that have happened? You had a long slide to get them way out from the road. And the bog should have kept them right where they were."

It was true, Rufus could out shot put the best of them. Not that he had ever competed, but he liked to watch track and field events on television, and he'd learned how to throw. He tossed heavy rocks as a fun sport.

Should he tell her? Mama had always told him he'd be in less trouble if he told the truth. "I slipped one time."

"What?"

"I didn't get one as far out as the other ones. She was light so I threw her in, so I didn't have to use that slide. But I stepped on a rock and kind of tripped when I was doing it. So she didn't get out as far as the other ones."

"When did that happen, which one of our patients was it?"

"Number three." He raised his fingers, one at a time. "So it was five years ago."

Mama knew who he meant. “How far did she go?”

Rufus walked and stopped at about six feet.

“Oh, Rufus. Why didn’t you tell me?”

“I thought it was far enough, Mama. They shouldn’t have never found her with the sinker on, and all.”

11

I'd asked my brother, John Carl—who was also my new neighbor—to check on Queenie and Rex after I'd been at the Coyote Bog scene for eight hours. It was another four hours before I finally rolled into my driveway.

"We had a real cluster today. Sorry. Thank goodness for John Carl, huh?" I opened the door of the kennel in the backyard. Queenie rushed at me and I lifted my hands. "No kisses. I am way too gross. You guys go run off some energy."

Queenie was the younger of the two and full of vigor, common in English Setters. Rex, a Golden Lab, managed to keep up with her for a while, nonetheless. I'd had so much standing around time at Coyote that if I hadn't been in uniform with my non-breathable Kevlar vest and heavy-duty belt on, I might have joined them.

We hadn't a clue how many more bodies might be in the bog, so the medical examiner's decision to send their multiple-fatality vehicle saved them several trips.

"Time for a treat," I called out. Both dogs beat me to the garage service door, and we trooped into the house. After pouring milk bones into their bowls and filling their water dishes, I escaped to the laundry room that adjoined a three-quarter bathroom off the kitchen. I hung my duty belt and vest on hooks and threw my uniform and underclothes in the washer with an extra measure of detergent. I'd do a heavy-duty, hot wash cycle after my shower.

I set the water at a lower temperature than usual to cool my overheated body, stepped into the stall, and stood under the water spray while I soaped, lathered, and rinsed. Then I turned up the temp and let the water pound down on my tense shoulder muscles. They relaxed a little.

After I'd patted myself dry, I wrapped up in the towel, started the washer and headed up to my bedroom. My Peeping-Tom canine companions watched me put on a tee-shirt and shorts.

When I'd left the scene, Smoke was wrapping things up, but needed to check in at the office before calling it a day. After nearly fourteen hours at work, he deserved a decent meal. But what? I headed to the kitchen, downed a tall glass of water, opened the refrigerator door, and stared inside. I felt brain-dead and hoped a wave of inspiration would flow through me.

My cell phone rang so I ran to the laundry room where I'd left it with my things. Smoke. I pushed the talk button. "Yes, dear?" I said in a syrupy-sweet voice.

"Music to my ears, little darlin'."

I snickered. "I'm glad. You rang?"

"I had a hankering for some Chinese so I put in an order I'll pick up on my way home." Home. That was music to *my* ears. He was bringing Chinese *home*.

"Yum, see you when you get here."

The past ten months had been, hands down, the best of my life. Smoke and I had formed an immediate, special bond when I started as a rookie deputy with the Winnebago County Sheriff eleven years before. He was experienced and astute. He'd mentored me and taught me the ropes. The strange catch was he'd been friends with my parents. So as much as I trusted and admired him, I hadn't admitted the attraction I felt—even to myself—for a long time. When I did, things changed between us. My grandma told me after Smoke saw the desire in my eyes, he'd found me hard to resist. But resist he did.

Smoke had fought his yearning for a few long years until love finally won out. He needed me as his life partner and asked me to marry him. We hadn't quite worked out the details, but we would. I figured for a man committed to bachelorhood, a little extra time coming to grips with what marriage entailed was not a bad thing. As far as I was concerned, we were married in the eyes of God.

Add to that, the activities in the lives of my family members had swirled like mini tornadoes the past year. My paternal grandparents moved into a townhome in Oak Lea and gave their old farmhouse to my brother after he moved back from Colorado. I suspected one of the big motivators for John Carl's return home was the prospect of a loving, stable relationship with Sara Speiss, my best girlfriend, and a darn good Winnebago County probation officer.

After my mother's fiancé—our former sheriff—had broken off their engagement, a widowed friend she'd known since high school stepped in to fill the emotional gap. It wouldn't surprise any of us if he whisked her off her feet and married her before Smoke and I tied the knot ourselves.

My maternal grandfather was in his upper eighties. He had a sharp mind, but his body was wearing out. Decades of farming had taken its toll and inactivity in more recent years compounded the problem. My mother's care was the reason he still lived in his own home. John Carl and I helped, but Mother carried the bulk of the load without complaint. I'd been thinking we should hire a home health aide to give her some respite before she completely burned out.

With all that, the biggest life-changer for our family was when we learned that Dad had fathered another daughter, Taylor, he hadn't known about. The young woman he was briefly involved with hadn't told anyone, including her parents, that Carl Aleckson was the one responsible.

Learning about our father's affair was especially hard on Mother. She'd loved him practically since birth. Her emotional struggle was the main reason my paternal grandparents, John Carl, and I hadn't spent as much time with Taylor and her family as I would have liked. My sister, nieces, and nephew were pieces of my life I hadn't known were missing.

I downed another glass of water to rehydrate. Smoke marveled how I could gulp water down so fast. My secret: I kept it on the tepid side. Ice cold water was too much of an assault to the esophagus and took my breath away if I drank it too fast.

I set plates, silverware, serving spoons, and napkins on the table in the dining room. Smoke would want to shower first, but I'd be ready when he was.

Sara Speiss sent me a text asking me to call her when I was clear. "Hey, Sara. You heard?"

"Oh. My. Gosh, Cork. Yes. But we didn't get a lot of details at the office. Old folks with religious marks on them, in Coyote Bog?"

Word always got around, no matter what. “Speaking confidentially, that’s about it, in a nutshell. I can barely describe what it was like. Shocking, seeing the first body, then the second, then the third, and up to the seventh. I mean, I’ve seen pictures of bog bodies. And you know the couple we recovered from the Whitetail Lake? They were unnaturally preserved, too. But in this case, the branding on the bodies gave the recovery much darker overtones.”

“I can’t even imagine,” Sara said.

“We’ve got seven unidentified victims, and we don’t know how long their bodies were in the Coyote Bog.”

“Where do you start?”

“We sent deputies out to canvass the neighbors, but the houses are few and far between on that stretch of road. Not all the residents were home, so we’ll hit them tomorrow,” I said.

“You’d think a person would report it if they saw someone dropping a body into the swamp.”

“You’d think. One challenge is this might stem back decades. We’ll get a better idea of the time frame when the M.E.’s office finishes up. Doctor Patrick said they may enlist the services of a forensic anthropologist.”

“The work they do amazes me.”

“No kidding. While we waited for folks at the scene, we talked about finds in other countries. Smoke said one of the most famous was found in Denmark in the nineteen fifties. They estimated he was over two thousand years old and perfectly mummified. Amazing. They dubbed him Tollund Man,” I said.

“I’ll have to look him up.”

"Me, too. Scientific methods are improving about as fast as other technologies, and they can test new things on bodies found a hundred years ago."

"Let's just say I admire scientific minds because I don't have one."

"You have great people skills, and that's not true of all the science-brain people I know."

"Yeah. Thanks. You've had an unbelievable day, so I'll let you go. Hopefully you can unwind."

"Hopefully. Smoke will be here any minute. He has a way of making things better."

"Take care, my friend."

"You, too."

I wandered around the house until I heard the garage door lift and headed to the kitchen. Smoke came in looking and smelling like he'd just stepped out of the shower. He set the bag of food on the counter and drew me into his arms. We held on tight for a long moment.

I moved my face along his neck until my lips found his for a promising kiss. "You could have showered here."

"I cleaned up in the locker room at the office so we could do this as soon as I got here." His lips brushed mine then moved in for another deep kiss. Until the dogs, impatient for his attention, whined and broke the spell.

"All right, you two. So, Rex and Queenie, how did your long day together in the kennel go?" He scratched the tops of their heads and under their necks, and they lavished in it until he stood up. "Now that I've properly greeted my favorites, I'm looking forward to a cold beer."

"Coming right up." I fetched two bottles of Grain Belt, a local light beer, from the fridge and handed him one. We twisted off the tops, clinked the necks of our bottles together, and took a swig.

"Now that's what I'm talking about," he said.

I picked up the bag of food, carried it to the table, and pulled out the containers. Smoke lifted the lids off and stuck spoons in them. Beef and broccoli, chicken almond ding, shrimp fried rice, vegetable egg rolls.

"You got enough for another meal, too. Leftovers, yay."

"I felt starved and actually stopped myself from ordering even more, believe it or not. Everything on the menu sounded good."

"Like grocery shopping when you're hungry."

"That's what I did all right."

We dished up, said grace, and dug in like you'd imagine after fifteen—closer to sixteen—hours since our last real meal. Randolph had pizza, sandwiches, and snacks delivered to the crime scene, but all I could manage was a granola bar. Death scenes kept my appetite at bay.

I swallowed a mouthful. "So will the highway guys pick up where they left off on their project tomorrow?"

"No. I talked to Wendell Peltz, and he thought they'd give it a day of rest and resume on Wednesday. The rain is supposed to hold off all week. He told me he hoped we'd be able to work in a time to debrief his men tomorrow, before they get back at it."

"That'd be good. But Kenner can't do the debrief, not with his son in the middle of all that trouble."

"You're right on. Speaking of Jaxson, they've got him in a holding cell until his first court appearance. So the other inmates don't know who he is. I tried calling Mike, but when he didn't pick up, I sent him a text to let him know we were keeping his family in our prayers."

Smoke wasn't a church-going man and kept his faith mostly to himself. His words touched me. "I'm glad you reached out to him. They've been in my prayers all day."

Smoke shook his head. "It doesn't look good for the other kid. It can take a long time to heal from a brain injury."

"Scary." I drew in a calming breath. "Smoke, you've been through the training, maybe you should step up to the plate, do the debriefing."

"Ah." He put his fork down and leaned back in his chair. "We've had discussions about my continually full other kind of plate. And that was before one of the largest cases I can remember was heaped onto it."

"Yes, but there are some freaked-out guys who need to get back to work. And they're about as touchy-feely as the deputies are so that puts them more at risk for more long-term effects of untreated stress."

"Valid point. I'll run it by the chief deputy early tomorrow, see if we can't pull something together." A yawn that looked like it started at his toes and ran the length of his body grabbed hold of him. He used both his hands to cover his mouth. "Ahhh, man. I am completely done in." Another deep yawn.

I got up, moved around behind him, and slid my hands to the front of his chest. "Go to bed. I'll put the leftovers away."

"That'd make it two nights in a row I slept here."

"I hope it's not too long until we're together every night."

"We must be close to having that talk." He stood and pulled my body against his in a tight embrace, then dipped his head lower for a tender kiss that melted the whole of my insides. He lifted his face and rested his chin on the top of my head. "We'll clean up the kitchen together."

"No way. You took care of dinner. I'll have it done in a jiff."

After I'd finished my chores and the dogs were ready to settle in for the night, I felt drawn to do a little research on bogs. I slipped into the den office with a cup of chamomile tea and honey, sat down at my computer, logged on to the Internet, and did a search on bogs in my state. According to the Department of Natural Resources website, Minnesota had over six million acres of peatlands that covered about ten percent of the state. More than any other state, except Alaska. Bogs in Minnesota were called boreal peatlands. Raised bogs, water tracks, and spring fens were the most common in northern Minnesota. Peatlands existed on every continent, including the tropics. I learned the deeper, more dense peat bogs had lower hydraulic conductivity than clay. Hmm.

I expanded my search to other countries where noted bog bodies were among the more than 1,000 uncovered over the centuries, mostly by peat diggers. The first recorded find was in Holstein, Germany, in 1640. And the others were mainly from England, Ireland, Netherlands, and Denmark. The most well-preserved bodies were found in raised peat bogs.

I looked at photos of bodies with reconstructed faces: Lindow Man, Yde Girl, Grauballe Man, and others. But it was Tollund Man, the one Smoke had mentioned at the scene, that drew me back. He lived and died in Denmark around 300 B.C. and his body was found by peat diggers in a bog just over six feet deep, in 1950. Because he was so well preserved, the initial thought was he hadn't been in the bog long at all. He had beard stubble and eyelashes and wore a hat made of sheepskin and wool. Tollund Man had a rope around his neck and it was debated whether he had been strangled or hanged.

Most agreed he was likely hanged as a sacrifice to the gods because his eyes and mouth were closed, and he was arranged in a fetal position before being placed in the bog. Bogs were regarded as spiritual, holy places for thousands of years, including during the Iron Age when Tollund Man was killed.

Did the bad guy responsible for the seven bodies in Coyote Bog do the same thing to his victims? Kill them as a sacrifice? Christian symbols were branded on their bodies, but that would go against Christian belief.

I studied Tollund Man's face and the creases around and between his eyes. What had caused the deep frown forever frozen on his face? Was he reacting to the air supply that was cut off? Or perhaps he'd been praying in earnest for a miracle rescue, or a quick and painless death. I surely would be, with a miracle as the number one request.

I minimized the page that held his image and checked out others buried in bogs instead of the ground, and the suppositions why. Many were presumed to be accidental falls, perhaps after imbibing too many drinks. Some were thought to be those not allowed to be interred in consecrated grounds, for one reason or another. Others were supposed murders when evidence of a heavy blow to the head or other trauma was present. Many had been weighted down.

Had our bad guy studied the same things I was reading about, and fantasized about doing something similar? He'd weighted some of his victims down. The thought chilled me to the core. I shut down the computer and did a check of the doors and first floor windows, ensuring they were locked, then I climbed the stairs and left the hall light on to find my sleepwear. Smoke's breathing was slow and steady. The dogs were asleep on their rugs and barely stirred. I quietly pulled pajama bottoms and a tee-shirt from the dresser drawer, changed, turned off the light, and climbed into bed. When Smoke didn't move, I thought he must be caught up in the throes of REM sleep. I said my prayers and drifted off to sleep with a smile of contentment.

12

I finished my report on the Coyote Bog discovery and recovery and dropped it in the hanging plastic holder next to Chief Deputy Randolph's office door.

The atmosphere in the administrative clerks' area was heavy, like a low-hanging cloud hovered over them, ready to spill. Lots of fidgeting and pen tapping among the troops. The son of their beloved boss was in trouble, facing serious charges, and they were duly concerned.

Dina, Sheriff Kenner's administrative assistant, stood, waved me over to her desk, and quietly uttered, "I can't get Jaxson off my mind."

"Me neither. It's gotta be a nightmare for him and his family."

"You can feel how we're all on pins and needles here, wondering what'll happen at his first court appearance today. Sheriff stopped by a while ago. He wasn't in uniform and looked rough. Really rough, hadn't even shaved. I doubt he slept a wink last night. I had trouble sleeping myself. I've known Jax since he was born." Dina wasn't a gossip; she was anxious.

I'd seen Jaxson at the annual summer employee picnic over the years and had watched him grow up from a little kid to a young adult. "It's awful, all the way around."

My eyes moved to others in the administrative pool who watched us. They clearly wanted to be in on the conversation, but the sheriff had a rule about not congregating at others' desks, and they respected that even in his absence.

I reached over and squeezed Dina's hand. "I better get a move on. Take good care."

"You, too."

I made my way around the desks for a few minutes, giving words of encouragement to the clerks and answering their burning questions about the bog bodies. When I got to the small office the sergeants shared, I phoned Todd Mason.

"What's up, Sergeant?" he said.

"Todd, wondering if you've had a chance to run a check on the cross pendant."

"Brian was looking earlier but got interrupted. We'll let you know when we have an answer."

"Thanks. See you at the debrief?"

"We'll be there."

Smoke had pulled together a debriefing session, mainly for the highway department workers. When the men from the water agencies caught wind of the discussion at the scene, they'd asked to be included. Why not? Every one of us needed effective coping skills for good health, and critical incidents pushed us to the edge. Smoke reserved C-118, one of the smaller conference rooms in the courthouse, across the corridor from the sheriff's department offices.

I popped into the room and saw a larger group assembled than I'd anticipated. Most sat at tables pulled together to form three sides of a square, effective for open discussion and interacting with others. The way some of them squirmed and darted looks at Smoke, it seemed they were eagerly anticipating magic words that would flow from his mouth to their ears and banish all their fears. It was a therapy session and a process to help put the traumatic incident into a new perspective, by working through it and following sage advice.

Randolph and Smoke stood in the front of the room, chatting with Wendell Peltz and Ron Sutton. Smoke had written key points on the whiteboard and held a stack of handouts.

The three road crew men: Bart, Andy, and Nick sat side by side at the table opposite the entrance, not saying much. The water agencies guys, Thomas Bauer and Corey Frank, sat together, kitty-corner from the others, their eyes on Smoke and Randolph.

Deputies Vince Weber, Todd Mason, and Brian Carlson walked in behind me. And a surprise, Roy Swanson from the M.E.'s office joined us a minute later. He'd likely grabbed hold of the idea that working through his traumatic first day as a death investigator would be beneficial. I greeted him and the others, adding a welcoming smile. We were an unlikely team, thrown together by one of the most bizarre cases we'd ever had.

Randolph sat next to Thomas Bauer and the rest of us took seats across from the highway guys. Smoke looked around, making eye contact with each person. My heart did a little ping-ping when it was my turn. We strived to be professional at work, leaving our personal relationship at home, but in unguarded moments, my feelings won the battle over reason.

Smoke gave the stack of handouts to Weber who sat closest to him. "Take one and pass ′em down." The top sheet highlighted what Smoke would cover and we'd use it as a reference to follow, jot notes on, and refer to later.

"Show of hands: who has been through a critical incident debriefing?" Smoke said.

The six of us from the sheriff's office, including Smoke, raised our hands. As did Roy Swanson.

Smoke nodded and directed his attention to the ones who hadn't. "When we experience critical incidents, it impacts us. Naturally. We need to process what we've been through, learn to effectively cope so it doesn't leave us with long-term physical or psychological problems. Make sense to everyone?"

Everyone nodded.

"Cops respond to emergencies on a regular basis, and a lot of those calls are downright distressing. We need to manage that stress, process it. We can't let it wreak havoc on our well-being, or we'll end up with post-traumatic stress disorder. I've known emergency responders who've had to leave jobs they loved because of it."

He paused, let that sink in, and said, "Many of you guys here aren't cops, but you got caught up in about the most unlikely deal any of us could've imagined. So, take a look at your handouts. We're going to work our way through the seven steps. Number one is assessing the impact it has on you, given your age and past experiences.

"Number two deals with your feelings of safety. Three is the one we'll spend the most time on because it's important that each one of us gets our thoughts and feelings off our chests.

Ventilate and defuse. After a critical event, your mind keeps playing it over and over, hoping it will start to make sense so you can quit thinking about it. In number four we'll go through possible psychological and physical reactions to be on the lookout for."

I considered defusing the most valuable component of debriefing for me, personally. Verbalizing the thoughts and emotions I had when dealing with the crisis helped take the sting away. Talking about it was half the battle, because it wasn't always an easy thing for me to do. I internalized way too much.

Smoke continued, "In number five we'll conduct a review of the incident, evaluate where we're at in the healing process, and what we can do to manage any problems. Number six deals with closure. Moving on. There is a list of support services, if any of you feel the need to talk to a counselor. And working through number seven, thoroughly reviewing the incident, will assist in both the short term and the long haul, so you're comfortable getting back to work, and on with your lives. Sound like a plan?"

Yes. I thought about my last debriefing session after two critical incidents Vince Weber and I experienced on the same day. First, we'd physically prevented a woman from taking her own life. Later, someone deliberately tried to run us down with her vehicle. It wasn't my worst day as a cop, but it was close. Besides a debriefing, I'd had many sessions with a psychologist, one who'd helped me through other traumas. She facilitated my recovery, as did love and support from Smoke, my family, and friends.

As we worked through the steps of our session, it was clear the people most impacted by the recovery of the bodies were the three highway crew members who were at the initial discovery. The rest of us came in after the fact. For me, the discovery of the bodies wasn't as traumatic as wondering what the victims had endured in the events that led up to their deaths. And how we'd uncover who had committed the heinous acts against them.

I was grateful that everyone participated and shared the worst of their thoughts and fears. There'd been times I'd wake in the middle of the night in terror from unresolved issues following a critical incident. When I thought I was fine, that I was over it, that my coping skills were intact.

The session was intense, so Smoke gave us a ten-minute break every hour, allowing us to walk around, get a beverage or snack, make phone calls, check messages. On our third break, Smoke and I happened to be in the squad room sorting through our mailboxes when Deputy Bob Edberg came in. He threw his memo book on the desk next to a computer.

"Hey, Bob," Smoke said.

"Hey. Finished with the debrief?" His mouth was turned downward.

"We're on break for ten," Smoke said.

I touched Bob's arm. "What's up?"

He ran a hand through his hair. "Ah, it's not a work thing, it's my mom. Either she's hiding money and valuables, or we got a problem with one of her caregivers." Bob's mother had lived with him forever. Her physical health had been poor for years, and she'd recently received a diagnosis of dementia. I admired Bob for his continued, devoted faithfulness, ensuring his mother was well cared for.

"I know I don't have to ask you, but I have to ask you: did all the home health aides check out a-okay?" Smoke said.

Edberg's shoulders lifted. "They're all contracted through a licensed agency, so the answer should be yes, but I have not personally run checks on any of them, no."

"You shouldn't have to. How many do you have coming to your home?" I said.

"Four, no, five. Because I work so many weekends and I'm off a lot of weekdays, not like most folks out there, so they have to rotate the aides to make it work. It's a screwy schedule, as you know. Two of them trade off on the weekends."

"You're a good judge of character, and none of them were on the questionable side?" I asked.

"No, and my mother hasn't had any complaints, said they've all been good to her. She even has a favorite. One of the weekend aides."

"One way to find out what's going on is to install a motion-detection camera. We've done that a time or two before," Smoke said.

Bob grinned a little. "We have, at that."

"Check the equipment room. A couple weeks ago we purchased some that are alarm clocks, dubbed nanny cameras. About as low profile as they get," Smoke said.

"Want me to start a complaint so you have the number when you check out the cameras?" I said.

"I guess so. Sure," Edberg said.

"Give me a list of the items you know are missing and I'll include that in the report. We'll be wrapping up the debriefing in about an hour, right, Detective?" I said.

"Should be, yep."

"How is it going?" Edberg said.

"Pretty darn good. Bringing the bog bodies out of their graves was a shock to everyone, of course. But not like some of the criticals we've had, like when kids are involved. Those tear me up," Smoke said.

"I'm with you on that," Edberg said then turned to me. "I'll put together the list of the jewelry and money I know is missing."

"Good. It won't take five minutes to write up what you know so far. You don't have an identified suspect you're trying to catch in the act so the report will be short. The supplemental might get more involved, based on what you find out. I'll text you the complaint number." I paused for a minute and studied the defeated look that'd returned. "Sorry you're going through this, Bob. We've been fortunate none of my living grandparents have dementia. Not yet, anyway."

"Thanks. I know how hard it was on you and your family when your gram had it."

"Yeah, very tough. But she didn't suffer long, at least."

Edberg nodded and sat down in front of the computer. Smoke laid a hand on his shoulder for a moment, then we headed back to the conference room. By the time Smoke had tied everything together, even the youngest highway worker was more relaxed, said he wasn't overly worried about encountering anything close to that on the job again. What were the chances?

"A few reminders: eat good food, don't drink too much alcohol. That only seems to help for a little while and then it's hell to pay. And don't be afraid or embarrassed to ask for professional help if you need it. We're here for each other, right?

"For those of you who don't have my cell phone number, it's listed on the bottom of the last page of the handout. Do *not* hesitate to call me if you have a question or want to run something by me, whatever. Day or night. Sometimes we need a middle-of-the-night-go-to-guy. Thank you, each one of you, for your active participation," Smoke said in closing.

We all stood and picked up the notes and list of resources for reference. A warm feeling of pride flooded through me as I watched others shake Smoke's hand and thank him for the session. Smoke wasn't perfect, but he was close to it. In my book, anyway. The room gradually cleared then I helped Smoke gather up the extra papers, erase the whiteboard, and shut off the lights.

We talked as we walked back to the sheriff's department offices. "I didn't tell you earlier, but I spent my first hour this morning running checks on missing people in the county, starting with the current year. Remember the one from last year, the gentleman who walked away from his care facility?" he said.

"Sure. We used dogs, drones, and an army of people, but it seemed like he had vanished into thin air. What was his name again, Wright?"

"Oscar Wright."

"Oh, yeah. Man, it'd be both good and bad if it turns out he's one of the recovered victims."

"No doubt."

"You'll keep searching the files?" I said.

"Yeah. I hope the M.E. will have something for us in the next day or two, but we need to start somewhere. I'll pay a visit to the neighbors by Coyote, the ones who weren't home yesterday. Probably means it'll go into the evening."

"Let me know when you're heading out there and I'll try to meet you. For now, I need to get a complaint number for Bob's deal. It sounds like calls have been pretty steady for the deputies today, so I'll grab something from the vending machine, go over reports, and get out on the road to assist. Want me to get you a sandwich, something else?"

"Nah, but thanks. I'll catch up with you later."

"Oh, and Detective Dawes?"

"Yes, Sergeant Aleckson?"

"You did a fine job with the debrief today. I have to say I was very impressed."

His cheeks colored, surprising me. "I'm not Sheriff Kenner, but I guess I held my own."

"You did. Speaking of the sheriff, his son should make his first appearance today."

"I heard that but didn't check the time on the court calendar. He maybe went already," Smoke said.

"I'll swing by Dina's desk to check."

"I'll go with you."

Dina hovered by her desk and her blotchy, tear-streaked face alerted us she had bad news. But it wasn't just bad—it was the worst. "The boy Jaxson hit died a while ago from his head injury. They're changing the charges from first degree assault to homicide," she managed between sobs.

Smoke put an arm around her shoulders. "Dear God."

The air rushed out of my lungs and I couldn't respond. A young man's life had ended senselessly in a fight, and Jaxson Kenner's life would never be the same. Nor would a long list of other people's whose worlds had changed forever.

13

Mama and Rufus

"**R**ufus, now remember, you're not to talk to anyone. If someone asks you a question, pretend like you don't understand or that you can't talk"

"Yes, Mama."

She was dressed in her uniform. "It's time for me to go to work. If you stay home, you need to keep the doors locked. Don't answer if anyone knocks and keep very quiet, like you aren't here. If you go out to check on things, like we talked about, then make sure you lock the door behind you."

"Yes, Mama."

"I don't know where they took our patients and I have to tell you that it makes me very nervous and upset. I thought their bodies would be in the sacred ground forever, long after their spirits went to Heaven. It causes me great sorrow."

"I'm sorry, Mama."

"I know you are, Rufus. You're a good boy who made a bad mistake. I've been thinking about it and maybe we need to bring more than one patient home in the next week. I have my eyes on three, trying to decide which of them should be the chosen one. Maybe it should be all three."

Rufus didn't know what to say. One was bad enough. Three would be really, really bad.

14

I was reading the incident report on the Jaxson Kenner/Sawyer Harris fight when Brian Carlson phoned me.

"Corky, I tracked down the manufacturer of that cross pendant. A company called Christian Jewelry Designs, right here in Minneapolis, believe it or not. They've been in business fifty-six years and have made that particular design the last twelve. They sell to big box stores, including Kohl's and Target. We don't have a Kohl's in Winnebago County, but we have the two Targets."

"So they aren't rare, there could be a lot of them out there?"

"I asked them to check the records of sales to the Target stores here in the last twelve years. They agreed, but it will take them some time to go through the invoices," Carlson said.

"I guess that'll tell us how popular they are."

"I'm also going to see if the stores here can pull up their records, see if a number of them were purchased at the same time."

"Good idea, Brian. I'll tell Smoke what you've got so far."

"See ya."

I went back to the report. Witnesses said Sawyer had been "goofing around" with his car in the school parking lot, teasing other kids by pretending he was going to run into them. He'd taunted Jaxson and it angered Jax. When Sawyer parked and got out of his car, Jaxson yelled at him. Sawyer yelled back, acted like he was going to grab Jaxson's shirt, and then Jaxson punched him hard. Sawyer fell backward on the pavement, a fall that turned fatal.

Tears gathered in my eyes. A kid acting stupid, angering another kid with a short fuse, leaving one dead and the other facing prison time. It'd be difficult to prove intent, but Jaxson must have known his punch was forceful enough to land his opponent on the ground. I filed the report and reviewed a few more, unable to let go of the sorrow I felt over Jaxson's case and that Sawyer's life had ended so unnecessarily.

It was nearly five o'clock that afternoon when Smoke and I met at the first of the three addresses where deputies hadn't gotten an answer at the day before. As I pulled in behind him, I considered how startling it likely was for a homeowner to spot two squad cars in his driveway. It invoked the old, "Who died?" reaction.

A one-story, tidy rambler sat on an older farmstead site. The original house had fallen into disrepair and was torn down. An old barn still stood. As a young teen I remembered the newer house being built, about twenty years before. When farmers retired and sold their cropland, they often retained a few acres with the homestead and other buildings and lived there until they died or moved away.

According to Communications, the homeowner's name was Floyd Myren. I didn't know him personally, nor had I been called to his residence. I followed Smoke to the door and stood aside as he rang the bell. The only sound we heard inside the house was the bell's tone. We waited a moment then Smoke pushed the bell again and rapped on the door a few times.

"Doesn't appear to be home," I said.

"I'll have the evening car stop by." We started back to our vehicles. "Did you happen to see a copy of the *Oak Lea Daily News* this afternoon?" he said.

"I didn't."

"The Coyote Bog bodies' story made the front page. Chief Deputy Randolph has been fielding dozens of calls since the paper came out an hour ago."

"I imagine. I saw people parked by the barricade the few times I drove County Seven to Thirty-five today. Like they are now," I said.

"Yeah. When Highway gets back to work tomorrow, starts to rock and roll with their equipment, hopefully that will help keep ′em away."

"You think so? I'd bet it'll bring more in. Folks will be watching, on the lookout to see if Highway finds another body."

"You got a point there. So on to the next neighbor?" Smoke said.

"Sure."

"It's a pain in the butt the road's closed. And a nice perk we get to drive around the barricades." Smoke worked his eyebrows up and down.

"Agreed."

No homes sat on the south side of County Road 35 for a mile west or a half mile east.

"Let's head west to the next house and catch the other one on the way home," he said.

"All righty."

We got in our vehicles and drove to the nearest neighbor, about a quarter mile from Myren's.

A middle-aged woman opened the door, her hand clenched in a fist above her heart and her eyes as round as a full moon when she uttered, "Yes?" at barely a whisper.

Smoke poked me in the back, indicating I should take the lead.

I smiled. "Afternoon, ma'am. Ms. Borgen, is it?"

"Yes. Did something bad happen to my son?"

"No, not that I'm aware of." I studied her a second. "Sorry if we alarmed you. We're here on another matter."

When she let out a sigh of relief breath, it made me wonder if her son gave her cause for concern. On the other hand, I was not a troublemaker by nature, but my job duties gave my mother plenty to worry about.

"So what is it?" she said.

"You heard about the bodies found in Coyote Bog yesterday?"

She nodded. "I was gone all day, but I heard it on the news on the way home. I can hardly believe it."

"We're talking with area neighbors about any suspicious activity you may have observed by the swamp. Maybe someone was parked by the side of the road on that stretch, like a van, or a truck, an SUV, and it struck you as odd. Especially if it was after dark during low-traffic times."

She glanced up like she was trying to pull a memory out of the air. "Hmm. Nothing that I recall. When people are pulled over to the side of the road and don't have their flashers on, you don't think all that much of it. You think they're making a phone call or something."

"It could have been some time back. Years, even," I said.

She shook her head. "No. We haven't lived here long, just two years, but nothing comes to mind."

I nodded and pulled my memo pad, pen, and a business card from my breast pocket. "I'll need your name and date of birth for my report." She flinched slightly but gave me the information. I handed her the card and noted her discomfort. "And what's your son's name?"

It took a moment for her to tell me.

"Thanks. If you remember something, please give me a call."

"Okay."

"Oh, one other thing. Do you know Mister Myren, your neighbor to the east?" I said.

"I don't. And I think he only lives there in the summer."

"Why do you say that?"

"About the time we moved in, one of the other neighbors mentioned that he had retired and spent most of the year in Florida. I think he has someone looking after the place," she said.

"You don't know who that might be?" I said.

"No. When I drive by there on my way to work, I've seen a woman waiting to pull out of the driveway a few times."

"What time is that?"

"Early in the morning, six-thirty, thereabouts," she said.

"Do you remember what she drives?"

"It's tan, maybe silver. Smaller car."

"Ford, Chevy, a foreign make?" I said.

She shrugged. "I don't know my cars very well."

"Okay, we'll catch up with her. Thanks for your time."

When we reached our squad cars, I opened my door and with my back to Borgen's house, quietly said, "Kind of odd, huh? First, she thinks something happened to her son, and then she doesn't want to give up her ID."

"Ya gotta wonder. With a little digging, we may uncover something about the two of them."

"I'll run her, check for warrants, before I leave here."

"Sure. She gave us a lead about Myren, anyway. He's the listed property owner and a woman seems to be looking after the place when he's gone," Smoke said.

"I'll see if he has a listed phone number and try to get a hold of him that way," I said.

"Good plan. Let's check out that last place and call it a night."

"Meet you there in a bit." I climbed into my squad car, accessed the state system on my mobile data terminal, and typed in Mae Borgen's name. She came back clean and clear. Not even a moving violation on her record.

The young couple at the newer two-story house reported they had not noticed any unusual activity by Coyote Bog in the three years they'd lived there. We recorded their information, thanked them, and took our leave.

On the walk back to our vehicles, Smoke said, "See you at home." *Home.*

When I opened the kennel door to the backyard, Queenie and Rex begged for attention from Smoke and me, and then took off running and exploring. Smoke followed me to the deck where I plopped down on a chair to watch our dogs. He leaned over the deck's railing, stretched, and pulled out his phone.

"I need to give Kenner a call, assure him that he and his family have our support. That's about all we can give them right now." He rolled through his contact list, hit the call button, and started pacing while he waited for Kenner to pick up.

That made it tough for me to sit. I moved to the side railing and found myself rocking back and forth, moving my weight from one leg to the next. My heart sank for the Kenners. Jaxson's life had taken a nosedive into deep, dark waters and I wondered if he'd make it safely to the surface.

Smoke stopped abruptly and straightened his posture, like he was standing at attention. "Mike? . . . Yeah, I'm here with Corky and we wanted to check in, see if you need anything. . . . Oh, you did? Okay, well, that's good, good. . . . How's your son holding up?. . . And what about the rest of you, your wife, other kids?" Smoke was silent for some time, shook his head, then nodded, then shook his head again. "I'll let you go. You know we're here for you, anytime, whatever we can do."

My phone rang as Smoke ended his call. "Hello, Mother."

"Corinne, I can't believe what happened. Jaxson Kenner got into a fight at school. The other boy hit his head on the pavement and died."

"It's awful. Smoke was just talking to the sheriff, offering the family our support."

"Kenner bailed him out of jail," Smoke said.

"Oh. Mother, did you hear Smoke?"

"I did. And I'm glad, for Jaxson's sake. Denny told me, more than once, that he was worried about him, the way he'd get into little scrapes. Maybe because Denny thought it could lead to something like this." Dennis Twardy, former sheriff.

"Sadly, it can. And does. As bad as I feel for Jaxson and his family, I feel way worse for the boy who died, and what his poor family must be going through."

"Me too, dear. Like you said, especially for Sawyer Harris and his family," she said.

I unbuttoned the top few buttons of my shirt to let in a little air. "Mom, sorry to cut you off, but I gotta get out of my uniform and figure out something for supper."

"You don't have to worry about supper. I have a big bowl of pasta salad—you know I always make too much. I'll run some over, along with a meatloaf I'm about to take out of the oven."

"You really don't—"

"Of course I do. I made two meatloaves. You go get cleaned up and I'll be over in ten minutes or so."

"I guess if it will make you feel better," I kidded.

She chuckled then disconnected. I turned to Smoke and shrugged. "Mother wants to feed us."

"Thanks for not protesting too much." Smoke's lips lifted in a small grin then a shadow crossed his face, and his eyebrows drew together.

"So what did our sheriff say?" I said.

"It was hard for him to even talk. Or focus. He kind of rambled on about how he wishes he could fix things, start yesterday over again, bring the boy Sawyer back to life. I gotta say I'm pretty damn worried about him."

"With good reason. You'd expect him to feel that way, say those things. When tragedy strikes, people will do just about anything to make it go away."

"Yeah, we've seen that enough. I guess it was the defeat in his voice that unnerved me. I've never heard that before," Smoke said.

"Jaxson's in a bad place and Sheriff knows the drill. That makes it much worse."

"No doubt. Good thing his wife is a rock," Smoke said.

"For sure. What about Jaxson? How's he doing?"

"He won't come out of his room."

"Did Sheriff say anything about Sawyer?" I said.

"No, and I decided not to ask at this point."

I glanced at the dogs, in pursuit of a squirrel. "Mother will be here in a minute and she told me to get cleaned up."

"And we know you always do what she says," he quipped.

Oh, the paradox. "Ha, ha. I try to, but when it comes to my job it's my duty to follow what my boss tells me to do—not my mother."

"The point of my comment."

I ran upstairs and shed my uniform with a sigh of relief. My Kevlar vest was damp, so I hung it up to air dry. I stepped into the shower, wishing the distressing cares and concerns could be washed away as easily as the grime that clung to my skin. I towel-dried, dressed, and made it back downstairs seconds before Mother arrived.

When we heard her car in the driveway, Smoke went out through the garage and carried in the box she'd brought. "Kristen, this is a welcomed treat. Thank you."

Mother was about to celebrate her fifty-third birthday but looked a decade younger. At least. She had stayed trim all her life and a mere sprinkle of wrinkles appeared when she smiled. It was a wonder she didn't have deep frown lines with the way she fretted over me and my brother. And everyone else she loved.

She gave me a quick hug. "Enjoy."

"You know we will," I said.

Smoke touched her shoulder. "We surely will. Thanks again, Kristen."

Mother smiled and scooted out the door.

Smoke took my hand and guided me to the food that sat on the counter. "We're bound to feel better enjoying a delicious meal together."

And we did. As we finished the last bites, Smoke said, "You should get your mother's meatloaf recipe."

"She doesn't have one. She just throws things in and mixes it up."

"Any idea what she throws in?" He leaned in closer, like he was coaxing a confession out of me.

"Sure, I've watched her a bunch of times. Ground beef, of course, an egg, oatmeal, milk, Worcestershire sauce, garlic, some herbs, like oregano and basil."

Smoke chuckled. "Sounds like you know the recipe by heart."

"The ingredients, yes. But I have no clue what the amounts are." My cell phone rang, and I glanced at the display. "It's Edberg."

He lifted his eyebrows. "Unusual for him to call after work."

"Hey, Bob. What's up?"

"Sergeant, hope I'm not catching you at a bad time."

"Not at all."

"I wanted you to know the alarm clock cameras are set up in my mother's bedroom, the kitchen, and living room. I did a photo inventory of her jewelry and valuables, and planted money in a few places. We're good to go on the monitoring. If more stuff goes missing, we'll see if Mom is moving it or one of the caregivers is taking it."

"A good way to find out," I said.

"With Mom's health being what it is, it's the only way. She got downright anxious when I asked if she was sure she hadn't put her things somewhere else."

"You know what? If it turns out she's the one after all, you won't need to tell her. When you see where she put them you can put them back where they belong."

"Dementia's the pits."

Smoke and I chatted about Bob's situation and things in my family as we cleaned up the dishes. We saved further discussions on the bog bodies' investigation and the trouble Jaxson was in for another time. After he hung the dish towel on its hook, Smoke drew me into his arms. "I'm going to take Rex home for the night. With me being gone so much, no sense making it any easier for bad guys to break in and cart away all my belongings."

I didn't hide my disappointment. "It seems to me Rex thinks this is his second home. You can always install a security system, you know."

He moved his hands to my shoulders and pulled back for a better look. "No doubt. And that's part of the in-depth discussion we need to have another time."

My heart did a flip-flop. "As in?"

"Our engagement, our future together."

"What are you thinking?"

"That I love you more than life itself."

"Smoke, I—"

He put his finger to my lips. "I know, and it'll be okay." His endearing kiss dissipated my doubts and my fears, until it ended. He pecked the tip of my nose. "I'll call you before I go to bed . . . unless you call me first."

I nodded slightly. Queenie settled herself against my leg as we watched Smoke and Rex take their leave. "Is this the way it's going to be, Queenie? Sometimes we stay together, sometimes we don't? And then I act like a big, fat baby about it."

When Queenie whined, I reached down and scratched her head. "Smoke says it'll be okay and I have to believe him, right?" But the more I thought about the "in-depth discussion" Smoke wasn't ready to have, the more keyed up I got. "Man alive, I need to go for a run, shake some of this tension loose." Queenie stuck her snoot in my thigh. "You're off the hook tonight. And I'll make it snappy."

I slipped on my running shoes then headed to the office den where I stowed my off-duty Smith and Wesson in a safe. It was ready to go in its pancake holster and I attached it to the waistband of my shorts. After suffering a critical incident on a run, Smoke insisted I arm myself. And it was the smart thing to do. I'd been in danger any number of times and being armed gave me a measure of assurance.

Queenie whined and shook her head back and forth, hopeful I'd change my mind. "Sorry, girl, not this time."

I walked the tenth-of-a-mile length of driveway, turned right on the township road, broke into a brisk jogging pace, and breathed in the cool evening air as the sun dropped lower in the sky. I needed to keep my outlook positive. My life in general, and my life with Smoke in particular, was very good.

Granted, Smoke was still working through issues, like a failed past relationship that left him scarred and scared. And things about our commitment caused him unease: he'd been a friend of my parents in high school, I was twenty years younger, and we both served with the Winnebago County Sheriff and handled many cases together. But there was no canoodling on the job.

Although making detective was viewed by many as a promotion, Smoke and I technically held the same rank. He'd been a supervising sergeant prior to his assignment to the investigative unit some years back.

I ran past my mother's old farmhouse—the same one that she, and her father before her, then John Carl and me after her, had all grown up in. She'd been gifted it when Gramps and Gram Brandt built a smaller rambler down the road. Gram had died several years before and as I passed their house, I prayed Gramps would make it safely through another night.

I reached the next crossroad and turned around for the return trip, sprinted a short distance, and then slowed down to what I estimated was an eight-minute-mile. I was home in record time.

"Well, I guess I need another shower," I told my waiting pooch.

15

I was about to knock on Chief Deputy Randolph's doorframe Wednesday morning when I heard him say, "I know the sheriff will make damn sure Jaxson honors the conditions of his release."

"Yes, he will," Smoke said.

I poked my head inside. "Good morning. You wanted to see me?"

Randolph stood, waved me in, and sat down again. "Yes. Come in, Sergeant, and close the door."

I took the chair next to Smoke. His smile was relaxed, no sign of tension there after our curt discussion the night before. Maybe I'd read too much into what he said before left for home.

"We got an update from Doctor Patrick. She spoke with Doctor Nancy Snyder, the one and only forensic anthropologist in Minnesota," Smoke said.

"The only one, seriously?" I said.

Smoke lifted a shoulder. "I didn't realize that, either. Besides handling requests from medical examiners around the state when remains are found under a variety of circumstances,

Snyder has also been working with the state archeologist on a large project, trying to identify remains from the large collection of bones they have at the state."

"Isn't that something?" Randolph said.

"Snyder is happy to assist Doc Patrick in estimating the ages the victims were at the time of their deaths, but it's unlikely she'll be able to pinpoint exactly how long they've been in the bog. It'd be a wide range," Smoke said.

"Hey, they do that kind of thing all the time on the crime shows," I said.

Smoke raised his eyebrows. "That's because the writers know people like to believe in magic. Back to Snyder, before we enlist her services, we're forming our own plan of action."

My ears perked up. "As in?"

"We're reopening the unsolved missing persons' cases from the last decade, starting with the most recent and working backward from there," Smoke said.

"Makes sense to me," I said.

Randolph nodded. "The best place to start."

"I reviewed the Oscar Wright file again since he was the most recent elderly person to go missing. I located his daughter and set up a meeting with her. Are you ready for a road trip?" Smoke said.

"Where to?" I said.

He chuckled. "Not far, Harold Lake."

"Isn't that where Oscar lived?"

"Yep. Daughter Claire works at the café in town and told me the morning rush is over. It gives her a thirty-minute window she can get away and talk to us. We'll collect her DNA while we're at it, submit it to the lab."

I stood up. "Ready when you are." Smoke had been on another case when Mr. Wright disappeared and wasn't the lead detective that worked it. Nevertheless, it was all hands on deck in the effort to locate him and everyone in the department was involved in some aspect of the search.

Randolph nodded. "Catch you both later."

Smoke lifted his hand in an after-you gesture and we headed to his unmarked squad car. "I swung by Coyote Bog on my way in to work today," he said.

"So did I."

"It's near impossible to stay away from crime scenes."

"They keep drawing me back, for sure. The dead tell their stories to medical examiners and I keep hoping something like that will happen for us. Like the bad guy will be there, and it'll be the break we need," I said.

"Wouldn't be the first time that's happened." We climbed into the car. "After the rocky start with construction two days ago, the road project's back on track, moving right along. Our county guys should finish up the ditch clean out today and the company they contracted with will take over from there," he said.

"Ron Sutton was there when I pulled in. I asked how his guys were doing and he told me the debriefing you did helped them—all of them—a lot."

"That was the goal and I'm happy to get positive feedback. We need our people to stay healthy."

"For sure. To let you know, I did a check on Floyd Myren. Mostly to find out who's watching his house, see if that person's ever noticed anything going on around Coyote Bog," I said.

"What'd you find out about Myren?"

"He doesn't have a landline and I couldn't find a cell number. I'd hoped to give him a call, get the name of the mystery woman his neighbor saw. Myren's only listed address is the one here by Coyote."

"It's possible he rents a condo, something like that, in Florida," Smoke said.

"That's what I figured. Mail still goes to his place here. Has a local bank, automatic deposits of both social security and VA benefits. Plus, his utility payments and insurances are set up on automatic withdrawal. The bank only has his local address on file, and an email address. His phone number on file is the landline he dropped."

"You can email him, I guess."

"I will."

"Find out anything on his family?" Smoke said.

"I located obituaries on his wife, his daughter, and a brother where he was listed as the survivor. He outlived all of them."

"Hmm."

"It's curious, anyway," I said.

"That it is."

"Back to Oscar Wright's case. I remember a lot, but maybe not all the details."

"I'll give you an abbreviated version. It was a weird deal, really. He was at the assisted living facility in Harold Lake because of his dementia. But his daughter said in the report that it hadn't gotten to the point where he needed to be in the memory care unit.

"On that Wednesday in May, Oscar was in the day area for an afternoon program. According to others who were there, and noticed, he got up and left about halfway through it. They figured he either needed to use the bathroom or wanted to go lie down in his room, something like that.

"A nurse saw him talking to an older woman in the hallway when she passed by, and going by the time frame, that nurse was the last one in the facility known to have seen him. They couldn't find a single person that saw him leave. It seemed he had vanished."

"And they think that older woman somehow spirited him away?" I said.

"Maybe lured is a better word. It's a logical conclusion, but why, and where did they go? The nurse gave a decent description of her. Caucasian, small in stature, gray hair, high cheekbones, narrow chin. And she wore glasses with big frames."

"I remember our team came up with a composite sketch and posted that, along with Oscar's photo, in the area newspapers. But no one came forward to identify her."

"Since none of the staff or residents knew her that begs the questions: who was she and what was she doing at the care facility?" Smoke said.

"Obviously not working there or visiting a friend or relative who lived there. If that were the case, someone would have known her."

"Correct. Nor was she identified as one of the volunteers. That's what led to the conclusion, as you noted, she spirited Oscar away. That belief was shared by everyone else who worked the case." He turned and flashed me a smile that set my heart aflutter. An unguarded moment no one was there to witness.

"Oscar may have known her from somewhere," I said.

"And they walked off into the sunset together?"

I shrugged. "Given her size, she couldn't have strong-armed him to go with her."

"That's a fact. He was six foot one, weighed about one eighty," he said.

"The great unknown, all right."

Claire Bolton's small bungalow was two blocks from her work. When she opened the door, I recognized her right away. Retirement age, tall, friendly, and chatty. Smoke and I showed our badges and she waved like it wasn't necessary. We all knew each other. "Come in, come right in." Claire touched each of our shoulders as we stepped across the threshold. I silently added "a toucher" to her description.

She pointed the way to the kitchen, and we sat around the table. The room was clutter-free, the walls a pleasing shade of yellow, in sync with the owner's sunny disposition. Smoke slid a business card across the table, and I did the same. Claire glanced at them, then at us. "You said you might have some information about my father's disappearance."

Smoke cleared his throat. "I don't want to mislead you, or give you false hopes—"

"You think Dad is one of the people they found in Coyote Bog." She locked her eyes squarely on Smoke as she folded her hands and squeezed them together tightly.

Smoke kept his voice low and soothing. "That's the possibility we need to check out. To either verify that he is or he's not one of the bodies."

Tears filled her eyes. "Oh, my dear Lord in Heaven. Does that mean someone killed him? Who would do that to an eighty-year-old man? Dad was a big, loveable teddy bear." Tears sprang from their ducts and rolled down her cheeks.

"Back when we couldn't find him anywhere, I was afraid he'd wandered over to the lake and fell in. But the sheriffs couldn't find him, so I kept thinking maybe he's alive after all. Like he hitchhiked somewhere and couldn't find his way back home. I've been caught up in a kind of hell." People without answers grasp at all kinds of straws.

"We don't yet know the cause of death of the folks we found," Smoke said.

Claire shook her head back and forth.

"I can only imagine what you've been through. I'm so sorry," I said.

"That goes for me, too," Smoke said.

"Claire, I'd like you to take a look at something." I pulled out my phone, found the photo of the cross pendant found in Coyote Bog, and held it up for her to see. "Do you recognize this necklace?"

She squinted for better focus and shook her head. "I don't."

Smoke gave her a moment then drew the DNA kit from his breast pocket. "This test will tell us if you're a blood relative of one of the male victims. If you are, we'll be able to identify your father's remains."

"I don't know. I mean I want to know, but I don't." Red blotches formed on her cheeks.

"It's not easy, any way you look at it. But if it turns out we've found your father, you'll be able to put to rest all your what ifs," Smoke said.

Claire nodded. "What do I need to do for the test?"

"Open your mouth. I'll swab the inside of your cheek and then we're done." The sample was collected and sealed in no time. "We'll let you know as soon as the lab has the results. They'll expedite it, but even so it can take a few days. Meantime, do you remember the names of your father's dentist and doctor?" Smoke said.

"Um, yes, I do." She provided the information and I recorded it in my memo book. They were both in Harold Lake.

Smoke put his hand on hers. "Is there anything we can do, contact anyone to help you?"

"Like your pastor or a friend?" I said.

She shook her head. "Thanks, maybe I'll talk to my priest later. For now, I just want to get back to the café."

"You sure you'll be okay going back to work?" Smoke asked.

"Way, way better than sitting here driving myself crazy thinking about this."

"In my time with the sheriff's office, we've had a few missing persons' cases where the person was never found. I've said this before, but if someone I knew and loved disappeared, not knowing what happened would push me to the edge," I said.

"Yep, so make it a point to never disappear."

"We'll make a pact." We drove in silence until I was the one who broke it. "In Oscar Wright's case, at this point, how can we piece together what happened, why he left the facility? We're missing key evidence."

"That's a sad fact, to be sure. I pulled files of two other elderly people who also went mysteriously missing in the last few years and were never located. One was four years ago, the other was three. We'll review them, see if we can find another common thread, besides all of them having dementia. The department explored the possibility of a connection between the cases back then, but didn't find one," Smoke said.

"Hmm, it might turn out that there is, after all. And the connection might be something more sinister than the three of them just wandered off on their own."

"That's what I'm thinking."

"Are you going to run Claire's DNA swab to the lab first thing?" I said.

"No, I'll have one of the deputies take care of that."

The Midwest Regional Crime Lab was about an hour away in Anoka County and about ten miles from the Midwest Medical Examiner's Office.

16

Smoke and I carried selected files to the squad room so we had a table to spread out the reports. A sense of both reverence and sadness touched me whenever I studied the faces of victims—no matter the circumstances—but especially if it involved a criminal act.

I read the file on Silas Petty, the man who'd gone missing three years before, and passed the sheets to Smoke.

He scanned through them to refresh his memory. "Mister Petty supposedly drove away from his house one week before his seventy-ninth birthday, on May fourteenth. Didn't bother to lock up his house—"

"And that led to two trains of thought. One, he planned to return a short time later, but got confused and something caused him to keep going. To where, no one had a clue. Or two, he knew he wasn't coming back, and left the house open for easier access. Again, no one had a clue where he would have gone," I said.

"And he didn't leave a note."

"No note, and his vehicle was never found."

"His disappearance tripped some dissension in the family, and finger pointing by the two sons who lived out of state. They called out their uncles, said they were close and should have made sure he wasn't left alone, even for a short time. But according to his doctor, Silas hadn't progressed much in the disease at that point; wasn't considered a danger to himself, didn't wander.

"The brothers who lived here didn't think he'd reached the point of needing around-the-clock care. They hired caregivers to be with him part of the time and took turns spending the night with him, so he wouldn't be alone. Since one of the brothers saw him every day, they could keep an eye on him, watch for any changes," Smoke said.

"I read that and thought what a great help they were to their brother. Poor Silas didn't want to leave his house and go to a nursing home."

"It made us detectives and his doctor wonder if something had shifted in his brain that affected his reasoning, made him drive off into parts unknown. Or maybe he'd run away on purpose. For reasons that he considered were good ones."

"That's what his brothers suggested must have happened. That he ran away to save his family from whatever lay ahead as his condition got worse," I said.

"The brothers had known him longest, but Petty's sons thought they knew their dad better than their uncles did. Both of Silas's brothers reported that he'd never given any indication he'd been thinking about losing himself. Then again, how many times have we heard similar things over the years? Truth be told, those who know the person best usually are right. But there's always the exception when the indicators aren't there, or they don't get picked up on," Smoke said.

"True. Like the guy last month who got a terminal diagnosis from his doctor, drove home, and took his life without even telling his family the news. They had to piece it all together."

"A shocker for them."

"Back to Silas Petty's sons, I see one is in Chicago and the other is in Boston. At least that's where they were three years ago," I said.

"That makes collecting DNA an issue. We'll see if Petty's brothers are still in Winnebago County and take it from there. I see no reason to contact the sons or the sister who's in Iowa at this stage of the game. Get them all riled up and then have it come to naught."

I picked up a sheet of paper and waved it back and forth. "Besides the fact that he was never found, his bank account wasn't tapped into."

"Nope. Another common thread in the three cases."

I thought for a minute about some statistics I'd read. Half of all people with dementia wander off at some point, either because they get disoriented or have some sort of mental disconnect where they believe they need to go somewhere specific, like to a job they haven't had in years, as one example. A long list of reasons was cited.

I laid Silas Petty's file on the table.

Smoke picked up the other file and scanned it. "Agneta Keats, age eighty-one, missing for just over five years now, disappeared on May ninth."

"Wait a minute. All three of them—Oscar, Silas, and Agneta—went missing in May?"

Smoke nodded. "They did, and in fact the detectives discussed that coincidence after Oscar disappeared last year, but couldn't come up with any particular reason. Aside from, in Silas's case, it was his birth month. That was it. And what could be the tie to the other two?"

"So you think it was an odd coincidence?"

"You know how I feel about that. But with no dots for us to draw lines to at the time, what would the significance have been, what did we miss?"

"None of the three knew the others, correct?" I said.

"Correct. And they had been receiving different levels of care. Had they been in the same facility, the Minnesota Department of Health would have been all over it. As would we, of course. Missus Keats was in an assisted living apartment. She was there the first time they made rounds, gone on the next."

Smoke studied Agneta's photo and passed it to me.

It had been a recent church picture. She was dolled up with a professional hair comb, blush on her cheeks, and color on her lips. I smiled at her sweet face. "Is it possible she's one of the female victims? I couldn't match her face up with any of them with any level of confidence." I set the photo on the table next to Silas Petty's and would make copies of them later.

"No. Same deal regarding the photos of our male victims, trying to match them to one of the bodies we recovered."

"If we had photos of the victims for a side by side comparison, maybe then."

Smoke lifted his shoulders in a small shrug. "Maybe. But a person's appearance definitely changes when their body goes through the adipocere, or mummification preservation, processes."

"For sure."

We read through the pages for a time then Smoke said, "Agneta Keat's disappearance generated even more controversy than Silas Petty's. Some of the family members thought her son did away with her for the life insurance. Unresolved disputes in the family stemmed back a couple decades. Our investigation verified the whereabouts of their not-well-liked brother, proved he was hundreds of miles away during the time frame in question. Even with no evidence of foul play, no body to prove Agneta was dead, one sister in particular was still not convinced."

"I remember how that piled on even more stress for the family. The insurance company couldn't pay the claim without a body, so the brother had nothing to gain at that time," I said.

"Correct. Minnesota law allows presumption of death four years after a person goes missing, if there's been no contact. The family likely filed a petition with the court by now. Especially given Agneta's age and health at the time of her disappearance."

"It's sad. Presumption of death still doesn't give real closure."

"It does not."

"All three of these folks were getting care from providers, two in facilities. The detectives looked for a caregiver in common, but never found one." I said.

"That's right. After Oscar Wright disappeared and we were faced with three disappearances of elderly folks in four years, we left no stone unturned. Definitely suspicious, but evidence was sorely lacking. We went over employment records looking for a common denominator, came up dry." He studied Agneta Keats's photo and set it down. "Well, let's figure out who we should contact in the families, let them know what we're working on, that we'll be collecting DNA samples."

His cell phone rang as he was looking at Keats's next of kin list. "Detective Dawes. . . . Really? I'll be right out to get her." He disconnected and raised his eyebrows when he said, "Talk about them and they will come."

"What?"

"Agneta's accusing daughter, Loretta Keats, is at the front reception desk asking to see me."

"Get *out*."

He nodded and smiled. "I am about to get *out* to meet her. See you in Interview Room A in a few."

"I can't wait to see her in person." The files and papers sprawled across the table would be secure until we returned.

I leaned against the door of the interview room, holding it open for Smoke and Loretta Keats.

Loretta was in her mid-sixties and looked to me like she was on break from performing the duties of someone in a noble profession—or something equally important—to attend to personal business. Dressed in a business suit, she exuded confidence. Her eyes captured mine as she reached for my hand and gave it a firm, single shake. Her calming presence took me by surprise. After reading the statements she'd made after her mother's disappearance, I'd expected someone more irate, edgy.

We stepped into the room. When Smoke waved his hand at a chair, Loretta sat down. We took seats on the opposite side of the table.

"How can we help you, Miss Keats . . . Loretta?" Smoke said.

She drew in a long stream of air through her nostrils. “I’ve been thinking about this for two days, since I read about the bodies you found in Coyote Bog . . .”

Smoke laid his forearms on the table and leaned forward. “You wonder if one of the victims could be your mother?”

“She was never found.”

“That’s a fact.” Smoke paused. “You had some suspicions back then, about your brother in fact.”

She gathered another breath and lifted her chin, jutted it out slightly. “Lawrence was an addict. From the time he was a little kid really. He let chemicals, and gambling, and bed hopping control him, take over his life. He was usually desperate for money. A bad seed, like our father. The apple did *not* fall far from that tree.”

She shook her head a few times before going on. “My father and brother are the main reasons I never married. My father was not a good person but he somehow managed to trick my mother into believing he was. And she was a *smart* woman. The truth came out eventually.

“Lawrence’s primary weakness was gambling. I didn’t want to take the chance I’d marry someone who turned out to be like either one of them.” She brushed at nothing visible on the table. “Sorry, I got off track. To answer your question, yes. I thought my brother killed my mother because she stopped gifting him money.”

“The report said you thought your brother did it for the insurance money,” Smoke said.

“That’s what I thought at first, until I found out that the insurance company wouldn’t pay the claim because her body hadn’t been found. Until so many years had passed. Then I started thinking he killed her because he was mad at her. She’d given me her checking and savings account books a month or so before she disappeared. I wouldn't tell him where they were, as much as he tried to pry the information out of me." Her calm demeanor was slipping away.

"That must have aggravated him to no end. Did he hurt you or your mother, trying to persuade you?"

"No, thank God. I would have pressed charges, had him thrown in jail. And then Mom disappeared." A loud, anguished wail escaped her lips. The unexpected cry unnerved me, made my neck hairs stand on end.

Smoke cleared his throat, an involuntary response when he was caught off-guard. I'd witnessed it a handful of times over the years. He reached out and pushed a box of tissues closer to Loretta.

She pulled out two tissues in quick succession and patted her eyes and nose. "I'm sorry and embarrassed. If I'd known that was coming, I would have tried to stop it."

"There's no need to apologize. With all you've been through, you need to let it out." Smoke rested his hand on Loretta's wrist a moment. "Why don't we get back to why you're here."

She nodded. "I need to find out if my mother is . . . is . . . one of those people."

"Of course, and we can help you with that. As it turns out, we've been reviewing missing persons' files and your mother's is one we're looking at."

"So you *do* think my mother was one of the bodies you found?"

"At this point we just don't know, and we can't speculate. Not until we run DNA tests to prove or disprove that. We'll need a sample from you. The lab will run the tests, see if there's a match to one of them."

"Okay."

"I have a collection kit in my cubicle. We'll get it before you leave," Smoke said.

"Oh, is that how it works? My sisters and I thought we'd have to go to the medical examiner's office . . . you know, where *they* are."

"Have any of you mentioned this to your brother?" I said.

"We can't do that. He was killed in Las Vegas last year and they still haven't figured out who shot him. My sisters and I think it must have been someone he owed a lot of money to." She shrugged. "I don't feel as badly as I should about his death. I feel much worse about the way he lived than the way he died."

"Loretta, our sergeant has a photo of a pendant she'd like you to have a look at, see if you recognize it." Smoke said.

I found the photo in my phone and handed it over. Loretta raised her eyebrows and shook her head. "No, it doesn't look familiar at all."

"Okay," I said as she handed me the phone.

"**H**er family had some issues, huh?" I said after we'd gotten Loretta's sample and she was on her way.

"Major ones, at that." Smoke picked up Silas Petty's file and pulled out a sheet. "Back to the third—and last—reported disappearance we've got on an elderly person in the last decade."

"You think we should meet with Petty's brothers first, collect the DNA and then contact his sons and sister if there's a match?"

"That's what I said, but I wonder about the sons. Will they be angry if we keep them out of the loop a while?"

"Maybe so. You know, Smoke, I need to remind myself not to get overly optimistic for these families. We've had enough disappointments on cases when those hopes have come to naught."

"Yes, we have." Smoke picked up the office phone in the squad room and dialed Silas Petty's brother's number. He was talking to Warren in short order and gave him an overview of the events, from the discovery of the bodies to the ensuing investigation. After several minutes, he closed with, "Thank you," and hung up.

I'd picked up a lot of their conversation. "I can't believe he hasn't heard about the bog bodies."

"He and his wife have been at their daughter's house in South Dakota. They'll be back home tomorrow. He said his brother Richard is up north opening his cabin for the summer. And their sister is still in Iowa, although neither brother has a lot of contact with her."

"So we'll get Warren's DNA when he's home?" I said.

"Tomorrow afternoon is the plan. He'll talk to Richard but wants us to get a hold of Silas's sons, let them know what's going on."

"I heard that you verified their contact information."

"And I don't see a problem waiting until after we meet with Warren, collect his DNA, and then bring the boys in on this. We'll have one more step in the process to report to them." He glanced at his watch. "Meantime, as long as we're in a holding pattern here, let's make copies of the photos of the three victims, along with their doctors' names and contact info. We'll run Loretta Keats's sample over to the lab then stop by the M.E.'s office, deliver what we got, check on their progress."

17

After we'd submitted the DNA sample to the evidence technician at the Midwest Regional Laboratory, we headed to the medical examiner's office. When I stepped into the reception area, my eyes were drawn first to the tasteful art on the walls and then fell on the smiling receptionist. Smoke had phoned ahead so she expected us.

"Hello, Detectives. Doctor Patrick is in her office. I'll let her know you're here." She phoned the doctor then buzzed us into the inner area.

"Thanks," Smoke said as he opened the door for me. I led the way down the hallway.

Dr. Bridey Patrick's door was open. She had a pile of papers on the desk in front of her and waved us in with the pen she held. "Have a seat," she said.

As we settled onto the visitor chairs, Patrick reached over, selected three documents, and laid them out, side by side. "We've completed autopsies on the first three bodies found in the bog and, as it turns out, they have two things in common.

"All had Alzheimer's—at various stages. And we were not able to positively determine a manner of death in any of them."

Smoke leaned forward. "Why's that?"

"Aside from the brandings, the bodies showed no other signs of violence. No defensive wounds. The brandings were done post-mortem."

"Thank God," I said.

Patrick continued, "John Doe One showed signs of cirrhosis of the liver, however it was not marked. John Doe Two had small areas of calcified plaque in his aorta. Jane Doe One's gallbladder had been removed."

"The gallbladder removal is a good lead, could help narrow things down," Smoke said.

Patrick nodded. "Yes, it is. Aside from the conditions I mentioned, all three were relatively healthy given their advanced ages. That being said, we can only estimate— within a fairly broad range—how old they were at their times of death."

"You're saying anywhere from seventy to one hundred?" Smoke said.

"No two people age exactly the same, of course. In older adults we see degenerative changes in the joints, spines, and bone tissue. The external aging differences we observe among individuals can be applied to what we see internally as well. I've been surprised to learn a healthy, spry older person is ninety when she looks not a day past seventy. And vice versa."

Smoke nodded. "You got a point, Doc."

"Doctor Patrick, we looked at the missing persons' files going back ten years and Winnebago County has records on three elderly folks who were never found: a male, one year ago, another male three years ago, and a female four years ago." I pulled copies of the files from my briefcase and handed them to her.

She studied each face in the photos. "These will be helpful, if it turns out they're three of our decedents. I can't say they are the ones we've autopsied. We need to enlarge the photos, take measurements. The contact information for their doctors and dentists are good resources, too."

"We've spoken with family members of all three and collected DNA samples from two so far, and we'll get the third one tomorrow," Smoke said.

"Very good. We'll see if their DNA matches any of the victims. If not, you may need to go back another decade or more in your files," Patrick said.

"There's also the possibility the victims were not from Winnebago County," I said.

"That is a distinct possibility. In that case, we'll enlist the services of the forensic anthropologist to help determine their ages to broaden the search. And you'd check with other counties in Minnesota, of course."

"We would." Smoke rubbed the back of his neck. "Doc, back to the cause and manner of their deaths. What is your unofficial opinion?"

"It's not conclusive, but it's possible they were suffocated. Suffocation leaves no marks. All three had degrees of bloodshot eyes, a telltale sign of suffocation and asphyxia. However, as part of the aging process, bloodshot eyes are not uncommon among the elderly. Even if we were able to determine that they died of asphyxia, it's possible it was accidental."

"You don't believe that, Doc," Smoke said.

"What I know is that we could not rule, with conviction, the deaths weren't natural, or accidental, or homicides, or suicides. That leaves us with undetermined."

"Natural, suicides? What are you saying? Someone branded them and threw them in a damn swamp!" Smoke said.

"Branded *after* death. Each one had Alzheimer's. Perhaps they'd decided they didn't want to put their families through all that their disease might entail and heard of someone who would help them commit suicide. Not knowing what would happen to their bodies."

"That's a big stretch, Doc."

"I agree."

"What would be your accidental scenario?" Smoke said.

She shrugged. "They were staying in a house where the furnace failed, filled the air with carbon monoxide, and they were asphyxiated."

"More of a stretch. How about the natural ruling?"

"Perhaps someone was caring for them, and after they passed, he branded them. And then improperly, and illegally, disposed of their bodies."

Smoke shook his head. "Where do you come up with this stuff?"

"We've had cases with similar circumstances to the first examples I gave. Not ending with seven elderly people found close to others in a bog, of course. Keep in mind we don't know who these people are, nor do we know how long they were in the bog. As I said at the scene, it could be as long ago as sixty years," Patrick said.

"True," Smoke said.

"You're free to take the weight plate and cord that was attached to Jane Doe One so your office can investigate. Also, our preliminary reports of all three. We'll send the sleepwear to the regional crime lab for testing, but it's unlikely they'll be able to collect any useful evidence from them, in my opinion," Dr. Patrick said.

"I agree. Sergeant Doug Matsen in our crime lab can track down when and where the cord and the weight were manufactured, where they were sold," Smoke said.

"We have the names of the doctors—and the dentists—of two of our missing persons, Oscar Wright and Agneta Keats. Shall we contact them and run the medical conditions by them, ask if either had what you found? We'll get DNA from Silas Petty's brother tomorrow, ask for the names of his doctor and dentist then," I said.

"That'd be fine. When we've completed all seven autopsies and have the DNA reports from the lab comparing the victims with the known family members, that will give us positive identification. Or not. Dental and medical records would verify the findings."

We followed Patrick to a room where the items were packaged and marked. Smoke put them in a box and carried it to his car.

I opened the trunk for him. "I'll get this stuff checked into evidence when we get back. Hopefully Doug can come up with some answers," I said.

"Good deal. Man, this is only day three, and it seems like we've been on this case for weeks."

"I think it's all the worry over Jaxson Kenner. And his father."

"You're probably right about that," he said.

We drove without chatting for miles. My thoughts jumped from Jaxson and his family, to Sawyer and his family, to Bob

Edberg and his mother, to getting positive identifications on those found in the bog. And then to Smoke, and what our future together looked like.

Smoke shifted in his seat. "I viewed the tapes from the Oak Lea High School parking lot fight."

"Did it match the report?"

"It did. Jaxson wasn't solely at fault, but he made a bad choice when he struck Sawyer like that. He packed a punch and Sawyer went down hard."

"Given the circumstances, with the eyewitness accounts and the tape to back it up, they'll likely reduce the charges to second degree manslaughter," I said.

"Likely to, yes."

"I wonder when the sheriff will return to work."

"All the personal agony the family is going through aside, Kenner's in a tough predicament. He's the chief law enforcement officer in the county and his son faces felony charges," Smoke said.

"I suppose there'll be some citizens who'll ask him to resign."

"No doubt."

Smoke pulled into the department parking lot seconds before his phone rang. He looked at the phone's face and raised his eyebrows. "It's the sheriff." He managed to pull off an upbeat voice when he answered. "Hello, Mike. . . . *What*? . . . Corky and I will be right over."

My heart picked up its pace before he disconnected. "Tell me."

"Jaxson ran away and Sheriff wants me to find him."

"Oh, no."

The Kenners lived in Oak Lea and Smoke drove the three miles in a flash. Mike Kenner opened the front door of his sixties-vintage rambler and pulled us inside. He looked like he'd run a marathon. Red faced with sweat rolling down his head and neck, damp tee-shirt. His wife, April, was sitting on the living room couch with her head in her hands. She looked up when she heard us come in. Her eyes were nearly swollen shut and her face and neck were flushed.

I went over to her and offered some comfort by giving her a warm hug. She cried even harder.

"We don't know what to do. I'm going to have to report him as fleeing from justice if we don't locate him ASAP," Mike said.

"How do you know he ran away?" Smoke said.

Mike retrieved a piece of paper from a side table and handed it to Smoke. "His note says so."

I moved within a couple of feet of Smoke and read, I'M SORRY FOR EVERYTHING. TELL SAYWER'S PARENTS THAT. PLEASE. I CAN'T STAND THE THOUGHT OF GOING TO PRISON SO I NEED TO START A NEW LIFE SOMEWHERE. The note wasn't addressed to anyone and wasn't signed.

"Did he take one of your vehicles?" Smoke asked.

"No," Kenner said.

"Where would he go?" Smoke asked.

"We don't know. Somewhere he can walk to, unless someone picked him up. I don't want the world to know about this until we can figure something out. If we call his friends, they'll know something's up and word will spread faster than a rushing river."

Smoke laid a hand on his shoulder. "Mike, you need to start there. You don't have to say much, just that you're wondering if they've seen Jaxson today, if they've talked to him, know where he might be."

"He wouldn't see any of his friends after he got out of jail. He holed up in his room and refused to face them," Mike said.

"He may have changed his mind, needed help from one or more of them," I said.

"Do you know what he took with him?" Smoke said.

"It's what he didn't take that has us worried most. He left his *phone* behind. But he took his iPad, along with a big, black camping backpack, some clothes, his hiking boots, rain gear," Mike said.

"What about money? Does he have access to any?" Smoke said

Mike rubbed his hands on his cheeks. "I'm not thinking straight. I never thought to call the bank to see if he withdrew money from his savings. I'll do that now."

When Kenner left the room, I sat down beside April again and Smoke took a seat in an armchair. I looked up at the photos on the wall, a picture-perfect smiling family of five engaged in a variety of activities: horseback riding in the Rocky Mountains, hiking on a Northern Minnesota trail, canoeing in the Boundary Waters Canoe Area.

April was naturally quiet, a trait that complemented her gregarious spouse's personality. But she was ready to talk. "People always say, 'I never imagined this could happen to me,' when something bad happens. I felt sorry for them when I'd hear their stories. And now, here we are, faced with one of the worst things imaginable. We have a big black cloud over our family and we don't know how to make it go away."

Smoke reached over and laid his hand on hers. "It's about impossible to imagine how that cloud will lift, but it will.

Someday. It might take a while. You're good people and you'll get through this together. With as much help as you need from your friends."

Tears rolled down April's cheeks as she tried to smile.

"Is there anything in particular you need, like driving your daughter where she needs to be, or maybe I can do some grocery shopping for you?" I said. Their oldest son was away at an eastern college.

"Not that I can think of right now, but thanks."

Mike came back into the living room. New beads of sweat had broken through his pores. "Jaxson withdrew eleven thousand dollars from his account."

"*No*," April said.

"That's a lot of money for a teen to have," Smoke said.

"He's always been a good saver. Plus, he worked the last two summers and liked to watch his account grow."

April's voice cracked when she spoke. "And now he's using it for his getaway."

"What are the conditions of his release?" Smoke said.

"The usual. That he remain law-abiding, not use drugs or alcohol, and not leave the state," Mike said.

"Mike, have you looked at his phone, checked it for recent calls?"

"Yes, the ones that he got today, but they all show up as missed calls. So he didn't take any calls, or phone anyone."

"May I have a look-see?" Smoke said.

Mike retrieved it from the dining table and handed it to Smoke. "His passcode is J-A-X-1-8-0."

"Thanks." Smoke pushed buttons and scrolled through both incoming and outgoing calls and text messages. He pulled the memo pad and pen from his breast pocket, sat down at the table, and started to write things down. Mike, April, and I took seats at the table and watched him work. "You're right, no outgoing calls or messages from Jaxson today, and several calls and texts he didn't answer. But a number of exchanges with friends yesterday. I count eight friends. He's had the most communication with Ava, but they aren't romantic messages. Does he have a special girlfriend?"

"No. Ava is one of his best friends, but they haven't dated. As far as his phone is concerned, our rule is his mother and I can look at his messages if we feel it's warranted. And as rebellious as he's been at times, he watches what he posts. I know he Snapchats, and those images disappear after you send them, and messages are gone in twenty-four hours."

"Actually, the messages don't completely disappear. They're hidden deep in the devices. A digital forensics examiner could find them," I said.

"I guess I should have known that," Mike said.

"The school resource officers talked about it. That's how I first found out," I said.

"If we need to dig deeper into his snaps, we can. Back to his friends. I don't see a single message that mentions Jaxson running away. Maybe he had a phone conversation with someone yesterday. I want you to call all the contacts in his phone, see if they know where he is."

Mike grimaced. "I don't know—"

"I respect that you want to keep this quiet, but if we can locate Jaxson before he leaves the state—if that's what he planned to do—he'll be in far less trouble. If it turns out none of his friends know where he is, I'd put out a statewide Attempt to Locate," Smoke said.

"How can this be happening?" April said.

"Where does Joseph go to college, again?" Smoke said. Joseph was their older son, a straight A student majoring in engineering.

"Brown University in Rhode Island." Ivy League.

"That's right. Does he know Jaxson left? Would Jaxson go to his brother?" Smoke said.

Mike shook his head. "No, to both questions. You know they've had their struggles. And Joseph wouldn't harbor a fugitive, not even his brother. It would go against his straight-as-an-arrow grain."

"How about other relatives, friends he's met at camp?"

Mike shrugged. "We'll make those phone calls. April, will you be able to help me?"

She wiped her nose and nodded.

"Smoke and Corky, this will take a while, so go take care of what you need to on the bog case. I'll let you know what we find out and we'll take it from there."

18

Mama and Rufus

"**M**ama, on the news they're still talking about the people we buried," Rufus said.

"I think it's best not to watch the news, Son."

His eyebrows squeezed together. "But what if someone saw us?"

"No one did because we were very careful. I kept my eyes on you every minute, from a safe distance. You always took care of the burials nice and fast. That's my boy. If someone had seen you they would have told the sheriff."

"Okay."

"I'm not worried about this and you shouldn't, either. But there is something important I need to remind you about. If anyone talks to you, you must remember not to use your given name. Do you remember that, Rufus?"

"I ′member."

"That's good. You're a faithful son and I don't know what I'd do without you."

"I don't know what I'd do without you, Mama."

Mama put her arms around her son and laid her head on his chest. That always calmed his fears.

19

On the way back to the office, I said, "As awful as all this is for them, it seems like Mike and April felt a tad better after you gave them that assignment. Something concrete to do. Plus, one of the phone calls might help find their son."

Smoke tapped the steering wheel a few times with the heel of his hand. "Jaxson needs a Come-to-Jesus meeting for all the hell he's putting his parents through."

"I think he's had a few of those meetings over the years. The extra sting is, he was in serious-enough trouble and now he's just dug himself a deeper hole."

"Mike said he wasn't thinking straight, and I have to agree. When he asked me to search for Jaxson, it was like a friend who was asking for a simple favor. And it's not simple by any stretch of the imagination. I'm happy to do what I can within the parameters of the law. But with the charges Jaxson faces, I'm doing nothing on the QT."

"You're right. If Jaxson isn't reported missing, using department resources for a private search is unethical and likely illegal," I said.

"Yep, as much as I'd like to help my friend and his family, that's not the way to do it."

It was closing in on 4:30, quitting time for office personnel in the sheriff's and other county departments. Smoke and I carried in the weight and cord recovered from the first autopsied female victim. We filled out the information on the evidence tags and put them in a locker. Then I followed Smoke to his cubicle and sat down.

He glanced at his watch. "A little too late to check in with Mister Wright's and Missus Keats's medical doctors. Remind me when we meet with Warren Petty tomorrow, to find out who Silas went to."

"Sure. What time was he coming in?"

"Nine."

"I feel like I should be doing more work on the investigation while we wait to hear back from Kenner," I said.

"Sergeant Aleckson, your shift officially ended almost two hours ago so why don't you take off. Remember what you said about resources and our limited supply. I'll call as soon as I hear from the sheriff," Smoke said.

"Okay." I wanted to ask Smoke if I'd see him later, if he'd come to my house, if he'd invite me to his, but it wasn't the right time or place to discuss our personal life. I stood, gave him what I hoped was a reassuring smile, and lifted my hand in a wave as I left.

Queenie was more than ready to get out of her kennel, and after she lavished me with kisses, took off after a squirrel. As fast as Queenie was, squirrels were great escape artists and it was high up the tree before Queenie reached the base. I watched her run then called her in.

When she had fresh food and water, I ran upstairs, shed my uniform, and changed into jeans and a tee-shirt. "Well, girl, how about we take a ride? It's been a few days since we visited Gramps and I know he misses you."

Queenie followed me into the garage, and I opened the door of my classic red 1967 Pontiac GTO. She jumped in the backseat and we headed to Gramps' house. He sat in his favorite chair watching the early news. His face brightened when Queenie ran over to greet him. I was close behind with a kiss.

"Two of my favorite girls," he said.

"How's it going, Gramps?"

"Good, good. Your mother is bringing dinner over when she gets done with work. She sure spoils me."

"She loves cooking, especially for you."

We talked for a bit. Then a chill ran through me when thoughts of the bodies recovered from Coyote Bog filled my mind. Victims at the M.E.'s Office, a number who still awaited autopsy. It struck me that someone had victimized vulnerable elderly men and women, in varying stages of Alzheimer's, the same disease that took my gram. What kind of a person did that, and why?

Smoke phoned as we left Gramps' house. "Kenner just called, said they talked to each contact in Jaxson's phone, but no one had seen him or talked to him today."

"That supports what you found in his phone. So now what?"

"After some persuasion, I convinced the sheriff to get an Attempt to Locate out. He agreed to contact Communications, so they'll have Jaxson's height, weight, other details to put in it. I didn't get into it with Mike, but we don't know the boy's state of mind. I'm concerned that if he feels trapped, he might do something foolish."

"That crossed my mind," I said.

"I'm on my way back to their place to see if we can come up with some possible destinations, start checking them. It'll be dark in a couple of hours and that'll make it more of a challenge."

"Anything I can do?"

"Check on Rex?" he said.

"How about I bring him to my house?"

"That works. Catch you later." If he meant that literally, it sounded like a fun promise to look forward to.

I wasn't sure if Rex was happier to see Queenie or get freed from his kennel, but the two of them ran around until I called out, "Car." I barely had the seat pushed forward in my two-door before they hopped in. "We're taking a little detour before we head home."

I turned west on County Road 35 and followed it to County Road 7. The road construction equipment was at rest on the side of the road, ready to be fired up again in the morning. I turned south on 7, did a U-turn, and pulled onto the shoulder. The dogs whined. "Hey guys, I just need to sit here for a bit."

I had driven by Coyote Bog nearly every day in my years on the job and tried to grasp the fact that bodies had been laid to rest there, not far off a well-traveled county road. For how many years? Again, what would possess someone to bury his victims at that site?

My eyes swept over the area. How had a person deposited the bodies into the bog? Perhaps he floated each one out on an inflatable raft, deflated it, and as the body sank, pulled the raft back to shore. One possibility. Whatever the method, it'd have to be done in the middle of the night when the people on the road were few and far between. But it was still a risk. Deputies were on patrol twenty-four hours a day.

My eyes traveled to the house on the hill, up from the bog. Anyone from that vantage point would have a bird's eye view of the area. But they'd have to be looking out at the right time. And if they'd seen anything suspicious, they should have reported it. Right? Rex whimpered and Queenie joined in. "Okie doke, we'll get you home."

As I shifted into gear, a silver four-door car rolled to a stop at the end of Floyd Myren's driveway. I hadn't seen it parked near the house. And since most of the drive was lined with trees, I didn't spot it until it was almost at County Road 35. Was it the person who kept an eye on the house?

"Hang on, my furry friends." I whipped the car around to face south and drove a half mile to County Road 107, the appointed detour road. I turned west and speeded up, hoping I'd meet the house checker and get her license plate number. When I reached County Road 6, it was obvious I'd lost her. "Well, I had to try."

The dogs barked, alerting me Smoke was home. I was in the kitchen, and they beat me to the door. After they got a moment of his attention, I stretched my arms around him and felt the tension locked in his tight muscles. I rubbed his shoulder areas to loosen them a bit. "You had another long day. It's after eight."

"No doubt. We got things rolling on the search for Jaxson so that's good. Speaking of good, can you keep that up for about an hour?" He dipped his head and found my lips for an inviting kiss.

"Have you eaten yet?"

"I must have had lunch, but what it was escapes me at the moment," he said.

"There's leftover meatloaf and pasta salad."

"That will hit the spot just fine."

"You relax and I'll have it ready in a minute." As I pulled the dishes out of the refrigerator, Smoke reached around me and grabbed a beer. He sat at the breakfast bar counter sipping on it while the meatloaf warmed in the microwave. Then I set the warmed plate and cold pasta salad in front of him.

I wanted all the details on the search for Jaxson, but he needed to eat first. Instead I told him, "I was on Country Road Seven earlier and saw a silver car leave Floyd Myren's driveway. It looked like it could be a Chevy Cruze or a Ford Focus, but I couldn't tell from that distance. I figured it was the person who checks on his house. I hoped she'd come my direction so I could get an ID from her plate. But she took another route."

"You're awfully curious about her."

"She's the one who must have Floyd Myren's contact info. Myren's lived out there for years and he may have seen something happen at Coyote Bog late at night that struck him as odd. Maybe thought he should report it but didn't. Like a lot of other people."

Smoke pushed his empty plate away and leaned forward with his arms crossed on the counter. "Since Mister Myren comes home for the summer, he should be back any time now."

"He should. Most of the snowbirds I know are home by the end of April, but some wait till June when they're more assured of warm weather."

"Yep. Well, the search for Jaxson officially started late this afternoon. The Attempt to Locate went out. Mike called the county attorney, gave him the scoop. And sent an email to everyone in the sheriff's office."

"I haven't checked mine since I got home," I said.

"He also sent a message marked 'important' to the other eighty-six sheriffs in the state."

"With your help, huh?"

"Yeah, he's really struggling. We brainstormed about where Jaxson might go. Since he likes hiking in the woods and camping out, that was in the message to the other sheriffs—a request to check the county and state parks in their counties. And we've got deputies looking in all our parks," Smoke said.

"It's warm enough, so he doesn't have to worry about freezing if he plans on camping. He's got plenty of money to last a while."

"I spoke with Greyhound Bus Company in Minneapolis, sent them Jaxson's photo via email and asked them to be on the lookout for him. They agreed to pass on the info to their drivers. And I stressed that if they see him, they are not to confront him. Just give us a call and tell us where he's headed. We can get an officer to meet him at his stop."

"You got a lot done in a few short hours. I hope one of those contacts has a lead for the Kenners soon," I said.

"The air is so thick in the Kenner household you could cut it with a knife. Their daughter is staying with a friend. I think the stress is too much for her. Mike and April finally worked up the courage to phone their parents to tell them the latest downer. I left when they were talking to them."

I went behind Smoke, laid my head on his shoulder, and slid my hands around to his chest. "Smoke, how are you holding up? I know you always think you should be doing one more thing, or ten more things, during an investigation."

"I won't lie. I'm very worried about Jaxson and his family. Especially Mike. Besides the personal trauma, his career is on the line."

"He's been popular with the people in the county. You think they'll blame him for what his son did?" I said.

"I think it's more that Mike might feel he can't continue on as sheriff."

"Wow, not good. He's young, what forty-five?"

"Forty-six. I hope things will straighten out, but the Kenner family is in a bad place any way you look at it," Smoke said.

I did some deep tissue massage on the top of Smoke's shoulders, working my hands down to his shoulder blades. "Smoke, you told me we have to talk about our future. I know we've got a lot going on right now, but we always seem to have a lot going on."

Smoke turned around on the barstool to face me and took my hands in his. "Corinne, I have never lied to you. Although I wasn't always completely honest for some time about how deeply I love you."

"Why do I think there's a 'but' in what you're about to say?"

He kissed one palm and then the other. "There's not a 'but'. We're committed to each other and will officially tie the knot someday. Will you wait for me until I can do that?"

That was the last thing I expected him to say. *Wait for him until he can do that?* I wanted to cry, to run upstairs, to escape somewhere so I didn't have to answer such a conflicted-sounding question. What did "someday" mean? I took a step back. "Are you saying you're not ready to get married?"

He shook his head. "I don't know. I wish I knew, but I can't seem to get past the embedded fear that I'll somehow ruin your life. That you'd be happier with someone else."

That unfounded fear had reared its ugly head yet again. "Elton Dawes, my life would be empty without you. I don't know what more to say to put your heart and mind at ease. Falling in love, getting married, is a leap of faith. No one knows what the future holds, so we need to make the best of what we have today."

The corners of his mouth lifted slightly. "Are you sure you're not the wise elder between the two of us here? I know in my heart you're right. I just need to believe in my mind that you are."

I willed myself not to be impatient. "Take the time you need."

He buried his face in my neck. "I love you."

20

Warren Petty arrived ahead of our scheduled meeting time. He and Smoke were talking when I joined them in a conference room. "Sergeant Corinne Aleckson, Warren Petty."

Petty was a striking man with a neatly-trimmed white mustache and a full head of snow-white hair. He had a dark tan, maybe from a recent tropical vacation or golfing in Arizona. We shook hands and I took a seat next to Smoke.

"Warren and I had just started going over his brother's case," Smoke said.

"It's been a long three years. In fact, Monday, the day you got the bodies out of the bog, was the anniversary of the day he disappeared. Something like this can tear a family apart," Petty said.

"A sad fact," Smoke said.

Petty shared some memories of his brother then shook his head and sniffed a few times in quick succession. "Well, I guess I came here to give you a DNA sample."

Smoke withdrew the kit from his pocket and pulled out the buccal swab. He held it up. “Open your mouth and I’ll collect it with this.” A five-second task.

“I don’t know how they can run those tests from just a little spit,” Petty said.

“Science has come a long way during my career and every year they find better ways to do things with better results,” Smoke said.

“Mister Petty, I want you to take a look at this, see if you recognize it.” I found the cross pendant photo in my phone and handed it over.

Petty studied it and shrugged. “No, I don’t recall ever seeing it before.”

“It wasn’t something your brother owned?”

“No, he wasn’t a guy that wore jewelry. If he did, it wouldn’t be a crucifix. We’re Presbyterian and it’s mostly Catholics that wear them, if I’m not mistaken.”

I nodded then put my phone back in its holder. “Another question. We met with the medical examiner yesterday. They’ve completed autopsies on two of the male victims. One had cirrhosis of the liver and the other had calcified plaque on his heart. Do you know if your brother had either one of those conditions?”

It took a minute for him to answer. “No, I sure don’t. I don’t think so, not that he ever said.”

“Okay, we’ll check with his doctor. Do you have the name of his medical provider?” I said.

“Doctor Miller. Right here in Oak Lea, at the clinic.”

“And his dentist?”

“Doctor Crown—and I’m not kidding—at the Oak Lea Dental Group.”

His side comment made me smile. “Thanks. Dental records are often used in identifications, but medical conditions are another identifier. When we get the DNA results back for comparison, that will give us conclusive answers. We’ll find out if you’re a match to one of the victims,” I said.

“I’m hoping I am. Not that we want Silas to be one of the victims. But we want the *conclusive* answers you just talked about, Sergeant,” Petty said.

Smoke leaned in closer to Petty. “I’ll give your nephews a call, let them know about the bodies recovered from the bog, that we’ve reopened missing persons’ cases from the past decade. I’ll tell them I contacted you and requested that you provide a DNA sample.”

“Appreciate that. When my brother disappeared, we had a lot of mudslinging. Haven’t been able to mend the fences yet.”

“That’s not uncommon when tragedy strikes. Thanks for coming in, Warren. I hope we can get the answers your family needs to mend those fences,” Smoke said.

“Me, too,” Petty said.

Smoke escorted him out and I waited in the corridor until he returned.

“I want to get this sample to the crime lab, a-sap. These families have been in limbo far too long,” he said.

“As much as we’re counting on three of the bog bodies being our missing persons, and giving the families some closure, we have to be careful not to get overly hopeful, so it doesn’t cloud our judgment.”

“We always need to be on the lookout for that.”

“And why we rely on science for answers,” I said.

“Yep. Game plan strategy: I’ll see who’s available to run this sample to the lab. Will you check with the doctors, ask about the medical conditions? It shouldn't be an issue, given you're requesting it for missing persons' cases. And they'll know their patients went missing."

"Sure thing."

"I'll check with other counties starting with our neighbors, see if they've had elderly folks go missing in the last twenty years."

"After I make the calls and finish some paperwork, I'll join you."

"Copy that, Sergeant."

I spoke with administrators from the three medical facilities. One hesitated giving the information until I convinced her I wasn't asking for complete medical records. My request was to determine whether their patient had a condition Dr. Patrick found at autopsy.

While I waited for answers about the medical conditions, I worked on overdue performance reviews for the deputies I supervised.

All three clinics got back to me with answers in less than an hour. Agneta Keats still had her gallbladder. And neither Oscar Wright nor Silas Petty had cirrhosis of the liver or calcified plaque on the heart.

The letdown I felt forced me to eat the words I'd given Smoke a short time before. We needed to be careful not to get overly hopeful.

I found Smoke in his cubicle bent over dozens of papers strewn across his desk. He finished a phone call, pulled the readers from his nose, and vigorously rubbed his face with both hands.

"What?" I said.

"Have a look." He handed me a sheet of paper with all the county sheriffs' departments in the state listed. About a fourth of them were marked.

"You got a hold of all these already?"

"Yep. The checks are by the ones I've talked to. After our neighboring counties, I moved to the next tier. 'No' means there are no still-missing elderly persons in the last twenty years. Some were two-minute conversations because they didn't have any. And 'Yes' is obvious. I have those detailed on this sheet." He handed it over.

I sat down to read. "Hmm. One from Sherburne. Female, Mildred Dryer, age seventy-seven disappeared May fifteenth, five years ago. Another one in May?"

"You got it. Keep reading."

"Two from Meeker. A male and a female. Horace Kline, age eighty-one, disappeared *May* thirteenth, seven years ago. And Gloria Freiburg, age seventy-five, disappeared *May* eleventh, six years ago. Dang."

"Both counties are scanning the files and will email them over."

"If—and it's a wishful *if*—these folks are three of the bog bodies, and it turns out those missing from our county are another three, that would account for six of the seven bodies," I said.

"Since we share borders with Sherburne and Meeker, it makes sense the bad guy would use the same burial ground. They'll review the files, locate next of kin, and get the doctors' and dentists' names for their records," Smoke said.

"Six disappearances in May over the course of seven years is not a coincidence."

"You got that right." Smoke glanced at his watch. "It might take a while before we get those scanned files. Meantime, you want to work on the southern counties, starting with Watonwan?"

"Sure." I picked up the list. "I'll be in the sergeants' office."

"Thanks."

I contacted the thirty counties on my list by phone in little more than two hours. Some of the smaller, more rural, counties had older computer systems and a search was more cumbersome than for those with newer systems. Verifying the records was a formality in most cases because each county had staff who knew if they had a missing person that disappeared under questionable circumstances and was never found. From time to time, sheriffs reopened cold cases with the hope someone would come forward, or new evidence would be uncovered that cracked the cases.

"We had an elderly couple who seemed to vanish eight or so years ago, but they turned up a week later in Florida," one chief deputy told me.

The Blue Earth County Sheriff reported, "Yes, a man by the name of Hiram Scranton disappeared right around six years ago. Let me search the records, get the details for you." It took him a minute. "Here it is. Went missing on April fifth. Family said he was home one evening and gone the next morning when they went to check on him."

He cleared his throat and continued, "No sign of foul play. All of his family members and close friends checked out fine and were eliminated as suspects of any wrongdoing. Mister Scranton lived about a quarter mile from the Minnesota River and it was feared he made his way down there and drowned. We combed the river, sent in divers, but never found his body."

"That's sad. Would you mind sending us the case file? Like I explained, we have seven bodies to identify and it's possible he's one of the victims."

"I can do that, no problem. It'd be a real help to us if it turns out one is Hiram. After all this time, the family has lost all hope he's alive."

I gave him my email address and we disconnected. The difference between Hiram Scranton and the other suspected victims was he had disappeared in April, not in May. But that didn't automatically eliminate him from the list.

I found Smoke in the break room getting a cup of coffee from a vending machine. "Any luck so far?" he said.

"Maybe. A man from Blue Earth County disappeared in April, six years ago. They're sending me his file."

"April, huh? Could be. How far away is that, about sixty miles?"

"About that," I said.

"How many counties left on your list?"

"All done."

"Good deal. Same here. I got one more to add to the list of potentials, too. In Mille Lacs County, a woman disappeared in March, eleven years ago. I'll get that file, too."

"If one of the missing women from our county is not one of the three found in the bog, then I guess it's a possibility."

"I talked to Special Agent Kent Erley earlier about our case, asked his opinion of who we need to look for. Where to start looking for our bad guy." Erley was an FBI criminal profiler we'd consulted on a previous serial killer case.

"Cool, what'd he say?"

"He'd work up a criminal investigative analysis, a profile, and get back to me," Smoke said.

"We know it's someone with a very sick mind, so it'll be good to get his expert opinion."

"Yep." Smoke shook his head. "We got this big case going, trying to ID seven bodies and figure out who put them in Coyote, and I'm torn about where to focus my efforts."

"What do you mean?"

"I feel like I should be searching for Jaxson."

"Smoke, every sheriff's office and police department in the state is looking for him."

"I know, I know. And our deputies are combing every inch of the county. But for all we know he could be in Ohio or Oregon by now," he said.

"How about Oklahoma? With no cell phone number to trace, no credit card transactions to track down, it's tough."

Smoke's cell phone buzzed. "Dawes. . . . What's the name again?" He handed me his cup of coffee and pulled out a pad and pen. "Address and phone number? And description of the vehicle." He jotted down notes. "Can you send that out statewide, and to our deputies? . . . Thanks."

"Speaking of Jaxson?"

Smoke's grin brightened his face. "That was Communications. Jaxson bought a 2000 Ford Escort from a private party in Dellwood this morning. Paid cash, of course."

"He hadn't left Winnebago County as of this morning?"

"Guess not. But I'd say the chances that he's still here are slim to none. The person reporting caught the news a little while ago and when he saw Jaxson's face, he recognized him as his car buyer. At least now we know how he's traveling, what he's driving."

"Did Communications notify the sheriff yet?" I said.

"No. I'll give him a ring after I talk to the PR. Let's head to my desk." I held onto Smoke's coffee and passed it over after he'd sat down. "I think I'm gonna need this." He took a few sips, set it on the only cleared spot on his desk, and dialed the number he'd written on his notepad.

"Dan Greeley? . . . Detective Elton Dawes, Winnebago County Sheriff's Office. Thanks for calling in the tip on Jaxson Kenner. . . . How did he happen to buy your vehicle? . . . Do you have the number he called you from? Good." Smoke wrote it down. "What time did he leave your house? . . . Did you notice which way he headed, east, west? . . . Good deal. I appreciate your help, Dan." Smoke gave Greeley his phone number in case he thought of anything else and hung up.

"Seems like a fine young man," he said. "Greeley said Jaxson headed east on State Highway Twelve. Whether he plans to hide in the Twin Cities or keep right on going is the question. In any case, he's had a five-hour head start. I'll let Communications know his direction of travel before I call Mike."

Smoke put the call on speaker phone. My heart picked up its beat when the sheriff was on the line. Smoke relayed the latest information then Kenner dropped a bombshell, his voice quiet and shaky. "Jaxson must have taken the Smith and Wesson M and P pistol I keep in a locked dresser drawer for April, in case she ever needs it. Never told the kids it was there, didn't even cross my mind to check on it. Then it was like someone whispered in my ear. I looked and it was gone. I don't know how he found the key."

Smoke silently mouthed, “Damn.”

“We’re beside ourselves, sick with worry over what might happen next.”

Smoke pinched the area between his eyebrows. “Jaxson’s been through gun safety training, hasn’t he?” Smoke said.

“Sure, when he was twelve.”

“Good to know.” He paused then added, “We need to tell the agencies looking for him about the gun and alert the FBI, in case he’s crossed state lines. I’ll handle that.”

Kenner’s voice cracked. “None of this seems real.”

21

Mama and Rufus

Rufus stood by, watching his mother make beef and cheese sandwiches for their lunch. She put three on a plate and handed it to him.

"Thanks, Mama." She made him do things he didn't like, but she took good care of him and fed him well.

"Well, Son, I still have my sights on the three patients I told you about, the ones who are more than ready to start their heavenly journey. The time is closing in and the date is coming up soon of when one must go. I'm still trying to decide if we shouldn't send all three."

"Mama, you've never done that before. One at a time. One a year."

"I know that, Rufus. That's been the plan, but everything changed this week when they stole those who were waiting in the bog until it was time for them to be taken up."

That didn't make sense to Rufus. He thought when Mama made him put the patients in the bog they were already on their way to Heaven. He'd finished one sandwich but had lost his appetite and slid his plate aside.

"Son, you can't be full, already? One sandwich isn't enough for you to keep up your strength."

Rufus was full up to his chin and didn't care one little bit about his strength.

22

Smoke drove his pen into a stack of papers on his desk.

"I'll make the call," I phoned Communications, let them know Jaxson was likely carrying a gun and asked them to pass the information to other county sheriffs, state agencies, and police departments in Minnesota.

"I have a bad feeling about how this is going down. Jaxson's a fugitive from justice and now come to find out he's likely armed besides," Smoke said.

"I've had a pain in my side since Sheriff told us about the gun. It's gotta be terrorizing for them."

"No doubt about that. I'll give Sam Magnus, the FBI agent I know at the Minneapolis office, a call. With Jaxson in their national system, we'll have a better chance of tracking him down."

"Contacting the FBI twice in one day, for different reasons, is a first. Sheriff's right, none of this seems real," I said.

Smoke was speaking with Special Agent Magnus when my cell phone buzzed. Bob Edberg. I stepped out of his cubicle to answer. "Hey, Bob, what's up?"

"Sergeant, I got home from work and checked the video equipment. The health aide that was here today was snooping around in my mother's bedroom. Looking in her drawers, her closet. She's one of the regulars, one my mother really likes."

"Did she take anything?"

"Not that I know of. I planted a hundred dollar bill in a dresser drawer and it was still there. It looked like she was rearranging things in Mom's underwear and pajama drawers. I kept thinking she was going to get something for my mother to change into, but she didn't."

"That does seem odd. I'd feel creeped out if someone went through my personal things for no good reason."

"I do, for my mother's sake. My first reaction was that I should call the agency, tell them I don't want her to come back, and why. But the more I thought about it I wondered if I should let it go for now, watch to see if she does something else," Edberg said.

"You said your mother likes her. Do you think she's taking good care of her?"

"I do. She plays board games with her, reads to her, feeds her a good lunch, seems attentive. When I'm in the area, I stop at home on my lunch breaks, see how things are going. I've met Melody—that's her name—several times. She's getting up there in years, wears orthopedic shoes for some sort of foot issue, but seems capable enough."

"As long as she can outrun your mom."

Bob chuckled. "I think she can."

"I'm not sure how to advise you, Bob. The thing is, Melody could have taken the money and didn't."

"And if she had, it'd be a no-brainer. We'd charge her."

"Let me ask you this, who does your mother's laundry?

"I do."

"If you want to question Melody, without tipping her off about the cameras, you could make a comment that your mother's things were moved around in her drawers and see how she responds, what she says."

"That's an idea. She may have a good reason, other than she was snooping around."

"Bob, change of subject, we got some info on Jaxson. You should get the alert on your devices any minute."

"What is it?"

"Two things: he bought a car in Dellwood this morning. And Sheriff discovered a pistol he had hidden is missing."

"Lord almighty."

Smoke had finished his conversation with Special Agent Magnus and stared straight ahead, tapping his pen. "A damn fugitive from justice."

"What did Magnus say?"

"He'd get a Be-On-The-Lookout to other states. Troopers are as likely as other agencies to spot him on state highways. More likely on interstates. They'll see if they can track his location through his phone, although it's not always very accurate with prepaids, and even tougher if it's a burner."

"Jaxson could have thrown that one away and gotten a new one after he called the party in Dellwood."

"True."

"Smoke, I know you want to hop in your car to see if you can find him, but until the FBI or another department gets a hit on his location, or someone spots him, you'd be chasing your tail," I said.

“I know, I know.” He pointed at his computer. “Besides, Meeker and Sherburne both sent the files for us to review. I’ll get ′em printed.”

“It was Bob who called. An aide that he and his mother really like was snooping through her closet and dresser drawers today but didn’t take anything. He saw it on video.”

“Poor Bob and all he’s going through with the aides. What does he plan to do about it?” Smoke clicked print for the first set, and then the second.

“Monitor her, see if he can find out what she was up to.”

Smoke thought a moment and nodded. “Let’s get to work on these files.”

The workday was winding down for both of us. I had officially been off duty for some time but was unofficially assisting Smoke. We pored over the details of the files we’d received from the other sheriffs’ departments and compared them with the Winnebago County files. The ones from Blue Earth and Mille Lacs arrived shortly after the others and we included them with the documents spread across the table in the squad room. Smoke and I hovered over them, made our way around the table as we perused and took notes.

Smoke pointed at some of the papers. “Each of them disappeared in May of different years, except the two outliers in March and April. The one missing from Sherburne County and the two from Meeker County, all lived within ten miles of Winnebago County. It stands to reason they could be among the victims in the bog as easily as those missing from our county. The gentleman from Blue Earth may be one of the four men, but I’m not so sure about the woman from Mille Lacs, since we have three women from the area to consider first.”

"I agree. Let's organize them chronologically by their years of disappearance. If you read, I'll write them on the whiteboard." I picked up a dry erase marker.

"Okay, Oscar Wright disappeared on May seventeenth, one year ago."

"Oscar Wright, check."

"We don't have one missing from two years ago, so the next one is Silas Petty who disappeared on May fourteenth, three years ago."

"Silas Petty, okay."

"Agneta Keats, disappeared on May ninth, four years ago."

"Check."

"Mildred Dryer from Sherburne disappeared May fifteenth, five years ago."

"Got it."

"Gloria Freiburg from Meeker disappeared May eleventh, six years ago."

"All righty."

"Horace Kline, also from Meeker, disappeared May thirteenth, seven years ago."

"Check. Well, that potentially accounts for six of the seven victims. One for every year of seven, except for one two years ago," I noted.

"Something could have happened that thwarted our bad guy's efforts that year."

"True. But we still have the seventh body, that of a male."

"Hiram Scranton of Blue Earth went missing April fifth, six years ago. And Rozanne Olson of Mille Lacs County, disappeared March sixteenth, eleven years ago," Smoke said.

"Rozanne Olson is definitely an outlier. Hiram Scranton may be, too."

"We'll put them on hold, for now. I'll work with Meeker and Sherburne, see how they're doing in their quests for DNA samples from the families of their missing persons."

Prickly sensations crept up my arm and spine. "Smoke, it's May. As far as we know our bad guy is still out there. Has he got another body he plans to dispose of this month, or is the seventh body one of the males, someone who recently disappeared, and it hasn't been reported yet?"

"You gotta wonder. It'd be damn near impossible for him to get in there now with the road all torn up. But Highway says they're scheduled to finish the project before the end of the month, and it'd be smart to put surveillance on Coyote as soon as they pull up stakes."

"Definitely. Back to your contacts in Meeker and Sherburne, will you send them a picture of the pendant, see if any of the families recognize it?" I said.

"Sure."

I took a photo of the information I'd written on the board. "Are we good here?"

Smoke nodded. "We're good."

I erased the board and made copies of Dryer's, Kline's, and Freiburg's photos to add to those missing from our county. We put the documents back in their respective files, carried them to Smoke's desk, and called it a day.

"Wanna fool around later?" I said as we walked to the parking lot.

Smoke's spontaneous laugh came out as a chortle and helped break the pressure and tension we'd worked under all day. "Little lady, you knew exactly what to say to make me feel a hundred times better."

I grinned. "So do you?"

"How about we get to our respective houses, free our dogs from their kennels, and then decide how we want to spend our evening?"

That sounded good to me. "I got a frozen lasagna I could put in the oven. It's not homemade, but I found a brand that tastes pretty close."

"Well, heck, why wait to decide how to spend the evening? Lasagna sounds good and fooling around later sounds even better. Rex and I will be over as soon as I'm presentable."

I opened my car door. "See you then." I climbed in and watched Smoke's long legs carry him the twenty feet to his car. My heart picked up its beat with excitement that the evening would belong to us.

The aroma of the Italian dish wafted from the oven and made my stomach rumble. It had been a long time since lunch, whatever I'd eaten. When Smoke and Rex arrived, Queenie begged for Rex's attention and I grabbed Smoke. Locked in his arms, I felt secure. And filled with excited anticipation of how the evening would end wrapped in his arms. Our deep kisses sealed the deal.

Both our hearts pounded, his faster than mine. He pulled back slightly, captured my head in his hands, and massaged the back of my neck with his thumbs. He looked at me and his long dimples deepened when he smiled. "There are times your beauty takes my breath away. Did you know that, Corinne?"

"Yours takes mine away pretty much all the time."

He shook his head and smiled. "In that case, I'd say beauty is decidedly in the eye of the beholder."

"Whatever." I said in my best teenage-voice imitation.

"That smells like real food in your oven."

"It does. But it's not like you and I are the best judges of what constitutes real food."

"That's partially true because we both appreciate good old home cooking."

"We do."

I pulled the dish out of the oven and we heaped servings onto plates. We'd barely taken a bite when Smoke's phone rang. He looked at the dial. "It's the sheriff."

"Mike, what's up? . . ." Smoke pinched the top of his nose then rubbed his forehead as he listened. I struggled to swallow my mouthful.

Smoke cleared his throat. "Where are you now?" . . . "Corky and I will come and pick you up. Can you hang tight for the hour and a half or so it'll take us? . . . In the meantime, call if you need to." He disconnected and shook his head.

"What?"

"Sheriff's got himself in a helluva mess. He'd gotten a call from the Pine County Sheriff's dispatch reporting Jaxson's disposable cell pinged from a tower outside of Pine City. Sheriff had himself convinced Jaxson was in the Chengwatana State Park up there, at one of his favorite camping spots. He drove to the park and started poking around in other people's tents. Got himself arrested."

"Our sheriff got *arrested* for going into other people's tents?"

Smoke's exhale was loud. "He didn't get into much detail, but it sounds like he talked the deputy that arrested him into contacting the sheriff there, that he'd vouch for him. Sheriff Brown saved him from getting booked into the jail, but I don't know if there will be charges. Brown told Mike he had to have someone pick him up. They towed his car to the law enforcement center and are holding onto his keys. Mike said he's waiting with Sheriff Brown in his office. Oh, and he said, 'Jaxson's in the area' about three times."

"Brother. What about April?"

"He didn't mention her, so we can presume she's not with him. I hope he's letting her know."

"This is not the Mike Kenner we've known forever."

"No, it's not. And we need to get to Pine County, a-sap."

"Let's take my squad, then you can drive his car home," I said.

"What about our pooches?"

"They should be fine in the house for the hours we're gone."

On the way, Smoke and I volleyed Sheriff Kenner's bizarre behavior back and forth, tried to stay optimistic. We could only speculate on the details that had led to his arrest and what might happen as a result. Did Kenner's actions constitute more than trespassing? How many campers did he approach? If any of them pressed charges the Pine County sheriff would need to follow through with their county attorney to decide whether or not to prosecute. Elected officials were held to a higher standard and public trust was important. How would Sheriff Kenner's constituents view this odd, potentially criminal, behavior?

"Sheriff Brown must be worried about Mike's emotional state if he won't let him drive," I said.

"With good reason. Mike sounded excited, like he was high on something. That bothered me, considering he'd been arrested, and his car had been towed."

"I can't imagine him taking any drugs. Unless he got a prescription from his doctor. I'd say it's more likely he's excited because he believes Jaxson is in the area."

"Probably so. Hopefully so. That raises the question: does Sheriff Brown have his troops out on the lookout for Jaxson?" Smoke said.

"You'd think. And they've been informed Jaxson's got a gun."

"Yeah, that too. What's got me concerned is Mike's gonna try to talk us out of driving him home. He'll want to stay up there, keep searching for his son."

"I know he's a mess, but even so, he's gotta realize the seriousness of all this. He could get banned from the county. If push comes to shove, there's two of us, and one of him," I said.

That coaxed a half-hearted chuckle out of Smoke. "You're up on your defensive tactics, little lady?"

"You know it, but I sure don't want to have to try them out on our sheriff."

"Nope."

"And it'd take both of us to out-tactic Kenner," I said.

"Probably."

The sun was setting when we pulled into the Pine County Law Enforcement Center parking lot. "There's Mike's personal vehicle," I said. It was easy to spot in the mostly empty lot.

Smoke phoned Kenner to let him know we'd arrived. The sheriffs waited for us in the lobby. I was taken aback by Kenner's appearance and hoped he didn't notice my reaction before I forced a small smile. I might not have recognized him if I'd run into him on the street. Smoke cleared his throat, gave himself that few seconds to think of what to say.

Sheriff Kenner looked like he'd wandered around for days. How had he gone downhill that fast? Unshaven and unkempt, his hair was matted down on one side and stuck out on the other. Dirt clung to his face, with lines, likely made from sweat, running down it. His clothes were dirty and stained, as was his exposed flesh. Bloodshot eyes, swollen half-shut, with a bit of a wild look in them. Blood had dried on the skin of his arm around a small cut.

No wonder he'd been reported. His appearance was enough to scare the most seasoned campers. Why hadn't Sheriff Brown told him to clean up?

"Thanks for making the trip," Sheriff Brown said then shook our hands.

"Glad to do it." Smoke finally had words.

"Yes, thank you," Kenner said.

Smoke put a hand on his shoulder. "Sheriff, you've been out in the woods. It'd be a good idea to wash up before you go home to your wife."

Kenner looked down at his arms without changing his expression. Did his brain register how he looked? He shrugged. "Okay."

Sheriff Brown pointed. "The restrooms are right around the corner there." After Smoke had led Kenner away, Brown said, "I tried to get him to clean up, offered him a shower and change of clothes, but he said he was fine. Obviously, he's not."

"No. So what led to his arrest?"

"He was out in the state park looking for his son. There aren't many campers out there yet, not like after Memorial Day. Tried to get people's attention outside their tents. If they didn't answer, he'd stick his head inside, thought maybe his son was in there, keeping quiet because he'd recognized his dad's voice," Brown said.

"He had the vehicle description and plate number of the car his son bought. I wonder why he didn't locate that first, and then check out a nearby tent?"

"Not everyone drives a vehicle to their campsite. Some hike in. Sheriff Kenner said when he didn't see his son's car, he thought maybe he hid it somewhere, in case authorities knew what he drove."

"I guess that sort of makes sense," I said.

"He called the number of his son's prepaid phone a number of times, thought he'd hear it ring at one of the sites, but didn't."

"So he decided to do physical checks instead."

"We had three calls before the deputies got out there and found him. Of course, they had no idea what in the hell was going on, who he was. Mike didn't seem all that coherent, repeating how he had to find his son, knew he must be in one of the tents," Brown said.

I shook my head. "Thankfully, you identified him. And we appreciate that you kept him out of jail. At least for now."

"I sent the deputies back to get statements from the complainants without revealing who their trespasser was. None of them wanted to press charges; they were just glad we'd gotten him out of the park, taken him into custody. I made it very clear to Mike that he cannot go back there on his own. I told him we'd search for his son. He made me promise to let him know if they got any more pings from his son's phone. I said I would. He needs counseling and about twenty-four hours of sleep."

"We'll see what we can do. The ironic thing is our sheriff is an expert when it comes to critical incident debriefings and walking people through the process of what to do, who to talk to," I said

"When it's your kid who's in trouble, all bets are off the table."

Sheriff looked and smelled like a new man when he emerged ahead of Smoke from the restroom. He'd shed his outer shirt and his white undershirt appeared surprisingly clean. His dark blue jeans needed washing, but the color camouflaged the dirt. His eyes were less swollen, maybe from a cold-water splash.

Sheriff Brown handed Smoke Kenner's keys. We extended our thanks and were on our way. Smoke's worries were confirmed when we neared Kenner's Ford Expedition and he said, "We should swing through the state park, take one last look."

Smoke laid a firm hand on his shoulder. "Mike, you're my boss. More importantly, you're my friend. There is no way in creation we are going anywhere near that park tonight. We all need to get home, get some rest. And see what tomorrow brings."

23

I pulled in the Kenners' driveway behind Smoke. The garage door lifted, and I watched the two get out of the Ford. The inside door opened, and April stood waiting to receive Mike with open arms. He raised his hand in a goodbye wave to Smoke then joined his wife.

I read April's lips when she said, "I'll close the overhead door." After Smoke cleared from the garage, she pushed the button. As the door went down, Mike's arms tightened around his wife, and my eyes filled with tears. One more blow for them to deal with.

Smoke climbed into the passenger seat and let go of a loud, "Huh!"

"That bad?" I backed out of the driveway.

"Those ninety minutes were among the longest of my life. Mike was on the phone with April at least half the time and spent the rest of it plotting ways to search for Jaxson. I'm exhausted."

"Is he in total denial about his actions in Pine County that actually got him *arrested*?"

"There's more to it than that. He was in the pits and now he's on a mountain top. Depressed, now manic. You can only skyrocket so far up before you crash. Scares the hell out of me, what's happening to him," Smoke said.

"You need to run all this by the chief deputy."

"I know. I feel like I'm between a rock and a hard place. Mike called me and not his chief to rescue him. But Randolph's the acting sheriff and has got to know about this, pronto. I told Mike that. All he said was, 'Yeah, I'll tell him.'"

"And you'll fill in the rest of the story with your observations and other details?" I said.

"Yes."

"You think he and April will be okay tonight?"

"As long as he doesn't talk her into any lamebrain scheme, like scouring the Pine County area in search of their son," Smoke said.

"She didn't go with him last time."

"April didn't know he was going."

"That's so not cool. Her finding out after the fact," I said.

"Nope."

Queenie and Rex must have sensed Smoke and I were over-the-top weary, so they laid down and watched as I pulled the uneaten plates of lasagna out of the fridge and put them in the microwave. "Thank you," Smoke said when I handed him one.

We gobbled down our food like it was our last meal. "There's more in the casserole. Ready for seconds?"

"You bet. I'll count it as my midnight snack."

"It's getting close."

We finished it off, then he said, "You know what I'm thinking?"

"You could fall asleep standing up?"

"Not quite. It's more along the lines of we head upstairs, crawl under the covers, and set aside the cares and concerns of the day."

And that's what we did. Despite all the turmoil we were caught up in, we concentrated on each other and expressed the love we shared in the sweetest way possible.

I woke up Friday morning to little knocking sounds on the roof. Like racquet balls dropping from the sky. It took me a second to realize they were raindrops. Large ones. Would the rain delay the road project on County 35 at Coyote Bog? In the four days since the gruesome discovery a part of me waited for *that* call, the one notifying the sheriff's office the road crew had found another body in the bog. It kept me on edge. With seven unidentified bodies with the medical examiner, I prayed that number wouldn't grow to eight or more. We'd assembled a viable list of elderly people who'd disappeared over the years, but the M.E. had not yet linked them to any they had autopsied.

I rolled out of bed and found Smoke in the kitchen drinking coffee. Queenie's and Rex's coats were damp; they'd been outside to do their business.

"Good morning on this rainy day, sunshine." Smoke stood and took me in his arms. I welcomed his sweet kisses.

"Morning. I wish we could spend this dreary day in bed."

"That's a thought. A very tempting one." He squeezed me tighter then lowered his head and nibbled on my neck.

His cell phone rang. "Sorry." He pushed the talk button. "Detective Dawes. . . . Good to hear from you. What's up? . . .

That's good news. . . . We'll see what the DNA tests show. How about the pendant, did either family recognize it? . . . Appreciate the info."

He disconnected. "That was Detective Gale in Meeker County. They got DNA swabs from the children of Horace Kline and Gloria Freiburg, along with their medical records. They delivered the DNA swabs to the regional lab yesterday and will get the medical records to the medical examiner today."

"Wow, nice and fast."

"They lucked out that the families are in the area. And you know how motivated officials involved in missing persons' cases are to solve them," Smoke said.

"Yes, I do."

"But no one recognized the pendant."

"Dang it."

"I'm heading to the office shortly. First off, I need to talk to Sheriff Brown in Pine County, see if there's any indication Jaxson's still there."

"And what about our sheriff?" I said.

"I'll find out if he's talked to Randolph yet."

Deputy Bob Edberg phoned me a little after 8:00. "The PCA who was going through my mother's drawers yesterday is the same one there today. I decided not to call her out on it, see if she displays any other odd behavior first. I'll make a point of stopping home a couple of times during my shift, if it works out."

"That'd be good, Bob. With the nanny cameras on, you can always check them, too."

"I wished I'd thought of that before ′cause it relieves a lot of the stress," he said.

"Too bad you need them, but good to have them when you do."

"Right on."

Smoke and I met in Chief Deputy Randolph's office at 8:40. Smoke had scheduled a conference call meeting with FBI Special Agent Kent Erley at 9:00.

"I talked to Mike earlier and just got off the phone with Sheriff Brown in Pine County a few minutes ago. It sounds like the two of you got caught up in quite the ordeal last night," Randolph said.

Smoke shook his head. "We gotta find Jaxson a-sap, before our sheriff does anything else dumb or dangerous looking for him."

"I agree. No more pings from the prepaid phone Jaxson bought. All the counties have the number to check, and I've requested they call it every hour. I'm counting on them to see it through."

"My question is whether Jaxson will stay in Minnesota or make his way to another state. He said in his note he wanted to start a new life. What does that mean?" Smoke said.

"That'd be a good question to ask the special agent when we have him on the line. What he thinks Jaxson might do," I said.

Smoke glanced at me and grinned. "Now you're thinkin'." He turned back to Randolph. "Clayton, I think you should get a team from Human Services, rather than from our office, to go over to the Kenners' house. Have them spend some time helping them work through all this. Mike can't see he needs help. And if it gets much worse, I'm afraid he'll end up in the emergency room on a seventy-two-hour mental health hold."

"A social worker and public health nurse might be just the right ticket," Randolph said.

"I've watched a number of them do crisis interventions, mostly in child protection cases, but they're well trained and very competent," I said.

"Yep." Smoke's phone rang. He pushed the talk button. "Detective Dawes. . . . Yes, Sheriff. . . . That's encouraging. Any hit on the pendant? . . . We figured it was a long shot. When the regional lab has the results, we'll both be notified and take it from there. Thanks, and have a good one."

Smoke disconnected and nodded.

"Not our sheriff?" I said.

"No, Morris from Sherburne. We might be catching a break here. They got a hold of Mildred Dryer's son yesterday, collected his DNA, and delivered it to the lab before they closed. Here's the capper: her son said she had her gallbladder removed about ten years ago."

My heart picked up its beat. "Oh, my gosh. But his mother did not own that pendant?"

"Nope. Not that he knows of, anyway."

"I wouldn't know all the jewelry pieces my mother has," Randolph said.

"No, but a distinctive pendant you would. She'd be apt to wear it a lot," I said.

"You have a point." Randolph drummed his desk with his fingers. "Identifying a victim and a break in the case would be the brightest spot we've had so far."

"You know it," Smoke said.

I said a silent prayer our first victim recovered from the bog was Mildred Dryer.

24

Mama and Rufus

When Mama came through the door that morning after working an extra shift, an overnight, Rufus was afraid of what she might have to say. If she'd made up her mind about how many patients she was planning to send on their heavenly journey. He had been praying there wouldn't be more than one.

Mama had a look that scared him. She'd had it when she left for work the night before and still had it when she came home. Like she was feeling fierce, or something. Her skin was dark pink. She was frowning and kept staring straight ahead, like she saw something. He didn't have the right words for how she looked, but it meant something was going to happen to one of her patients pretty soon.

It was close to the time Mama would bring a patient home, and the whole thing filled Rufus with fear. If only he had a way out, away from Mama. He loved her, and she loved him and treated him good. Except when she made him put her patients in the bog.

He'd lost his appetite and hadn't eaten the sandwiches Mama left for his late-night snack. It was the first thing she noticed when she opened the refrigerator that morning. "Rufus, are you ill, coming down with something?"

"I don't feel so good, Mama."

She put her arms around him and held him a while. "There, there. You'll feel better when our patient is sent on her heavenly journey, won't you?"

"Yes, Mama."

25

Randolph nodded at Smoke and me, clicked the speaker on his phone, and dialed Erley's number.

After brief introductions, Smoke got down to business. "Special Agent Erley, when we talked yesterday, I gave you a quick rundown of what we've got going on here in Winnebago County. To recap, the body of an elderly woman was accidentally recovered from a bog during a road construction project. An angel had been branded into her forehead and crosses were branded into the back of each wrist, post-mortem.

"On further investigation, while looking for artifacts that might help identify her, we found another body with the same markings. That prompted us to continue our search and we found five more. All branded with the same symbols. But no other signs they had been physically abused.

"The medical examiner's office has completed three autopsies but has not found a definitive cause of death, so the manner stands as undetermined in all three at this point." Smoke said.

"There is no question of foul play regarding those bodies. Undetermined is the worst ruling for investigators working a case when you suspect it's a homicide, to be sure." Erley said. His voice was clean and clear.

"You got that right. Our question is, where do we start looking for the perpetrator? We have an idea of what would motivate a person, or persons, to do something so bizarre, but we'd appreciate your expert opinion," Smoke said.

"This is the first I've heard of an angel of mercy—or angel of death—that actually branded his or her victims. That adds another layer to this."

"A disturbing one," I said.

"Yes. Angel of mercy serial killings are rare. Still, there've been over forty documented cases in the U.S. alone since nineteen-seventy. The offender decides the victim is no longer a contributing member of society and needs to die. Or the victim is suffering from an illness, or disease, and should be released from his misery.

"There are varying elements in the profiles for these killers, but they share the commonality, almost always, of being employed in a hospital or other care facility where they have easy access to their chosen victims. They may be doctors, nurses, aides, or a custodian."

"Custodian, really?" Smoke said.

"Yes, but that's the exception. In the case you're working, victims were found outside of a facility. In fact, in a bog. That's significant. The victims' identities have not been confirmed, but you have a degree of confidence that three of them were from your county and went missing over the last four years. All had dementia. Two lived in assisted living facilities and one was still in his home, receiving care there. There are three more reported missing from neighboring counties and the oldest case goes back seven years," Erley said.

"Correct," Smoke said.

"You also told me that you'd gotten a list of employees from the assisted living facilities during the time frames two of them disappeared, and from the healthcare agency that the Petty family used."

"Correct. We did not find anyone that had worked at all three places," Smoke said.

"Unless that person used different identities and worked at the facilities at a time other than when the victims disappeared," Erley suggested.

"Hmm. Something to consider. We'll expand the scope of the investigation. So who are we looking for?" Randolph said.

"A person who had a dysfunctional childhood with a controlling, emotionally abusive parent, likely the father. Felt inadequate. Although most serial killers are male, when it comes to healthcare serial killers, about half are female. He or she did not form strong emotional bonds, was socially isolated. Craved attention and love but not given much. Didn't learn what constituted a healthy relationship. Likely had an inappropriate, harmful relationship as an older teen or young adult, that led to further isolation.

"Chose a career as a caregiver to satisfy the longing of being needed by others, loved by them. The more, the better. Then something major happened that caused a psychotic break. It led to the delusion she had been given divine authority to end the suffering of those she deemed had a diminished quality of life. A new calling of sending people to a better place. The angel and crosses indicate that place is Heaven where there is no suffering. I'd say the break happened in the month of May, given that's when your people went missing. Why the offender disposed of the bodies in a bog is an unknown, and I can only speculate," Erley said.

I cleared my throat. "I read about different reasons people were buried in bogs in past centuries. For thousands of years, many considered bogs spiritual places and some killings were thought to be done as sacrificial offerings. Others were buried there because of their criminal acts, or suicide. Different things prevented people from being buried in what they considered was the consecrated ground in cemeteries. Different trains of thought. Others were put in bogs after they'd been murdered. Killers did it to cover their crimes by burying the evidence."

"After Detective Dawes phoned me, I did some research on bogs myself since it's the first case I've been brought into where victims were found in a bog. As I said, I can mostly speculate on the significance. The religious symbols branded on the victims led me to believe the offender was either offering them as sacrifices or buried them in what he or she thought was sacred ground," Erley said.

"Either one is a logical conclusion. Kent, you've referred to the offender as 'she' a couple of times. Should we be looking for a female?" Smoke said.

"When I started working on the investigative criminal analysis, I knew it could be either or both based on the statistics. Possible victim Oscar Wright was last seen leaving the facility with a petite woman. Had she been responsible for his death and the deaths of the others, she would not have been able to dispose of the bodies by herself. She had to have help. The question in my mind was, was she the assistant that lured the victims, or the boss that called the shots?

"As I worked through the analysis, I concluded the offender is a woman who took on the role of controller after her psychotic break, most likely caused by a violent act, one she was forced to take part in by the parent—the father—who dominated her. Her father may have been her first victim after that break."

Smoke and I exchanged a look. Was his body the seventh one?

Erley continued, "Her assistant is closely tied to her, closely related. Either a much younger brother, or a son. The woman with Mister Wright was described as older, so what is her actual age? I'd say fifty at the outside. Maybe forty-five. Not what I would describe as older, but she disguises herself to go unrecognized. She comes across as trustworthy and caring, and in fact does enjoy caring for people. All her victims had dementia and that's why she chose them. She's been operating in the healthcare field and collecting victims without being caught for at least seven years. Likely changes her appearance with each new job, uses a variety of identities, has figured out ways to pass background and job history checks. Likely lives near the Coyote Bog so she can keep an eye on it."

"And knows by now we've uncovered her secret offerings. How will she handle that?" Smoke said.

"She'll be distressed the bodies have been removed and will either ramp up her efforts in Winnebago County by adding more bodies to the bog or relocate to another area and start over."

"You think she'd keep burying people in the bog with the increased risk of being caught?" I said.

"She doesn't believe she'll get caught. She's under the delusion she has a divine calling. She's been flying under the radar unnoticed for years, doesn't expect that to change. One last thing to consider: your people have all gone missing in

May. One may have been buried this month already, or she has yet to bury another."

"Maybe that's the seventh body. Someone who hasn't been reported missing yet." Smoke looked at his watch. "It's the seventeenth today."

"Or she is still narrowing in on her next victim," Erley said.

Every muscle in my body tightened. Smoke and I had discussed the same possibility. Randolph, Smoke, and I exchanged grimaced looks.

Randolph leaned forward. "Special Agent Erley, I'm impressed how detailed you are, how you figure it all out. The female you describe is downright scary."

"Scary and dangerous. As far as creating a profile, some say it's as much an art as it is a science. Much of it is based on what we've learned from interviews with serial killers and other violent offenders. Patterns emerge. Some people raised in dysfunctional and abusive households are less impacted by the adverse experiences than others are. Some break, some don't. Much of that rests on their personalities and the level of the abuse," Erley said.

"Understood. We've seen that in both offenders and victims through the years. Back to the offender. We're looking for a petite woman in her mid-forties and a younger man who works with her. She has a variety of looks and identities," I said.

"Yes."

"We appreciate all your help, Kent. And if you have a little more time, I'd like to run something else by you," Smoke said.

"What is it?"

Smoke told him about Jaxson and the details about his crime and escape.

Special Agent Erley asked questions about his family members, friends, and activities.

Randolph, Smoke, and I filled in as many of the blanks as we could.

"Tell me what the note said again, I'll write it down."

Smoke pulled out his notebook and read, "I'm sorry for everything. Tell Sawyer's parents that. Please. I can't stand the thought of going to prison so I need to start a new life somewhere."

Erley was silent a moment then said, "He's remorseful. That's a good thing, if it guides him to make the right decision. If he isn't found first, it will be one of the things that brings him back. That, and his love for his parents. Even if he doesn't always act like it. You described their family camping trips and other activities. He has a large number of friends. He's not a loner, so being on his own will get old after a while.

"He hadn't left the state after many hours, and that tells me two things. Deep down, he knows he's going to turn himself in at some point, or he'll get caught before he can. And he'll be in less trouble if he stays in Minnesota. That may or may not be true. But that's what he thinks based on the conditions of his release.

"The more important aspect is that he's comfortable in the great outdoors and knows remote areas in your state, such as the Boundary Waters. He could lose himself up there for a long time, provided he has shelter and provisions. He's got a pistol to help keep him safe from wild animals. It wouldn't take down a bear, but it might scare one. That's about all I got."

"What you've given us actually makes me feel better, more encouraged about Jaxson," I said.

Smoke and Randolph agreed they felt better, too.

"We appreciate your insights, Kent," Smoke said.

"You're welcome, and feel free to contact me again, if you need to." After our goodbyes, Smoke hung up the phone.

"If Jaxson hides in the Boundary Waters, or one of the other state parks in Northern Minnesota, we may have to wait for him to resurface. There isn't good cell phone coverage in a lot of that area so the chance of getting pings would be hit and miss," I said.

"That's an issue, to be sure. Our chief here has asked dispatchers in the state to check Jaxson's cell number daily. Maybe one will get a hit," Smoke said.

"Our next course of action, Elton?" Randolph said.

"You'll want to fill in the other detectives and command staff about what Erley told us. About the angel of death killer, likely a healthcare worker, and what he said about Jaxson."

"Yes. I meant after that."

"Like I suggested earlier, have a mental health team pay the Kenners a visit. It'll help April as much as it will Mike. Maybe more so. She knows better than any of us how out of character Mike has been," Smoke said.

"Agreed," Randolph said.

"Corky and I will get a list of employees who worked at the facilities and agencies used by our three missing folks. We'll go back seven years, for now. Hopefully, they'll have employee photos of any that might've left. Chief, if you can get a judge to sign court orders today requesting the employers provide us with the basic information, we'll get on it. I'll give Sherburne and Meeker a report on what Erley said so they can check out who provided health care for their missing," Smoke said.

"If we're looking at the same offenders, they must have gotten started in the other counties then moved over to ours, given when their people disappeared," Randolph said.

"But when did they dispose of the bodies? They could have kept them for some time until they died. Who knows?" Smoke said.

Randolph shook his head. "'Who knows is an understatement about now."

Smoke sat down at his desk to contact Meeker and Sherburne Counties and I went to the sergeants' office to phone the assisted living facilities where Agneta Keats and Oscar Wright lived, and the home healthcare agency Silas Wright used. I spoke to the human resources staff at each, explained that we were working on a sensitive case, and requested limited employee records over the past seven years: names, birth dates, addresses, dates of employment, photos, and any notable performance issues. And that we'd have a court order to present to them. All agreed to provide the information and assured me they'd be ready in two to three hours.

I'd barely finished the last call when Smoke popped his head around the corner of the open door. "The lab has two DNA matches."

"What?"

"The first two victims we recovered. Turns out they've been identified as Mildred Dryer from Sherburne and Horace Kline from Meeker. I haven't told the chief or the other counties yet."

The news brought me to my feet. "Seriously? I know it doesn't take long to get the results when they run a known person's sample. I'm trying to process that missing persons from Sherburne and Meeker—ones we only learned about yesterday—are not only two of the victims, but they're the first ones identified."

"That struck me, too. Ironic. The lab is notifying the other counties, and I'll give them a call myself shortly."

"I actually hoped one would be Mildred Dryer, after we found out she'd had her gallbladder removed." I shook my hands to relieve some of the emotional tension that was building inside of me. I felt a sense of joy for the families that would get closure and disappointment for the Winnebago County families who would not.

"You okay?" Smoke said.

"Yeah." I pulled the six photos of the missing from my shirt pocket and studied them for the hundredth time, it seemed. "I've carried our missing people with me for days, added the others yesterday." I handed one to Smoke. "Mildred. She was what my mother would call a 'handsome woman'. Stately." The image of her lying in the bucket of the excavator, dressed in a gown, branded with symbols would be with me forever. "She'd lost weight since this picture was taken, but I can see how she could be the first recovered victim."

"I agree. Not that the M.E. needs to since they have a DNA match, but I'm convinced the facial image in this photo would match the facial image of the first body," he said.

I pulled Horace Kline's photo from the stack and had another good look. He held a beer and wore a big grin on his ruddy face. "And Mister Kline. He looked skinnier coming out of the bog, too. Compared to how he looks in this photo." I held it up.

"Drinking a brewsky. Must've also imbibed a lot of hard stuff along the way that contributed to his cirrhosis."

Smoke's phone buzzed. "The M.E.'s office." He pushed the talk button. "Detective Dawes. . . . Good, very good. . . . We'll wait to hear from the lab, see if we get more matches. Did you pin down a manner of death on either one? . . . Well, we'll go with that, for now." He disconnected.

"They completed two more of the autopsies?"

He nodded. "When the bodies of the four kids who overdosed on fentanyl-laced heroin at that party came in—horrible deal—their cases took priority. Of course. Now they're back to examining our victims," Smoke said.

"The M.E.s deal with a lot of the same tragedies we do, but in a different way."

"No doubt. Doc Patrick said if nothing pressing comes in over the weekend, they're geared to finish up with the last three Coyote Bog bodies."

I crossed my fingers. "The families of our missing folks are waiting. It'll be good to have answers, one way or the other."

"Yep."

"To let you know, human resources from all three places will have the employee records and photos ready in a couple of hours, or so. It helps that none of them have large numbers of staff, and many of the employees have been around forever," I said.

"That will help narrow down our list of suspects. If someone has been at the same facility for twenty years, that means she isn't changing jobs every year. On the other hand, our offender likely is."

"Or is working part time at a couple of places," I said.

"We'll see what we got when we get there. Meantime, I'll update the chief and make those follow up calls to Sherburne and Meeker. They'll want to make notification before word gets out to the world, so we'll keep it private until they give the nod. I'll circle back later."

"My goal between now and then is to finish the job evaluations for the deputies I supervise."

Smoke cracked a grin. "You still working on those? It's not like you've been busy or anything."

I raised my eyebrows and lifted my hand. "Bye."

26

Meadowbrook Assisted Living in Harold Lake and the Home Health Comfort Care Agency in Oak Lea both had the documents ready when we arrived. Smoke presented each with a court order to keep on file for their legal protection. They provided copies of employee records going back seven years, that included names, birth dates, addresses, dates of employment, photos, and any notable performance issues, as I'd requested.

Ridgewood Care Center in Oak Lea was our last stop. The human resources director had questions but respected the position of the sheriff's office.

"What I can tell you is, we're conducting an investigation based on information we've received, and we'll see where it leads. Meantime, we ask that you keep this confidential," Smoke said.

"I will. Of course. But I have to confess that it gives me the chills to think someone who worked here could have been involved in such a horrible crime." She had no doubt figured out the reason we were there. "I mean, we do a good job checking backgrounds, school records, and get letters of recommendation from past employers, as well as personal references. A thorough job," she said.

"I'm sure you do," Smoke said.

"Thanks for your help," I said.

On the drive back to the office, I said, "I've been wondering about Mae Borgen, the woman who was so skittish when we paid her a visit. When she talked about going to work early in the morning, I should have asked her where she worked."

"She came out free of holds or wants when you ran a check on her."

"I know, but she lives near Coyote and can keep an eye on things, like Special Agent Erley said. She has a son, a possible accomplice. And she's around the age Erley mentioned as likely. When we get back, let's compare her driver's license photo with the employee photos we got," I said.

"Sounds like a plan."

Smoke and I settled in at the large table in the squad room with the printouts, notepads, highlighters, and pens with black, blue, and red ink. "We got our work cut out for us," I said.

"Yep."

Deputies Todd Mason and Brian Carlson came in. They both looked worn out and it hit me that I was too. "Detective, Sergeant, with those stacks of paper and writing supplies, I'd say you're about to have more fun than you deserve," Mason said.

Smoke's eyebrows lifted. "You got that right."

"Has this seemed like the longest week in all of our years working together?" Carlson said.

Some weeks seemed like a month long. At least. "Now that you mention it," I said.

"About sums it up," Smoke said.

"We started out Monday morning with that awful deal at the bog, and then the sheriff with Jaxson and all. Sad. Monday feels like it was two weeks ago," Carlson said.

"I hear you, man. But with Jaxson taking off, it'd be fine with me if time stood still until they found him," Mason said.

We were silent for a time then Carlson said, "We were in the crime lab going over things with Doug Matsen when we heard you were back at the office. Doug'll be here any minute to report on the weight and cord found on the first Coyote victim."

"Good deal," Smoke said.

"I have an update on the cross pendant. Christian Jewelry Designs, the manufacturer, got back to me this afternoon," Carlson said.

"And?" Smoke said.

"They finished checking their invoices and have the number of pendants they sold to the Target stores in our county." Carlson pulled out his notepad and flipped it open. "They read the numbers to me over the phone and will mail the copies."

"The old-fashioned way," Smoke said.

Carlson smiled. "Yeah, the man I'm working with sounds like he's about ninety-five. Sharp as a tack, just takes him a while to finish a project like this." He read from his notes, "It's not a big-ticket item, but sales are decent. Their biggest shipments have been at Christmas, Easter, and around confirmation and graduation time. But what struck me, what didn't fit with the general trends, happened seven years ago.

Easter was April eighth that year. Anyway, after the Easter sales depleted the supplies at the Oak Lea store, they shipped twenty pendants there. And the next week they shipped twenty more. That's the anomaly. Never happened before or since."

"Either twenty people each bought a pendant, or ten bought two, or did one buy twenty?" Mason interjected.

"And the answer is, drumroll . . ." Carlson paused to tap out a staccato beat on the table with his hands. "One person bought twenty."

"We just came from that Target store. It was pretty easy for them to track down the sale," Mason said.

"And the purchaser?" Smoke said.

"Ah, no. That was missing from the equation. It was a cash sale," Carlson said.

"We wouldn't want it to be too easy for us, now would we?" Smoke said.

If he'd been closer, I would have elbowed him. "If our offender is the one who bought them, that's one explanation why none of the missing persons' family members recognized the pendant as belonging to their loved ones," I said.

Sergeant Doug Matsen walked in with his reports. "This must be the place."

"For blood, sweat, and tears," Carlson quipped.

"We hear you've made some progress," Smoke said.

Matsen nodded. "Some." He handed the reports to Smoke. "The twenty-pound weight tied around the first female victim is older, manufactured thirty-seven years ago by Murphy Iron, a company in New York. It was widely distributed and available at both large and smaller sports shops, so tracking down its sale at this point is not feasible."

"I'd suspected as much," Smoke said.

"On the other hand, the clear, vinyl-coated, three-eighths-inch thick, galvanized aircraft cable—that was a mouthful—was manufactured in Burnsville, Minnesota by Wilson and Jackson. Their coatings are available in vinyl or nylon, in clear, white, or black, and come in spools of fifty to two hundred fifty feet. The one we have is clear vinyl.

"The company wholesales their products throughout the United States and Minnesota, including six service companies and four hardware stores in Winnebago County. The companies have no retail outlets, but it's a popular item at the hardware stores. People use it for electrical projects, tie downs, safety fasteners, clothes lines.

"I took the cable to Wilson and Jackson and met with Jason Wilson. He was able to identify the lot and batch number, manufactured six years ago. Ten fifty-foot spools were shipped to the hardware store in Emerald Lake that April. So I called on them. They keep track of inventory to a point, but not in a computer program. They had cash register tapes from back then, but not who bought the coated cable. All that led to a dead end," Matsen concluded.

"You did your job and got close, anyhow." Smoke lowered his voice. "This isn't public information until they notify the families, but the first two bodies have been identified. Mildred Dryer from Sherburne County, missing five years. The one weighted down with the dumbbell plate. And Horace Kline, from Meeker County, missing seven years."

Carlson's eyes widened. "That kind of caught me off guard. Sherburne and Meeker?"

"Yeah, it came together pretty fast the last couple days. They also had missing folks and collected DNA from their families. The regional crime lab came up with a match this morning," Smoke said.

Mason lifted his shoulders in a slight shrug. "That's a good thing."

"I guess. Two identities made, five to go," Matsen said.

Smoke nodded. "Yep. Meeker has another one we're looking at, besides. Change of subject: did the chief talk to you guys about our conversation with Special Agent Kent Erley today?"

"He sent out an email memo with instructions not to leak the information to anyone outside the office until further notice," Mason said.

Smoke bounced his palm on a stack of papers. "What we got here is the employee records from facilities where the offender likely worked. We asked the HR reps to keep that confidential, also."

Deputy Vince Weber joined us in the squad room. "Huh. You're havin′ a party and didn't invite me?"

"Vincccccce!" Carlson said, like he was welcoming him to the *Cheers* bar.

"Funny one, Briaaaan!" Weber tossed his notepad on the table. "It's Friday—almost evening—for most folks, and if we didn't have one more day on our rotation, I'd say let's find the nearest *Cheers* and toss back one or two."

"I'm the detective on call this weekend, so I have a couple more days to go," Smoke said.

"Do what you can to hold down the excitement, Detective. If no big new cases come in, that would help us catch up. Tomorrow is our last day in Major Crimes this time around, and we have a bunch of loose ends to tie up," Mason said.

"It's been a taxing week, no doubt," Smoke said.

"One bright spot to cheer you up, guys. I'm almost done with your job reviews. Tomorrow, it could happen," I said.

"Yeah well, can you at least tell us if any of us flunked?" Weber said.

"None of you flunked. And I'll add that we have a fine bunch of deputies, and you three are among the finest."

Mason and Carlson said, "Thanks," in unison, like the team they were.

"Ah, gee, that makes my heart kind of go pitter-patter." Weber had trouble with praise, but his touch of sarcasm didn't hide his sincerity. "So what've you got goin′ on here?" He pointed at the project before us.

Smoke briefed him.

"Yeah, we got the memo about the angel of death. The worst kind of deal, right? Somebody who's supposed to be takin′ good care of people is killing ′em. And if that's not creepy enough, she branded ′em, and buried ′em in a bog. When I thought about it, what Erley came up with as a profile seems like it makes a lot of sense," Weber said.

"I agree," Mason said.

"So I got about an hour left on the clock. If you want, I can help you sort through those records," Weber said.

"That would be mighty fine," Smoke said.

"Carry on, then. We'll be in the Major Crimes room if you need us," Carlson said as he and Mason headed for the door.

Smoke handed Weber the stack from Ridgewood Care Center. I took the one from Meadowbrook Assisted Living, leaving Smoke with Home Health Comfort Care.

"How do you plan to tackle this?" Weber said.

"Last year, when Oscar Wright went missing, we got lists of employees from these places, but didn't find a common person who had worked at all three places. Special Agent Erley said the person may have used different identities and could have worked at the facilities at a time other than when our victims disappeared," Smoke said.

Weber's eyebrows lifted. "Huh."

"This is an elimination process. We're looking for a woman in her forties who uses different names and ages. Birth dates to correspond with them, and it could be a wide range. Maybe thirty to sixty? The witness—who was the last one known to see Oscar Wright before he disappeared—said the woman with him was Caucasian, older, small in stature, gray hair, high cheekbones, narrow chin. And she wore big glasses," I said.

"Huh, those could cover most of her face," Weber said.

"Yep." Smoke pulled out the composite sketch of the mystery woman created the previous year and slid it Weber's way. "For all we know, she's stolen other people's IDs that have characteristics similar to hers, makes it relatively simple for her to pull it off. She can't do much about her height, except to elevate it a couple inches, and spikes wouldn't be allowed in her line of work, naturally. We'll go through the records again, cross out the ones that are easy to eliminate, narrow it down from there."

Weber shook his head at the composite sketch. "Yeah well, if I ran into her what'd pop into my head is, she's an older woman who looks young for her age. Like your mom does, Corky."

"Thanks, Vince," I said.

"You make a point, Vince. Some older folks have few wrinkles, making them look younger. And when older folks are fit and spry to boot, they seem more youthful than their actual age. Both of you know it doesn't take much to alter one's appearance. Hair, head or facial, versus no hair on men. A gray-haired wig or a red-haired one. Makeup, glasses, padded bra, the list goes on," Smoke said.

"Vince, if you put on a big bushy wig, I might not recognize you," I said. He'd had a shaved head for as long as I'd known him.

"That brings a scary enough image to mind. Now I gotta think of something else to get rid of it."

I snickered at an imagined image of him with hair. "This composite can be our guide to start with. We'll compare it to the photos we have in the employee files. The detectives last year couldn't find anyone who knew her. That's suspicious in itself," I said.

We spent the next hour studying photos, checking birth dates, names, and dates of employment. Many were easy to eliminate based on a variety of factors, like those who were not Caucasian or female, or were far outside the age range. Longtime, full time employees were considered and set aside. The offender could have spent years at one of the facilities and then moved on to another. Erley said she wasn't necessarily working at a facility when a person went missing from there. She might have been employed there at an earlier time. We also considered that she had been employed full time at one of the facilities and part time at the agency at the same time. With the shortage of healthcare workers, it wasn't an uncommon practice.

We closely studied the faces and came up with a list of nine potentials to investigate. More than I would have guessed.

"It's the witching hour, gang. You want me to keep working?" Weber said.

Smoke glanced at his watch and blinked. "Three o'clock already? That hour flew by. No, go ahead and take off, Vince. Really appreciate your help, though. We got way farther in short order than I'd hoped."

"Sure. It was actually kinda fun. Catch you two later, then." He saluted and left.

I picked up another driver's license photo, studied it, and handed it to Smoke. "She doesn't fit, does she?"

"No. Not like the other employees we've singled out." He set the photo down. "Let's check the DLs of the ones that do fit, see if their addresses are the same as what's listed in their records. Find out what they look like on those photos. If the employee records haven't been updated, some of the photos could be several years old," Smoke said.

"And then we pay each one a visit, find out if they're really who they say they are?"

"Sounds like a plan. We also need to set up meetings with Meeker and Sherburne, compare employee records with what they got. But with tomorrow being Saturday, that may have to wait until Monday. I'll touch base with them again before quitting time, see where they're at in the process. We need to nail down the common denominator a-sap."

"Smoke, every so often this weird sensation runs through my body, like it's a warning. We need to identify the demented offenders and stop them before they strike again. And that could be soon."

"That sixth sense of yours has been right on, many times, Corinne. Special Agent Erley told us the killer—killers—won't stop until they're caught, and I think you've got good reason for that weird feeling."

I had another close look at the photos. One by one, I slid five away from the others. "What do you think?"

Smoke pulled his readers from the top of his head to his nose then picked up each photo, studied it, and set it down. He did the same with the four I had ruled out. He pointed to the five I'd selected. "We'll start with these, see where they lead us."

27

Smoke headed to his desk to make the calls and I stayed in the squad room to run the drivers' license checks on the five women in question.

The first one, age 47, had been employed by both Meadowbrook Assisted Living and Home Health Comfort Care until three years prior. A wave of excitement washed over me until I learned she no longer had a registered Minnesota driver's license or a Minnesota identification-only card. I ran an out-of-state check of her full name and date of birth. She popped up at an address in North Carolina. A search on social media captured her in a series of photos with family and friends. And a new career as a beauty consultant. One down with four to go.

The second one, age 44, had a valid license and was at the same address listed on her employment records. She had worked for Home Health Comfort Care for two years. Silas Petty had used their services but disappeared a year before she started there. Shoot. I checked four social media sites, and she didn't show up on any of them.

The third one, age 58, had started part time at Home Health Comfort Care four years before and was still employed by them. Had she been the one who reported Silas Petty wasn't home when she arrived for work? I felt a glimmer of hope. Her driver's license matched the address on her employee records. Dolly Corbin lived in Emerald Lake and was not on social media. Then again, neither was I. Even with the privacy settings, it concerned me that people I didn't want to see my posts might read them anyway.

The fourth woman had a different address than was listed on her records. She was still in Minnesota but had moved to Alexandria, about two hours northwest of Oak Lea. I found her profile on social media and noted her listed occupation was Nurse at Douglas County Jail. Apparently, she wasn't concerned who knew where she worked. I crossed her off the list of potential suspects.

The fifth woman was 46 years old and had worked part time for Ridgewood Care Center for four years, and on call for Meadowbrook Assisted Living for three years. Both fit into the time frame of when Oscar Wright and Agneta Keats went missing. Rhoda Barnes was no longer employed by either facility. She had a valid driver's license and lived in an apartment in Oak Lea. Bingo. She wasn't on social media, either. We could start a club. Or not.

I studied the photos again and noted that all of them fit the general description of the woman last seen with Oscar Wright—if they were made to look older. Except for the third woman. With her listed age, she qualified as older. I printed the information on the third and fifth women, the two I considered possible suspects.

Smoke joined me in the squad room and watched as I slid the DL printouts and employee records in individual files. I gave him the skinny then flipped each file open.

"We have two women who worked at all three places in the right time frame. I think they're likely one in the same person. That's why the detectives came up short last year when they were looking for commonality between the three who had gone missing over the last four years."

He looked at the files. "I think you're onto something. Nice job sorting through them all, narrowing them down."

"Sure. I need to check Silas Wright's file, see if Dolly Corbin was the one scheduled to work the day he went missing."

"No, that wasn't her name. It was something else," Smoke said.

"Okay. But that doesn't mean Dolly didn't get there before the other's shift started."

"I'm with you on that thought. I recall the other one was cleared after a pretty intense interrogation."

"We need to talk to Dolly Corbin and Rhoda Barnes," I said.

"Agreed. And I have an update from the other counties."

"What?"

"Meeker rounded up the employee records from the two facilities where their missing folks were living at and Sherburne from the one. They're going through them as we speak. Let's get these files of Corbin and Barnes scanned and sent over so they can do a comparison. They're as motivated as we are to flush out this angel of death. Special Agent Erley's profile put the frosting on the cake for all of us," he said.

"They'll be able to compare the addresses of any suspects, see if they match up with ours. That'll be a quick check."

“Yep. Between the two of them, their people disappeared seven, six, and five years ago. Before ours started, so the suspect may or may not have moved,” Smoke said.

“True, but she buried all her victims in Coyote Bog. At least seven that we know of. We need to visit both counties, discuss next steps. Maybe tomorrow?”

“We’ll make that work.”

I phoned Home Health Comfort Care, identified myself, and asked if Dolly Corbin was working that evening. She was not. In fact, she was on vacation for a week. We didn’t know if Rhoda Barnes was currently working as she hadn’t given that information to either facility when she’d left her jobs. Smoke chatted with Meeker and Sherburne, arranging to meet with one in the morning and the other in the afternoon.

After delivering the suspects’ information to Chief Deputy Randolph, we were on the road en route to Rhoda Barnes’ apartment. She lived in a complex on the northeast side of Oak Lea, a secure facility. Smoke rang the bell for the manager. A stocky young man appeared at the glass door a moment later. Smoke pointed to his badge. The man glanced at my uniform and opened the door.

Smoke extended his hand. “Detective Dawes and Sergeant Aleckson. And you are?”

“Max.”

“Max, we need to talk to one of the residents here, so we’d appreciate you letting us in.”

“Sure thing. What apartment?”

“Three-twelve. Rhoda Barnes.”

“I’m not sure that she’s home. I don’t see her much. I think she’s got kind of a weird work schedule,” Max said.

"Where does she work?" Smoke said.

"I don't even know."

"Have you been the manager here long?"

"Yeah, since we opened six years ago," Max said.

"And Rhoda's been here how long?"

"She wasn't one of the first to move in, but I think some time in the first year."

"Does she live alone or share the apartment?" Smoke said.

Max shrugged. "Ah, well, she might have visitors, I guess."

"Any particular ones?"

"Well, I guess I can't say. I haven't seen anyone come in with her. She's friendly enough, but quiet-like, so I don't know if she has any special friends or not."

"We'll see if she's in." Smoke offered Max his card.

Max took it and nodded. "Okay. Can I ask if she's in trouble or something?"

"We just need to ask her a couple of questions. Nothing to worry about," Smoke said.

"Oh, okay. That's good to know. Well, I'll leave you to it then."

Max watched us get on the elevator and disappeared from sight when the doors closed.

"She may or may not have visitors, huh?" I said.

"Must not have a lot of them. Max hasn't seen her with anyone over the years."

"He's hardly seen *her* over the years. Or apparently even really talked to her."

"Sounds like it," Smoke said.

The elevator doors opened, and we took a left, directed by the arrow for rooms 300-312. Each room had a doorbell, a nicer feature than the knockers on doors at some buildings. Bells that rang inside eliminated the loud knocking noise. Residents must appreciate that.

I pushed the doorbell. No sounds inside. I counted to thirty and rang again. I was in uniform, so I stood to the side. Smoke faced the small peephole in case Rhoda looked out. We listened for any activity but didn't detect any. After a minute, Smoke pointed his thumb toward the elevator. We headed there and hopped on.

We stopped by the manager's door on our way out. When Max opened, Smoke said, "You have my card. I'd appreciate if you call me next time you see Rhoda Barnes. Any time of the day or night."

Max nodded. "Sure thing."

On the drive to Emerald Lake, Smoke bopped the steering wheel with the heel of his hand. "If we don't hear from Max by tomorrow, I think we need a deputy stationed there, at least part of the time. You've sent a dose of your heebie-jeebies my way."

"Your gut and mine are both telling us she's our bad guy and we can't find her soon enough."

Fifteen minutes later we pulled into the parking lot of a four-plex apartment building in the small community of Emerald Lake. It was in a residential area overlooking a large brick church. "Seems that Dolly Corbin gets to enjoy some peace and quiet when she's home," Smoke said.

"And I hope she's at home enjoying that now. Until we disturb it."

"There are only two cars in the lot. Hopefully one belongs to her."

I ran both license plates, and neither vehicle did. "Nope."

"Doesn't mean she's not in, so let's go check," Smoke said.

On the way into the building we met a giant of a man on his way out. He half-nodded at us and walked away. I glanced over my shoulder and was surprised at the distance his long legs carried him in short order, even with his lumbering strides. It looked like he was headed toward the business district.

"Goliath," I said under my breath.

"With a little Frankenstein thrown in the mix," Smoke murmured back.

Smoke rapped on apartment 4, but no one answered. After another attempt, we looked at each other and shook our heads.

"Let's try the other apartments. Maybe someone can enlighten us," Smoke said.

I mouthed, "We should have stopped Goliath."

Smoke raised his eyebrows and nodded. The only person who answered her door was a rather frail older woman. After introductions, we inquired about Dolly Corbin, but she didn't know her or how long she'd lived there.

"I don't get out much or see my neighbors' comings and goings. My daughter comes over with groceries and we make supper a few times a week. It's the only time I like cooking anymore. When my daughter is here. As far as the lady you're wondering about, I've only seen her a couple of times. And I don't recall when the last time was. Quite a while ago, now. But I did see a large man coming out of that apartment one day last week when I was getting my mail," she said.

"Do you know who he is?" Smoke said.

She shook her head. "I said 'hello' to him, and he nodded. Didn't say 'hello' back. Then I said, 'did you just move in?' He had a blank look on his face, like he didn't understand me, and didn't answer. Haven't seen him since." She'd missed a second sighting of him by minutes.

"How would you describe him, other than he was large?" Smoke said.

"Well, he was wearing a loose tee-shirt. Brown eyes and dark hair and had a wide nose." She demonstrated the width by spreading her thumb and forefinger out across her own thin nose. "He looked like he lifted weights, you know, a body builder with big muscles."

"Any guess on his age?" I said.

"Well, he could be twenty-five, I suppose." Goliath.

Smoke handed over his business card. "We appreciate your help, ma'am. If you see either the big man, or the woman who lives in the apartment, would you kindly give me a call?"

She took the card and read it. "Well, I've never had to call a sheriff's detective before. I surely will if I see them."

After I climbed in the car, I said, "It's amazing how virtually anonymous people can keep themselves from others living in the same small complex."

"Seems to happen a lot. If our suspicions are correct that Barnes, aka Corbin, is the offender and renting both apartments, then we know she prefers to be as low profile as possible."

"Yes." I waved my hand at the parking lot. "The same two vehicles are still here, so that means Goliath didn't take one of them. Neither of the owners' descriptions fits his anyway."

Smoke started the car. "I need to talk to the chief, get the ball rolling to set up surveillance."

"I'll drive so you can make the call."

"Deal."

We got out, exchanged places, and I shifted into drive. Smoke brought Randolph into the latest loop. "We need to end this dark angel's reign of terror," Smoke said. They figured out the logistics of when to post deputies to keep watch on the two buildings, then disconnected.

"Chief said we're putting in too many hours, and we need to hang it up for the night," Smoke said.

"Then we will do just that."

Or so we thought.

Smoke dropped me off at my squad car and I was halfway home when he phoned. "You're wondering what to pick up for dinner?" I said. It was almost five o'clock, and I was ready to eat.

"Wishful thinking. I got a call from Sherburne County Communications. Jaxson's number pinged near the National Wildlife Refuge there."

"No way. Camping that close to home?"

"Makes you wonder. They got two deputies out looking for him, but there's over thirty thousand acres in the refuge. Even if they can get within a couple miles radius, it'd be easy for him to hide," Smoke said.

"For sure. There's no overnight camping at the refuge, correct?"

"Correct. But you think that would deter someone fleeing from justice?"

"Ah, no. Especially not someone with Jaxson's camping experience. What about Sheriff Kenner, does he know?"

"No. I called his home, talked to April, she said Mike is sound asleep. His doctor prescribed a medication that's working. Thank God. I filled her in and told her I'd keep them informed. She's on the edge of her seat."

"Poor thing."

"Also talked to the chief and got his blessings for the road trip. I'll pick up one of our less-than-pristine undercover vehicles and head up to the refuge." Smoke said.

"I'll come with you."

"Nah, you go home."

I pressed down on the accelerator. "Smoke, I need to. I'll change, get out of uniform. And borrow Gramps' old Buick. It won't be on the county's dime. I'll check in when I get there."

"Corky—"

"See you there."

The next twelve minutes passed in a blur. I changed, rounded up Queenie and Rex for a visit with Gramps, asked to use his car, and jumped into the old Buick for a longer trip than it'd had for who knows how long. As I drove away, I whispered something he couldn't hear, "Thanks, Gramps, for not questioning me when I make requests and don't give you reasons why."

Those instances had been going on for years—me popping in at odd moments with somewhat unusual pleas. And whenever possible, I enlightened him after the fact of what I'd been up to. Gramps had told me many times he was glad to help the Winnebago County Sheriff's Office with investigations. I smiled at the thought he lived random moments vicariously through me.

When my thoughts returned to Jaxson, I sobered up right quick. The forty-minute drive seemed to take forever before I turned off Sherburne County Road 5 onto Prairie's Edge Wildlife Drive, the entrance to the Sherburne National Wildlife

Refuge. I pulled over and sent Smoke a text, asking where he was. He responded with, *By the Oak Savanna Trail pull-off, a quarter mile down Prairie's Edge*. Close.

He sat in an old Ford Fiesta, one that qualified as a beater. I parked and hopped in with him. "Do you know where the deputies are?" I said.

"One is making his way on the Mahnomen Trail, and the other is on the Blue Hill Trail. On ATVs. Those trails aren't meant for vehicles, even ATVs, but they're pushing the limits to cover more territory. And they can check areas off the trails, if need be. They've been searching for close to two hours with no luck. I tried calling Jaxson's number, but he didn't pick up, surprise, surprise."

"What's our plan?" I said.

"If we knew for certain Jaxson was in here, I'd consider assembling a posse to search for him. On the other hand, I'm leery if he spots us, it might force his hand."

"Special Agent Erley said Jaxson recognizes getting caught is one of the possibilities."

"I know, but he's young and impulsive and that makes for a potentially volatile situation," Smoke said.

"So the four of us keep looking?"

"For now. If Jaxson's here, his car should be, too. Easy enough to hide it in the thick forests, but easier to spot than a person." Smoke looked at his watch. "We've got about two and a half hours before it's too dark to see well."

"The park closes at sunset."

"Damn. I have a sinking feeling the chances of finding him are slim to none, but we have no choice. We have to look. We'll head down the drive at a snail's pace. I'll keep a lookout in the immediate area, and you can do some distance scoping." He picked up the pair of binoculars from the seat and handed them over.

“Will do.” I adjusted them to line up with my field of vision.

The road was over seven miles long and at mile two, Smoke hit the brakes. I pulled off the binoculars and spotted the reason why. The gravel on the side of the road had been disturbed. “I’d say a vehicle drove off the road and into that field,” he said. We got out for a closer look.

I pointed at the marks. “And the driver tried to cover his tracks by kicking the tire tracks away with his shoes.”

“Looks like it.”

I lifted the binoculars to my face and searched farther into the field for signs that a vehicle had driven through. “I think the driver continued to try to cover his tracks by brushing them away for a short distance.” I continued to search, followed the lines. About a football field away I spotted a vehicle, mostly hidden among the trees. “I might be looking at Jaxson’s new wheels.”

Smoke reached for the binoculars, adjusted them, and found the target. “Yep. Let’s go find out.”

28

Mama and Rufus

"**R**ufus, you need to relax. You're too restless."

"I can't help it, Mama. Cops came to the apartment building today."

"What do you mean, Son?"

"It was a lady cop who had a uniform on, and a man who had a suit on, like the detectives wear on TV," Rufus said.

Mama tried to keep her voice calm so Rufus didn't get more agitated. "Where were you when they came to the apartment? You didn't answer the door, did you?"

"No. I saw them outside. I was leaving and they were going in."

"Did you talk to them?"

"No. I didn't say a word, like you told me," Rufus said.

A wave of relief washed over her. "That's my boy."

What were two cops doing at their apartment building? They couldn't have been there for her because they didn't know who she was.

29

The ride was a bit choppy to the grove of trees, but it wasn't far. Smoke stopped fifty feet short of where the vehicle sat. "Game plan. I'll creep over there and you keep watch for any movement. He might take off if he spots me," he said.

We got out and eased the doors semi-closed without slamming them. Smoke bent over at the waist and took long strides along the outside edge of the forest. I sank down on one knee and watched, ready to jump up and run if it came to that. I lost view of Smoke when he stepped into the treed area. About a minute later, he stuck his head out and waved so I jogged over.

He tapped me on the shoulder and pointed south and kept his voice low. "We won't go too far, maybe a diameter of about sixty feet, see if we can flush him out." He headed the opposite direction. After we'd covered the area with no sign of Jaxson, we met back at his car.

Smoke pointed at the unlocked driver's side door. "Where the hell is Jaxson? Keys are in the ignition. Phone's in plain view on the seat. I'll see if it's the same prepaid burner." He dialed the number and it buzzed until it stopped on its own.

"Where do you suppose he put the rest of his stuff?" I said.

"Let's check the trunk." Smoke pulled a protective glove out of his back pocket, slipped it on his right hand, reached in, pulled the keys out of the ignition, and opened the trunk. Empty. "Figures," he said.

"Two scenarios flashed through my mind. Jaxson left the phone in the car so we'd get pings in this massive refuge and wouldn't be able to exactly pinpoint where it was. And he left the car here because he suspected we knew he'd bought it, and figured it was time to ditch it. Then he took off for places unknown."

"On foot?"

"Unless he got someone to pick him up," I said.

"In that case we should find that person's phone number in his burner. And your second scenario?" Smoke said.

"He's in the refuge, camping, plans to return for the car, doesn't worry about it being discovered. Either he forgot the phone or didn't plan to use it."

"I'll see what's in his call history." Smoke put a glove on his other hand and started his search. It took a while then he said, "Great, I left my memo pad in the car."

"Give me the numbers. I'll type them in my phone."

"There's only one outgoing call and a ton of incomings. I'd say ninety from his parents."

"Tell me the outgoing one."

He read it off. "It's gotta be the guy he bought the car from."

"Yeah."

"I'll phone the Sherburne deputies, let them know our location." After he finished the conversation, he called out, "Where are you Jaxson? Turn yourself in so we can help you."

"If only he could hear you," I said.

"Randolph needs to weigh in on this." Smoke called him and gave him a play-by-play. By the time he'd disconnected, I had the gist of it. "Chief will send the K-9 up here. As it turns out, they're in Little Mountain, so they'll be here in about twenty minutes. Hopefully find Jaxson before it gets too dark. Randolph doesn't want the two of us to pull an all-nighter here," he said.

"Why not? We're meeting with the Sherburne detective in the morning anyway."

"Yeah, who needs sleep?"

Deputy Hizy joined us on foot. Deputy Walters was there minutes later. Smoke had asked them not to ride their ATVs in too close in case Jaxson was in the vicinity. We talked quietly for a bit then Smoke said, "How do you want to handle this? One of you should go with our K-9, help with Jaxson's arrest if they find him. But you're both welcome to do that, as far as I'm concerned."

"I'll phone our supervisor, he can make the call," Hizy said. He walked away and when he returned told us, "We'll both stay, in case you need the backup."

"Good deal," Smoke said.

"You guys have about the most famous case in the state going on in Winnebago. Maybe in the whole nation," Walters said.

"You mean the one besides the sheriff's son absconding?" Smoke said with a touch of sarcasm in his voice.

"Ha! Lots of buzz about those bodies found in that bog. What a deal," Hizy said.

"No question about that. We're in the thick of a strange investigation with lots of moving parts. The victims are at the M.E.'s office for autopsy, and we hope to get all of them identified. Sooner or later." Smoke couldn't share the details, but they'd find out soon enough the first body recovered was from their county. The one whose image was burned into my brain for the long haul.

Smoke's phone rang and when he glanced at its face, told the deputies, "Excuse us." He looked at me and moved his head slightly, indicating I was the one included in 'us'. He uttered, "The M.E.," as he pushed the talk button. "Detective Dawes." He listened then blew out a puff of air. "Wow. Good news and no news, which in this case is not good. . . . I'm in the middle of something right now, but I'll see if I can reach the detective in Meeker. . . . By Monday? . . . That'd be a relief. I hear the whole state, make that the nation, is waiting for answers. . . . Appreciate it."

He disconnected and shook his head. "They identified the fourth victim, and you heard it was Meeker's? Gloria Freiburg."

"I prayed it'd be one of ours. And the third?"

"Couldn't ID him from the DNA samples, meaning it's not Oscar Wright or Silas Petty."

"Man. You're not kidding about wanting answers. What was that about Monday?"

"They'll complete the last autopsies tomorrow and the lab should finish up comparing the DNA samples by Monday."

"They've got to be matches with the family members of Agneta, and Silas, and Oscar, right? The seventh body, the third recovered from the bog, could he be the one missing from Blue Earth County?" I said.

"Anything's possible. But given the fact he's been gone six years, same as Gloria Freiburg, I'd say it's not probable. And he disappeared in April, not May,"

"Not probable but not impossible."

"I'll give the Meeker detective a ring. It's early enough in the evening, he can decide if he wants to make notification tonight or wait till morning," Smoke said.

"I'll get back to our host deputies."

Deputy Hanson arrived with his canine companion, Booster, a Belgian Malinois. Booster wore his tactical vest and tugged on his leash. Hanson kept a firm grip on it. After a brief, "Thanks for the quick response," from Smoke we led him to the car Jaxson had driven. Smoke opened the driver's door and backed away, giving the team room to work. Hanson commanded Booster to pick up the scent. Booster sniffed the seat and floor, whined, and pulled on his leash.

When Hanson said, "Search," Booster didn't hesitate. With his nose close to the ground he went from the car, past us, around a tree, then out of the treed area to Prairie's Edge Wildlife Drive and headed west.

Smoke and I exchanged looks. "Whaddaya wanna bet Jaxson's no longer in this wildlife refuge?" he said.

We gave them a head start before the Sherburne deputies, Smoke, and I followed in our vehicles at the team's pace—about five miles an hour—and left a respectable distance between us. Toward the end of the drive, I turned to Smoke. "It looks like your hunch was right."

"Damn. Now the question is, did he head north or south?"

Hanson and Booster reached the county road and Booster indicated Jaxson had turned north. Hanson commanded Booster to "Stop," and waited as Smoke and I got out of the car and caught up to them. "Should we keep tracking?" Hanson said.

"Maybe a quarter mile or so, see if Jax headed back into the refuge. My guess is he kept on going. Or he wouldn't have gone down the drive to the county road in the first place," Smoke said.

"Right." They resumed the search.

Vehicles passing by slowed down and two of the southbound ones pulled onto the shoulder to watch the K-9 Unit move with their full attention directed at their assignment. It was not meant to be a spectator sport, but whenever the public caught view of the team working, it was. Big time.

Hanson and Booster went the distance then stopped. We couldn't hear Hanson's command from that distance, but we knew what it was. The search had ended. And we'd hit another dead end in our efforts to locate Jaxson.

Smoke turned to the Sherburne deputies. "Well, that about wraps up this leg of our journey. We need to determine the next step. Either we tow the vehicle tonight or post someone here, see if Jaxson returns for it. Do you have the name and number of the nearest towing company?"

"Sure." Deputy Walters pulled out his phone and recited the info. Smoke and I both plugged it into our phones.

"Thanks," Smoke said.

When Hanson and Booster returned, Smoke said, "I guess that's a wrap for tonight."

"Glad to help. Anytime," Walters said, and the deputies took off.

"You and Booster can hop in this fine vehicle and we'll give you a ride back to yours," Smoke told Hanson.

We got in and Booster energetically sniffed around as far as he could reach. If Hanson had let him jump into the front seat, he would have. I cringed, thinking about the possible activities that had occurred in the beater and what we might be sitting on.

"Detective, you sure picked the bottom of the barrel from our undercover fleet," Hanson said.

"Yeah. I hope I make it back to Oak Lea."

"You've got contact info for a towing company if you don't," I said with a smile.

Smoke glanced at me with one eyebrow raised. "Thanks for the reminder." He pulled to a stop by Hanson's squad car, and we all piled out.

"We were hoping we'd find Jax, but hey," Hanson said.

"It'll happen. Meantime, it's Friday night so it might get crazy for you," Smoke said.

"That's how she rolls sometimes. Catch you later." Hanson secured Booster in the backseat, climbed in himself, and drove off.

"Randolph's on the edge of his seat, I'm sure." Smoke picked up his phone and called him. Their conversation was brief. "He's sending a deputy to stand guard until zero-eight-hundred tomorrow. If there's no sign of Jaxson by then, we'll bring the vehicle back to the sheriff's garage."

"When Jaxson left it here, he did it on purpose. I don't think he's coming back for it."

"Nor do I, but Chief wants the bases covered. He'll brief the sheriff, hopes it'll give the Kenners some relief knowing their son is still in Minnesota, and pretty damn close to home."

"Good. Do you suppose Jax bought another phone and contacted a friend to pick him up?" I said.

"That crossed my mind. But would anyone be dumb enough to get involved and not contact the sheriff's office? Let's hope not. Looks like Jaxson will miss his high school graduation, and if one of his friends gets charged with harboring a fugitive, he probably will, too."

"What a mess."

Smoke looked at his watch. "Our relief should be here in a half hour, give or take. You need to head home, get your gramps' old vehicle safely tucked into its garage bed for the night."

I chuckled. "Yeah, it is pretty old. I hate to keep it out too late."

"Is anyone looking?"

I glanced around. "What?"

"You're not officially on duty. We're not in Winnebago County, and I need to do this." He pulled me into his arms and kissed me, intensely passionate. It left me breathless, on fire.

Both of our faces were flushed when we separated.

"I hope that's a promise of things to come." My words came out as a breathless whisper.

"I promise."

I had to keep my attention focused on driving and not on Smoke. But at times I caught myself and needed to redirect, not get distracted. It was after 8:00 p.m. and the sun was lower in the sky, starting its slow descent to set in about forty-five minutes. I'd be home by then, waiting for the love of my life to join me and live up to his promise.

Even though I headed south, and Jaxson had gone north, I kept a lookout for him. In case. Oak Lea's High School graduation ceremony was set for a week from tonight and Jaxson had forfeited his seat there, lost the right to claim his diploma with his proud parents and grandparents in the audience, cheering. I blinked away threatening tears. All week I had gone from grieving over what Jaxson and his family were facing to Sawyer's tragic death and his family's sorrow.

As much as the resulting tragedies from that school fight tugged at my heartstrings, I was drawn back, time and again, to the investigation of the seven victims recovered from Coyote Bog. Learning their identities, flushing out the killer, and helping the families find closure . . . those were the primary goals.

Gramps wore the pajamas I'd given him for Christmas, and I sat with him for a while, mostly to have some time together. The dogs laid by our feet, content to be where we were. "I really appreciate you letting me use your car again, Gramps. I topped off the gas tank on the way home."

"You wouldn't a had to do that, Corky. Did you put the Buick to good use?"

"I did. Smoke and I have been looking for someone for a few days and got a lead he was in a neighboring county," I said.

"That wouldn't be your sheriff's son now would it?"

Gramps had followed the news. "You may be onto something, but I can't say who it is at this point."

"I shouldn't have asked, put you on the spot like that."

"Gramps, you can ask me anything, anytime. But I can't always give you an answer."

That tickled his funny bone, and his laugh sounded a lot like Santa Claus's "Ho Ho Ho."

I gave him a parting hug. "Do you need anything before we go?"

"No, no, can't think of a thing. I'm glad you brought the pooches over. They sure seem to like me."

"What's not to like?"

Queenie and Rex were happy to be home and burned off energy chasing around the yard in the dark. Queenie had energy to spare. Rex was older, but didn't want Queenie to show him up, so he kept pace. I called them in, went upstairs, and filled the bathtub with warm water and foaming lavender bath salts.

I climbed into the tub, laid back, and stretched with most of my body submerged. I closed my eyes and inhaled the relaxing scent. It seemed like a year since I'd last soaked in the tub. After ten minutes of appreciating the lap of luxury, I got out, patted dry, lathered Smoke's favorite scented lotion on my body, and put on pajamas.

I'd gotten in the habit of parking my squad car in the driveway if Smoke was staying over so when I heard the overhead garage door open, I knew he was pulling into the open stall next to my GTO. We wanted to maintain a measure of privacy in our relationship, and if he spent the night, anyone who happened by didn't need to know about it.

I opened the door from the kitchen to the garage with Queenie and Rex on either side of me, their wagging tails slapping against my legs. Smoke's wide grin brightened his face. "Now that's the kind of welcome home I love best."

I stepped back to give him room. The dogs brushed up against him when he leaned over and captured my lips in his.

"Mmm, you smell good," I whispered into the crook of his neck.

"Showered at the office. But I don't smell as sweet as you do."

"Did you eat anything on the way home?" I said.

"Nah, my appetite has come and gone for the last five or six hours. But now that you mention it, is there something in the freezer we can nuke?"

"Probably." He gave the dogs some attention while I pushed containers of food around in the freezer. "Here are the choices. Leftover offerings from my mother include goulash, a chicken and wild rice casserole, or a hamburger, zucchini, and carrot casserole."

"My stomach rumbled louder as you listed each one. That zucchini one is especially tasty, if I remember right."

"Yes, it is. Coming right up." I loosened the cover of the container and set it in the microwave. As it thawed and warmed, I opened the fridge and looked for a side dish to go with it. "There's a cucumber salad I got from the deli that should still be good."

"Sure. And a beer?"

I found two bottles and set them on the counter, along with the salad. Smoke pulled the opener from the drawer and popped off the tops. He handed one to me and lifted his. "Cheers to a better day tomorrow."

"Hey, today could've been worse. We got IDs on three victims, got leads on where our prime suspect probably lives, and found out Jaxson was nearby earlier in the day."

"Thanks for looking on the bright side. Carlson was right with his longest week comment. It seems like we've been on the bog body investigation and looking for Jaxson for a month. At least."

I laid my head on his chest and put an arm around his waist. "I know." The microwave dinged. "Let's get some sustenance. We're going to need it later."

Smoke kissed the top of my head. "If you're referring to a particular promise I hinted at earlier, you are so right, little lady."

30

Mama and Rufus

"Rufus, I'll bring our patient home tomorrow, so she'll be ready to leave on her heavenly journey on the twenty-sixth."

"But, Mama, the road is all tore up. How will we be able to get there?"

"Not to worry, Son. The information I got from the county website said the project will be done by then. It's a short stretch of road. And even if it's not done, we'll find a way."

Rufus did not like that thought one bit. He didn't like any of it in the first place. "I'm scared about that."

"We will succeed, no reason to let it upset you. I've tried to let go of the way I feel about the disruption the road project caused, and the poor souls who were disturbed out of their graves. I'm waiting for direction of what we need to do about that. In the meantime, we'll get our next patient tomorrow, and maybe another one on Monday. I'm working out those details."

"Mama, I think one at a time is better."

"Hush, Son. Don't get caught up in negative thoughts that go against your mother's calling."

"Okay, Mama."

31

I opened my eyes Saturday morning to Smoke's smiling face, his sparkling eyes on me. Memories of our night together flooded my mind and warmed my body. He was the most loving lover. The way he coaxed passion from the deepest recesses of my soul made my toes curl. He awakened sensations so sweet nothing this side of Heaven could begin to compare to them.

He kissed my nose. "I was about to wake you, Sleeping Beauty. You go on duty in an hour."

"Do I have to?" I said in the whiniest voice possible.

"No, but knowing you as I do, I'm confident you want to."

I dropped the whine. "You're right. Somewhere out there's a death angel and her helper we need to flush out. And find Jaxson, wherever he is. Maybe hiding in plain sight."

We arrived at the sheriff's office less than an hour later. For all the balls the department had up in the air, as we walked down the corridors, it felt unnaturally quiet at 6:48 that Saturday morning. Chief Deputy Randolph was at his desk; other command staff and office personnel were off for the weekend. He expected us, but when we stepped into his office, it took him a few seconds to process we were there. His worry lines were deeper and the circles under his eyes were darker. I felt a measure of guilt that Smoke and I had rested peacefully through the night after we finally fell asleep.

"Clayton, you been here all night?" Smoke said.

Randolph rubbed his cheeks vigorously. "I can't seem to get enough coffee in me this week to make much difference."

"I hear ya. But you gotta get some rest. Caffeine only works to a point. If I was your boss, I'd make you go home."

"As soon as I tie up some loose ends, that's where I'm headed."

"You said you have some updates," Smoke said.

"Yeah. No sign of Jaxson, so we're bringing his vehicle in." Randolph looked at his watch. "Should be loading it in about an hour. Sheriff's on board with that and if he could drive the tow truck himself, he would."

"Poor guy, chomping at the bit to do something," I said.

Randolph raised his eyebrows and nodded. "Natural, I guess."

"I know what he can do. Jaxson left his burner phone in the car and likely picked up another one. He knows we had his number—his father called him umpteen times—and Jax must have figured we used it to track his whereabouts. We're concerned he may have phoned one of his friends for help. If Mike or April can call Jaxson's contacts again, ask them that, that'd be good. Or maybe even pay them a visit. It's easier to lie over the phone than it is face to face," Smoke said.

"I like that and will ask them." Randolph thought a moment. "I've had deputies posted at the two apartments with no luck."

"Seems to be the prevailing theme, unable to locate people we're on the lookout for."

"I've got four-hour shifts around the clock. That angel of death has got to show up sooner or later. If not her, then the young man the neighbor saw coming out of her apartment in Emerald Lake."

"You'd think," Smoke said.

"It's possible she has a live-in gig, caring for someone," I said.

"Perish the thought, but could be," Smoke said.

"You might get a new lead from either Sherburne or Meeker when you meet with them," Randolph said.

"Speaking of which, we better get on the road, Sergeant. They expect us around eight thirty."

We arrived at the Sherburne County Sheriff's Office at 8:22 and met with Detective Tanner, a seasoned officer close to retirement, in a conference room. "I paid Mildred Dryer's son an early visit. He was shocked but relieved, and real happy they'll be able to bury her next to her husband, his father," he said.

Detective Tanner gave us time to digest his words and the impact Dryer's recovery will have on her family. He opened a folder and pulled out a thin stack of papers. "Here's the employee printouts from the facility where Mildred was living. Based on the physical description you provided, we narrowed it down to two females." He slid the sheets to our side of the table.

I picked them up for a closer look and passed them to Smoke. He studied them then laid them on the table between us. I had the file with our suspect's photos and gave them to the detective. "What do you think?" I said.

Tanner examined them, looking back and forth from one to the other. "Yeah, I can see how these two could be the same person." He pointed at the employee record he had. "And a likely match to Jasmine Kerry here." The brown-eyed brunette was listed as age thirty-four, five years before.

"Yep. Corky?" Smoke said.

"My thoughts exactly. It says she worked there for a short time. Left in July, two months after Mildred went missing."

"I'd guess she hung around for a while to make it look less suspicious," Tanner said.

"You checked the address in her file?" I said.

Tanner nodded. "An apartment in Elk River. A young family living there now, so I ran her DL for a current address and searched for her other places, including the state prison system. No trace of her. Anywhere."

"Stands to reason, seeing how she's an expert at making others disappear," Smoke said.

Even knowing that, his words still sent a chill up my spine and down my arms.

I picked up the copies of the possible suspects. "May we keep these?"

"Sure, they're for you."

"Thanks."

It was my turn to drive. "Why don't you swing by the wildlife refuge? It's not that far out of the way," Smoke said.

"Sure."

He sat in the passenger seat looking at photos of our suspect in three different personas. "It fries me how this deadly chameleon, posing as a caregiver, has been operating in and around our county for years, undetected. Three elderly people went missing and every investigation led to a dead end."

"Dead end is the sad truth. But that's not what you meant. She managed to fool investigators when she was questioned, or when they checked out her whereabouts at the time of the disappearances."

"Hindsight makes things we missed look way too obvious," Smoke said.

"Hence the expression. People fly under the radar all the time. Take the Unabomber, for example. He hand-delivered his bombs, had over a hundred FBI agents working full time for a while trying to figure out who he was. Where he was."

"Yeah, I remember that it took seventeen years and it was his own slip-up that finally led to his capture. Quite the deal."

"So don't beat yourself up about what happened with past investigations. Dolly/Rhoda/Jasmine has been hiding under a rock for years," I said.

"There's still that nagging shoulda woulda coulda deal."

"That's because you care, and what makes you the best detective we've got."

Smoke made a "hmm" sound.

We reached County Road 5 and turned north. Smoke had been scouting for Jaxson since we'd left Elk River. So had I. "Let's take Prairie's Edge in," he said.

"You have a feeling we'll catch Jaxson returning for his car?"

"No, but stranger things have happened."

A few minutes later, we saw a hiker on the drive, and I held onto the hope the "stranger things" comment had come true. Smoke leaned forward, his body visibly tense. My heart rate sped up. The young man had a large black hiker's backpack that stretched from shoulder to waist and appeared stuffed full. He wore black athletic pants and a stocking cap, so we couldn't see his hair. From the back, he looked like Jaxson.

"Pull up closer behind him and stop," Smoke said.

When I did, he jumped out and called out, "*Jaxson.*"

The young man looked over his shoulder and turned around. Not Jaxson. "Sorry, I thought you were a friend of ours." Smoke lifted his hand in a goodbye salute.

The young man half-smiled and nodded. "No problem, man." The doubtful look on his face as he glanced from Smoke to the unmarked squad said it all. He was relieved he was not the *friend* we were looking for. The man turned and continued on his way. Smoke climbed back into the car.

"Between the polo shirt with the sheriff's patch, the gun on your hip, and the badge on the front of your belt, you didn't fool him for a second."

"I caught that the same second. Not that I was trying to fool him. If I'd had a chance to think about it, I could've said, 'I thought you were someone else.'"

"No biggie. Until he turned around, I thought he was Jaxson. Doggone wishful thinking," I said.

"Let's drive to where Jaxson's car was found, see if there's any evidence he was there after the tow truck hauled it away."

I stopped short of where tire tracks went in and came out again, from where the car had been parked. We got out and visually perused the gravel, looking for footprints near or inside the tracks off the road. Nothing evident. "Let's drive the rest of the loop, then head back to Oak Lea. Unless something exciting happens along the way," Smoke said.

Nothing did.

The Meeker County Seat was southwest of Oak Lea, and about twenty miles further from our county seat than Sherburne's was. After a homecooked meal at a Mom and Pop café in town, we met with Detective Gale at the sheriff's office. He was tall and lean with slicked-back hair and a pencil mustache. His dapper look reminded me of actors in 1940s movies. Gale escorted us to his office, and we took seats opposite him.

Gale brushed a finger across his eyebrow. "I have to say, everyone in the department from the sheriff on down is grateful to you guys. It feels like two giant gifts were dropped from Heaven. Who'd have possibly guessed that two of our cold cases—ones that we weren't currently investigating—would be solved by the Winnebago County Sheriff's Department?"

"Our highway department pulling a body out of a bog during a construction project opened up one of the most bizarre cases we've ever had, no question about it. When we broadened the scope of the investigation, we didn't have a clue where it'd take us," Smoke said.

"We shake our heads all the time, don't we?" Gale said.

"That we do. Getting down to why we're here. You've got employee records from the care facilities, photos?" Smoke said.

Gale slid five files our way. "Have a look. Our missing folks were at separate facilities. Like you did, when the second one went missing, we looked at a possible connection between the two, but didn't find one. The special agent coming up with the idea that one person was posing as multiples was a godsend for our investigation."

We each picked up a file. After a glance at mine, it was easy to see the woman did not match the physical features of the other three. "No," I said, and traded files with Smoke. When I saw the next photo, the nerves on the back of my neck tingled. "She fits." She had worked at the facility Horace Kline had disappeared from.

"Yep," Smoke said. "And you're right, this one doesn't." He set it aside.

I opened the third file and shook my head. "This woman's ears are visible in the photo. She has ear lobes, our suspect doesn't." I pointed at the second one's photo. "Nor does she. Some features are easier to alter, but ears are tougher, unless you get prosthetic ones."

"No need to bother if your hair covers them up," Smoke said.

The fourth file wasn't a good match, but we hit pay dirt with the fifth. "I don't believe it. Smoke, look at this."

"Damn."

"She used the same identity she did in Winnebago County, when she worked for the two different facilities. Rhoda Barnes. Geez."

I handed Gale the file with our suspect's photos. He laid the pages on his desk and I pointed at Rhoda's. "Same info, except the address. She lived in Dassel back then."

"A few miles from the Winnebago County border," Smoke said.

"Right." Gale spent some time reading through them and looking at the photos. "So, Rhoda Barnes is listed as forty-six. The file you have on Dolly Corbin says she's fifty-eight. And the first one you think is a match, the female we have an employee record for as Krystal Wiley, is listed as forty-one years old. When I look at them side-by-side, they could be the same person."

"Wonder where she came up with the name Wiley. Probably how she thinks of herself. Wily, scheming," Smoke said.

"Seems to be that, all right. According to her DL, Rhoda Barnes lives right there in your county seat. Oak Lea. Krystal listed her address in Dassel. Wow, the same address as Rhoda had," Gale said.

"One less address to check out," I said.

"Right. But Krystal is currently nowhere to be found. At least not in Minnesota," Gale said.

"No surprises there. We got the address for Barnes in Oak Lea, and a different one for Corbin in Emerald Lake. Both apartments have been under surveillance since yesterday. She hasn't been to either place, so I'm thinking she's either staying with someone, like her accomplice, or she's got another place somewhere else," Smoke said.

"What a cluster," Gale said.

I pointed at Kerry's file. "Another one to add to the mix, Detective. From Sherburne. Jasmine Kerry, age thirty-nine, advancing her age to what she'd be now. Not that any of the ages she used are likely true," I said.

He studied the record a minute and shook his head. "However you look at it, it's nothing short of amazing she can span her age twenty years. And people believe her," Gale said.

"Smoke referred to her as a 'deadly chameleon' earlier."

Detective Gale sucked in air through his nostrils. "Deadly. Chameleon. Yes."

32

Mama and Rufus

Rufus had been trying to think of anything besides what his mother had planned for the day. He did not want another patient to take care of.

It was scary enough to think of one. But the thought of more than one made him break out in a sweat. If he knew how to escape, he would. But Mama was smart and would find him wherever he went. And might send him on his heavenly journey for disobeying.

He was tired of keeping up with the apartments and homes they had, and all the different ways Mama looked and dressed. He wanted her to be herself, the way she used to be before his grandfather made her do something terrible. It changed her in a bad way.

The phone Mama had given him rang and he was afraid to answer it. She told him he was only to talk to her. When he saw it was her number on the phone, he pushed the talk button. "Mama?"

"Son, I'm checking to see if everything is ready there. Does the room look nice and is the bed clean?"

"Yes, Mama."

"Have you seen any highway workers on the road today?"

"No, Mama. You told me they don't work on Saturday."

"Yes, just wanted to be sure. See you later, Son."

"Okay, Mama."

The patient coming home with Mama would start the ball rolling on something he hated more than anything in the world.

33

"We've got all these different identities the offender has been employed under. We need to contact all the elder care facilities and agencies in the county, show them her photos, see if she's got a job at one of them," Smoke said.

"Yes. Let's check with Randolph, see if his office staff will assemble the list so we can contact them. I'll be off the next three days, back on Wednesday, but we can't wait that long. We need to find her before she nabs her next victim," I said.

We were on the way back from Meeker, a few miles outside of Oak Lea, when my phone rang. Bob Edberg. "Hey, Bob—"

"My mother's gone." His voice cracked.

"*What?*"

"I got home . . . nobody here."

"I'm with Dawes, not far out. Stay put till we get there," I said.

He disconnected without a response.

"Edberg needs us. At his house. His mother's not there and he's in panic mode."

Smoke pressed down on the accelerator, and instead of continuing straight on County Road 12 into town, he turned off on a township road. Bob had built his home on a five-acre lot in a development with four other homes on a small lake, more the size of a pond. It was two miles from city limits, but the wooded area was isolated, quiet, and seemed like it was deep in the country.

As we pulled into Edberg's driveway, I phoned Communications with our location. We found him inside, pacing and pounding a fist into his other hand, over and over. "They stole the nanny cameras," he said.

"Bob . . ." After uttering his name, I didn't know what else to say.

"First question. Any sign of a struggle, anything out of place?" Smoke said.

"No. I looked around inside then went outside to see if she was there for some reason, called for her, but got no answer. I came back in to do a better search and that's when I spotted the cameras were gone."

"Notice anything else missing?" I said.

"Like money, jewelry? Haven't checked."

"You had a care attendant here when you left this morning, right?" Smoke said.

"Yes, one of the weekend workers."

"Have you talked to her, or the agency since you got home?" I said.

Edberg shook his head. "I called you first."

"The name of the agency and the attendant?" Smoke said,

"Senior Home Care. Jasmine Wiley."

Jasmine Wiley. The first name from Jasmine Kerry and the last name from Krystal Wiley. It felt like all the air got sucked out of the room. Neither Smoke nor I responded for what seemed like an hour. Finally Smoke, in remarkably calm voice said, "Can you describe her?"

"Attractive, early forties, dark brown hair, green eyes, five three, five four, slender, maybe weighs one twenty."

"Corky, will you grab the files?" Smoke said.

My mind raced and my stomach churned on the way to the car and back again. We were about to drop the worst of the worst news on Bob Edberg. How many times had we done that in our careers to others? But with one of our own, our friend, it was especially difficult. Nearly impossible. Edberg was astute and likely saw the writing on the wall as soon as he'd discovered his mother was missing, before he'd called us.

Smoke and Bob were locked in a hug that put a lump in my throat. I quietly spread the files on the kitchen table and waited for Bob to gain enough composure to take a look. His hands shook as he pulled a pair of readers from his breast pocket and slid them on. He placed both hands on the table, arms extended, and leaned forward. I sensed he needed to keep distance between himself and the images.

"Does Jasmine resemble anyone in these photos?" I said.

His voice quivered. "All of them, to a certain extent. She looks most like Krystal, but a little older than her. Wait a minute, my mother's favorite caregiver, Melody Reed, is almost a dead ringer for this Dolly Corbin. But heavier, with blue eyes, not brown. Shorter hair." Edberg bounced his pointer finger up and down at the photo.

"*Melody*, the one you saw going through your mother's dresser drawers?" I said. *The angel of death posed as two separate caregivers for Edberg's mother?*

"Are you sure?" Smoke said.

"I can't swear to it, but I'd say so."

"This just got a whole lot more complicated. And we need to take it one step at a time. What we got here looks downright incriminating, but the first thing is to check with the agency, see if they've had contact with Jasmine Wiley, if they have an explanation. Do you want me to handle that?" Smoke said.

It took Bob a few seconds to decide. "No, I will." He pulled the phone from his belt, found the contact he needed, and hit the talk button. "This is Bob Edberg, Emma's son. I got home from work and my mother isn't here. If Jasmine Wiley took her somewhere, I need to know why. And if Wiley left before her shift ended, left my mother here alone, I need to know why. She didn't leave a note. I need to call her, if you'll give me her number. . . . Then have her call me. Pronto." He disconnected. "It's their damn weekend answering service. She said it's against company policy to give out their employees' private numbers."

"If we don't hear from her in five minutes, I'll call back, as a Winnebago County detective," Smoke said. "What does Wiley drive?"

"Toyota Camry, four-door, gray, about three years old, I'd say."

Smoke phoned Communications and requested they check on a vehicle registered to Jasmine Wiley. He held on while they searched, then shook his head. "How about Melody Reed, again no known middle name." After a minute, he said, "Thanks," and disconnected. "No registered vehicles come back to either one."

"Damn, why didn't I ever catch the plate?" Bob said.

"You had no idea you'd need it, Bob. We'll get her number and address," I said.

The service called back a few minutes later. Bob put his hand over the phone. "Wiley hasn't picked up and there's no voicemail."

Smoke reached for his phone. "This is Detective Elton Dawes, Winnebago County Sheriff's Office. I'm here with Deputy Robert Edberg. It's critical we get Jasmine Wiley's phone number, a-sap. I also need her address. And another one of your attendants—Melody Reed's—address and phone number. I'll speak to your boss, cover for you. . . ." He made a writing gesture and I pulled out my pen and pad. I recorded the numbers for the two women as he recited them. "Thanks," he said and hung up.

"The answering service lady said she doesn't have Wiley's or Reed's addresses but will get a hold of the administrator and get back to us as soon as possible. Sergeant, will you get the numbers to Communications, see if they can pinpoint the locations of the phones? And have them send a message to our deputies, tell them to be on the lookout for a gray Camry."

I passed the requests on to Communications while Smoke phoned Chief Deputy Randolph. "Chief will be on his way here as soon as he gets a deputy to help interview your neighbors, Bob. Should be here shortly."

Edberg took another look at the photos on the table, shook his head, took off his glasses, and brushed away sprouting tears. "This monster who hides behind all these disguises has got my *mother*."

I laid my hand on his shoulder. "We don't know that for sure. But if she does, we'll find her. That monster and your mother."

"You know it'll be all hands on deck until we get your mother safely home," Smoke said.

"Should we dust for fingerprints, look for touch DNA here?" I said.

Edberg shrugged. "With the number of attendants that take care of my mother, I'm sure their fingerprints and DNA are comingled all over the house."

"In this case, we know who the suspect is. At least we know her by the different names she goes by. You raise a good point about fingerprints, Sergeant, and most facilities require them with the background checks, nowadays. The problem is, I don't believe the BCA retains those cards after they've been checked. If she was in the criminal justice system, she would have been flagged before now," Smoke said.

"I think you're right. She'd have to sign a consent form for fingerprints to be taken in the first place. And she wouldn't do that if she had a criminal record," I said.

Chief Deputy Randolph knocked on Bob's door and identified himself as he entered. Deputy Vince Weber arrived a minute later. "Geez, Bob, really sorry here. We'll find your mother," Weber said.

Edberg nodded. "Thanks."

Smoke gave Randolph and Weber the lowdown, including the possibility Wiley had posed as a second caregiver for his mother. They checked out the additional photos we'd gotten from Sherburne and Meeker Counties.

"Yeah well, she fits right in with the ones we figured were the most likely suspects," Weber said.

"She's been clever enough to evade interrogations up till now, but that's about to change. We're surveilling the two apartments twenty-four seven. She's bound to show up before long," Randolph said.

"Vince, check the four neighbors' places here, find out if any of them noticed a gray car in Edberg's yard, or if they saw his mother outside with anyone, particularly getting into a car. If they saw the car leave, what time that would've been," Smoke said.

"My one neighbor's retired, and he's out puttering in his yard a lot. I'm counting on him," Edberg said.

"On my way," Weber pulled out his notepad and left.

"I'm gonna try Wiley's number," Edberg said. He hung up after a minute. "Maybe Reed will answer." No luck there, either. "Where the hell is she? Where did she take my mother? Mom can't handle a lot of stress. Things upset her for no good reason. It's gotten worse with the dementia. Much worse. The trauma she must be going through . . ."

Edberg sniffled and grabbed a few tissues from a box on the end table. He dabbed his eyes then pulled out his phone. "I'll try the numbers one more time."

Another exercise in futility, and his anxiety had climbed. I wanted to confiscate Edberg's phone, tell him that trying Wiley's and Reed's numbers was making him more anxious. On the other hand, he was doing something when doing nothing felt worse.

Weber reported back. "Two neighbors were home. One didn't see nothin′ and the one you called out, Bob, spotted a gray Camry leaving your driveway around fourteen hundred." One hour and thirty-eight minutes before. "Neighbor Jim didn't have a real good view, what with the sun in his eyes, but it looked to him like a woman was driving. Didn't notice anyone else in the car. Didn't see your mother outside before the car left."

"Was my mother in the car or not?" Edberg puffed out an exasperated, "huh."

"He coulda just missed seeing her," Weber said.

"Or, let's look at another possibility: Wiley left early. Would your mother have gone outside alone?" Smoke said.

"Not likely. She isn't very mobile. Her rheumatoid arthritis makes it painful for her to walk. But I know people with dementia sometimes wander. Like I said, I took a quick look out there, but we should do a better search to make sure she's not here."

"Sure, let's do that," Smoke said.

"Vince, appreciate you staying late, helping out, but we're covered here so you can go on home," Randolph said.

Weber nodded. "Holler if you need me."

The five of us trooped outside. Weber took off and Edberg assigned the rest of us a section to check. I had the backyard where the mowed grass ended at the lake. With no beach, tall reeds grew several feet out from the shoreline. I walked about a hundred feet one way, turned around, and covered about the same distance the opposite way. I closely examined the lake's bank and the plants growing out from it. No disturbance, no sign anyone had entered the water from Edberg's yard, or from the neighbors' yards on either side of him.

I stepped backward up the lawn from the lake for a broader view, scouting the rest of the shoreline. The tops of the reeds swayed back and forth in the breeze. Nothing appeared amiss. I turned to face Edberg's house and searched for anything out of the ordinary, like a thread from a piece of clothing caught on a low-hanging tree branch. Anything that would indicate Mrs. Edberg was out there. But spotted nothing.

We met back in Bob's living room to compare notes. Our silence was the unspoken word none of us had found a sign Mrs. Edberg had wandered outside. "Bob, if it's any consolation, there's no indication your mother fell in the lake." I left out the words *and drowned.*

Edberg's jaw clenched as he gave a single nod. "I'll try their numbers again."

My phone rang before he had the chance. Communications. "Sergeant Aleckson. . . . Where? . . . Thanks, Robin, we'll head down there." I disconnected and smiled. "Wiley's phone pinged in Bison Park, downtown Oak Lea."

"We're on it," Smoke said.

"Bob, you ride with me," Randolph said.

We were in our vehicles in seconds and left the personnel files for later. Smoke and Randolph activated the emergency light bars in their rear windows, then killed them when we got close to the park. I phoned Edberg, relayed they should take the park's north entrance, and we'd go in on the east side, in case Wiley was on her way out.

On the warm, sunny Saturday afternoon, scores of people were there, making the most of the near-perfect weather. Kids giggled and romped on playground equipment, groups sat around tables and on benches, teens tossed frisbees and balls. Walkers filled the pathway that ran along Bison Lake. Normal people engaged in normal activities. But the one we sought was not normal, by any definition, or stretch of the imagination.

"Jiminy, this is gonna be fun," Smoke said.

The main parking lot was nearly full. We parked in one of the few available spots, and Randolph found another. Smoke and I met them at his car. "Four of us walking around with guns and badges is going to get people's attention, put them on watch. And Edberg's uniform adds an extra alert," Randolph said.

"Might be a good way to flush her out. If she sees Bob, she's sure to run. Then we'll sic Corky on her. Out of the four of us, she's the best bet to catch her," Smoke said.

We took a minute to survey the crowds, searching for our suspect.

"When I saw her this morning, she was wearing scrubs. Light blue," Edberg said.

"I don't spot anyone in blue scrubs," I said.

"No. But there's a lot of people here," Smoke said.

"Sergeant, why don't you start in the restroom down below and check the lower pavilion. Detective, the upper pavilion and down toward the lake. Bob, you and I can walk around together, see if we spot her," Randolph said.

Ten minutes of effort, and all we got were curious looks and questions from people who wondered why we were there. But no sign of Jasmine Wiley. We headed back to Randolph's car. "We tried calling her number once in here, let's give it another try," Randolph said.

When we heard a faint ringing, I think all of us held our breaths for a better listen. I surely did. We spread out a bit and headed in the direction of the sound. It stopped ringing so Bob dialed again. We were within fifteen feet of the upper pavilion where at least twenty people gathered, but not one of them dug for a phone. As we closed in, we discovered the reason. The ringing came from inside a garbage container. "Damn," Edberg muttered.

"At least she left the phone on so we could find it," Randolph said.

"I guess," he replied.

"Bob, you got a glove in your pouch?" Smoke said. Every deputy carried a pouch on his or her duty belt with about ten protective gloves stuffed inside.

He fished one out and handed it to Smoke who put it on. We turned the container on its side for better access. I squatted down with Smoke and peered inside. He felt around until he located a brown bag with the phone inside. He stood up, reached in the bag for the phone, then held it in his palm.

A couple walked by and darted interested looks our way, quietly exchanging words.

Randolph righted the garbage container. "Let's get back to our cars. I'll let Communications know they can drop the search on this number."

"Pop the trunk and I'll grab an evidence bag," I told Smoke.

I found one in his storage case and he dropped the phone inside. "We'll check incoming and outgoing numbers then turn the phone over to our lab for a forensic investigation," he said.

"Why don't I ask the folks in the pavilion if they saw our suspect. If someone did, it'd help establish a timeline of when she was here," I said.

"Sure," Randolph said.

After going from table to table with no luck I threw in the towel. None of them had been there longer than thirty minutes, and no one noticed a woman in light blue scrubs by the pavilion.

When I gave the team my report, Smoke said, "Watching all the head shaking when you were talking to them, I figured as much."

Edberg kept his voice low and I had to strain to hear him. "I won't sleep until we find that evil devil."

34

Mama and Rufus

Mama carried in a box and handed it to Rufus. "This has been a fine day, Son. It proves we're on the right mission. Our patient's son put three new clocks in his house and thought I wouldn't notice. I figured they had to be cameras. What else would they be? No one gets three new clocks at the same time."

Rufus scratched his head. "Cameras?"

"To videotape people. They have them in daycare facilities and other places to check on attendants, making sure they're taking good care of those who need it. Of course, I always treat my patients very well."

"I know, Mama."

"This patient keeps talking about someone taking her things. I don't know if others did that or not. I never did, not until today. After I disconnected the cameras."

"Mama, maybe you shouldn't have taken the cameras at all."

"Rufus, don't you see? I had to. Otherwise they would've seen the patient leave with me. They don't know who I am, but still."

"Okay."

Mama smiled. "And I did something to keep them busy, in case they found out what my other cell phone number was."

Rufus didn't want to know but asked anyway, "What is that?"

"I hid it in a public park. That should keep them looking for a long time."

35

It was 4:40 when we gathered back at Bob Edberg's. I collected the files of our prime suspect in her variety of guises from the table.

"Why haven't we heard back from the answering service? It's been well over an hour," Randolph said. "What's the number, Bob?" He punched in each one as Bob recited them and then hit the speaker button.

"Senior Home Care." The female who answered sounded like she was fifteen.

"It's Chief Deputy Randolph, Winnebago County Sheriff's Office. We've waited way too long for someone to get back to us. What's going on?"

"Oh! I'm sorry. My shift just started at four-thirty, and I have a note to try the administrator again. The one on the shift before me left her a message but didn't hear back."

"I'll need that phone number."

"Oh! I guess that'll be okay. I don't know why she hasn't called back. She always does, like right away." All four of us recorded the name and number she gave on our memo pads.

When Randolph disconnected, he dialed the administrator's number and left a curt message. He pushed the end button with extra force. "What kind of a business is she running anyway? Her office is closed on weekends and that's when things always seem to go south. She's got to have a reliable way for people to reach her." He gave the tops of his thighs loud slaps.

Edberg's face was pale and strained. "We have to find my mother."

Randolph nodded. "Change out of your uniform and meet us at the office, Bob. We'll check Wiley's phone, have it interrogated for deleted calls and messages—"

Randolph's ringing phone interrupted. He looked at the face and walked some feet away. "Mike. How are you doing? . . . I guess the good news is, it shows Jaxson doesn't want to get his friends in trouble by asking for their help. . . . It's got to be about impossible for you to deal with this. . . . Mike, shifting gears, you should know what else we've got." Randolph gave the sheriff an abbreviated version of Edberg's mother's disappearance and that we'd launched an investigation. He left out details about the suspect.

After listening to Kenner for a moment, Randolph said, "Hang in there. Call if you need anything, okay? Later," and disconnected. "Sheriff and his wife got in touch with every one of Jaxson's friends and not a one has heard from him. Sheriff said he'd pray for your mother's safe return, Bob."

Edberg looked down and nodded.

A father and mother with a son out there *somewhere*. A son with a mother out there *somewhere* held by someone with depraved intentions. Nightmares that our friends were living, breathing every minute. We'd do everything in our power to find Jaxson and Mrs. Edberg before either of them came to further harm.

Randolph, Edberg, and I hovered around Smoke's desk and watched him push buttons. Mrs. Edberg had been gone over three hours. "Jasmine Wiley had this phone for one purpose only. To get calls from Senior Home Care. And they go back just two months. She only called in once," Smoke said.

"That's about the first time I met her, two months ago," Edberg said.

"What about Melody Reed? How long has she been coming to your home?" I asked.

"Hasn't been quite that long, maybe six weeks."

"Two recent hires," Randolph added.

Smoke's phone buzzed and he raised his eyebrows. "It's the M.E." He answered and pushed the speaker button. "Detective Dawes."

"Detective, Bridey Patrick." The chief medical examiner herself. On a Saturday.

"Doc. You have news?"

"Yes."

"I put you on speaker phone so Chief Deputy Randolph, Sergeant Aleckson, and Deputy Edberg can hear what you've got for us."

"That's fine. Those of us here at the office can appreciate what the families you're working with are going through while they await answers. So do the scientists in the lab. We completed the three autopsies this morning and the lab was able to positively identify all three victims."

We wouldn't have to wait until Monday. I uttered a silent prayer of thanks, knowing who they were before Dr. Patrick recited their names. “Oscar Wright, Agneta Keats, and Silas Petty.”

When Smoke bowed his head, it started a chain reaction and the rest of us followed suit. Three more families would have the closure they’d sought for a year or more.

Patrick raised her voice’s volume. “Are you there, Detective?”

Smoke cleared his throat. “Yes, yes, we’re here. You delivered a humdinger of a message and it needed to sink in.”

“I can understand that. We search for answers, all of us who work for victims and their families. That’s what makes us so diligent. Sadly, we don’t always find all the answers we want. In these cases, since the victims’ family members were available, we got the matches we hoped for. Very rewarding to identify the victims.” She paused. “With the exception of John Doe number two, of course. Any leads on his identity, Detective?”

“We have one possibility, a man reported missing six years ago in Blue Earth County. We’ll check that out first, get a photo from their sheriff’s office for comparison. If he looks like the victim, we’ll take it from there. If not, we’ll get an image of John Doe Two to the media outlets in our county, along with the surrounding ones. The sheriff’s office can post it on our social media sites. If need be, we’ll expand to the metro news channels.”

“It sounds like you’ve thought this through, Detective. We have photos, of course.”

“It’s fine to send them to the Blue Earth Sheriff, but we don’t want to post the originals for the public. We’ll need a computer-generated image for that.”

"I'll have the lab take care of that. We'll be ready to release the bodies early next week and will need the names of the funeral homes the families will be working with," Patrick said.

"Sure. We'll try to take care of that tomorrow. Right now, we're in the middle of something that's taken top priority."

Edberg let out a loud gasp. I moved behind him, put my hands on his shoulders, tightened my grip for a moment, and stepped away when he nodded. A signal he was okay. I knew as well as he did, he was not even a little bit okay.

"I'll let you get back to work," Patrick said.

"Thanks, Doc. For all you do. And how well you do it."

Patrick made a short giggle-like sound. "Thank you, Detective. Goodbye." She ended the call.

Bridey Patrick had a crush on Smoke and it bubbled to the surface every once in a while. Had she known Bob Edberg was in crisis over his mother's disappearance, I think she would have stifled her instinctive reaction.

"That's what we've waited for. Their identities. Sad news for three families, but a big relief at the same time." Smoke looked at Edberg. "I think you know this, but for all of us in the sheriff's office, nothing is more urgent than finding your mother."

Along with her wicked abductor. Abductors.

Randolph finally got a call from the Senior Home Care administrator, Courtney Wade. He clicked on the speaker feature.

Wade spoke with an authoritative voice. "Chief Deputy Randolph, my sincere apologies for the delay in returning your call. We've been out on our pontoon this afternoon and I didn't realize I'd forgotten my phone in the car. Not until I got back to it."

"We have a grave situation here and need the addresses for both Jasmine Wiley and Melody Reed," Randolph said.

"Sorry, I don't know them offhand. They're in the personnel files."

"We'll meet you at your office and have a look at those files, with your permission," Randolph said.

"You think they were involved in something criminal?"

"It looks that way. How soon can you get to your office?"

"Umm, fifteen minutes? I'm in Emerald Lake now," Wade said.

"We'll see you there." Randolph looked from Smoke to me. "You two are the best versed on the suspect. This whole investigation, really. You know where Senior Home Care is, right?"

"Sure," Smoke said.

Courtney Wade waited for us outside the large brick building that housed several businesses, in addition to the one she ran. Wade was in her forties, and under her no-nonsense demeanor, it seemed she liked to relax and have fun. Or she wouldn't have spent the afternoon floating around on a boat.

Smoke and I introduced ourselves, then Wade escorted us to her office.

"Your chief deputy was vague about what's going on, but my answering service staff said that Jasmine Wiley was not at the Edberg home when Emma's son arrived home this afternoon, and his mother was not there, either. That she's missing."

"Correct. We have reason to believe Wiley may intend to harm Missus Edberg," Smoke said.

"Whatever would make you think that?"

"Convincing evidence has come to light that indicates she's done it before. More than once," I said.

Wade's skin blanched. "Her background is clean, her references all positive."

"She's been living a lie, deceiving employers and other people for years," I said.

"Our clients love her. She takes wonderful care of them," Wade said.

"All part of her deception. If you'll find her file, along with Melody Reed's, we need to have a look," Smoke said.

"You think Jasmine and Melody are working together?"

"We think they are the same person."

Wade swayed and grabbed the edge of her desk for support. "*What*? How is that possible?"

Smoke waited a minute then shook his head. "The files. Please?"

Wade's hands trembled as she pulled out two drawers, thumbed through them, retrieved the records, and handed them to Smoke and me. We laid them on the desk, and each flipped one open. I recorded the listed addresses for no good reason. Maybe to look official, maybe so I didn't groan or roll my eyes. Jasmine Wiley, age 43, listed her address as the same one Rhoda Barnes had in Oak Lea. Melody Reed, 61, had an address that matched Dolly Corbin's in Emerald Lake.

Smoke lined their photos side by side and pointed. One look confirmed what we believed. She was the suspect we were searching for. One person with two identities, working for the same agency. "Do you see the resemblance?" he said.

"I guess they do look like they could be mother and daughter. I'd never seen them together, of course, and didn't notice it before. I see how they look alike in the photos, but they're so different from each other in person. Melody has an Irish background and you can hear the lilt in her voice. Jasmine has a slight eastern accent, Boston maybe. Their mannerisms are not at all alike. Melody walks with heavy steps, Jasmine is graceful, light on her feet."

"You've noticed details about both of them, sounds like," Smoke said.

"I like to get to know my employees as best I can. I make occasional site visits at clients' homes, check to see how things are. It's important our clients have caregivers they like, that they trust . . ." She stopped, looked down, and shook her head. "This is awful."

Smoke picked up the files. "Can we get copies of these? Or do we need to get a warrant?"

"I'll make copies. You're the law, as far as I'm concerned. If it turns out they're not involved with any wrongdoing, will you either shred them or return them to me?"

"Yes, ma'am," Smoke said.

We were on the road, rolling again. "Phone Randolph, tell him we're on our way, let him know about the same addresses situation," Smoke said.

"Sure." After the call, I said, "Randolph is asking Oak Lea PD to help surveille the Corwin/Wiley apartment here." I checked my notes then closed my memo pad. "How in the world does she keep track of all her identities? She must have a big flow chart, maybe separate closets with clothes and accessories for each one."

Smoke bopped the steering wheel. "That's a thought. As far as we know, she uses up to two, possibly three, IDs at any given time. Different jobs. How does she juggle everything? No clue.

She's damn clever, that's a scary fact, and has eluded the authorities way too long.

"I can't wait to see the look on her face when we slap cuffs on her wrists. And when the judge sentences her. And when she gets hauled off to prison with no chance of parole. She's been breaking bread and breathing air as a free person far too many years," he said.

"As has her accomplice."

"Yep. And if he's not with her, she damn well better 'fess up who he is and where he's at."

"We got a good look at the big guy who is likely the one working with her. And neither has shown up at either apartment, driving us all nuts," I said.

"They're hiding somewhere, that's a given. We found their secret burying place, removed the bodies. Ruined their whole set up. They could be scouting out another burial site," Smoke said.

"We have plenty of wetlands in Winnebago County to choose from."

"Unfortunately."

"We have to find Missus Edberg before they find a new spot," I said.

"Yes."

"I've thanked God over and over all week that our highway guys took on that project to fix the road over Coyote Bog. If they hadn't done the clean out, those bodies might never have been found. Their families wouldn't have found out what happened. For us, knowing the killer posed as a caregiver put us on a path to find her. Or, like Special Agent Erley said, she will keep on killing," I said.

"The major stumbling block right now is we know she's out there, but where? If we don't find her a-sap, it's a given she'll end Missus Edberg's life."

Icy chills surged throughout my body. "As afraid as I am for Jaxson Kenner, I'm terrified for Bob's mother. The seven victims recovered from the bog all lost their voices, couldn't tell their stories. Except to the medical examiner. We can't let Missus Edberg lose hers."

Smoke blew out a breath of air. "No."

36

Mama and Rufus

"**M**ama, the patient keeps asking where she is," Rufus said.

"You need to keep telling her she's in a good place and is going to an even better one."

"I told her that. But she keeps asking anyway."

"That's why she was chosen to be sent on her heavenly journey, Son," Mama said.

"And she said she hurts."

"I'll give her medication to help take her pain away."

"That'd be good, Mama. I don't want her to hurt."

"Neither do I, Son. Maybe you should drive to Maple Grove, or to the store you like in Waconia, and get some groceries. No one knows you there, do they?"

"No one knows me here, either."

"That's true. Would it make you feel better to get out of the house for a while? I will take loving care of our patient."

Getting out would help Rufus. He didn't like having patients around, even if it wouldn't be for long. None of them had names and that made him sad. He had to help Mama send people on their heavenly journeys and never knew their names.

"I have a good idea. They have nice theaters we've been to in both of those towns. Why don't you take in a movie, even two movies? It'll get you out of here for hours and might help you sleep better tonight. How does that sound?"

"Go to a movie? I haven't done that for a long time."

"I know. We've been too busy with moving and everything. Don't worry about groceries for tonight. We have plenty of food here."

Rufus whistled as he headed out the door. Mama said he could see two movies. And it'd be late when he got home, so the patient would be sleeping by then.

37

Back at the sheriff's office, Bob Edberg paced up and down the corridor, his head down, like he needed to keep watch a on his feet. He looked up when Smoke spoke his name.

"Chief's in his office talking back and forth with the surveillance deputies and Communications. Last I heard our guys have found reasons to stop three gray Camrys in different parts of the county. None of the drivers fit Jasmine's or Melody's descriptions. A teenage boy, a fifty-something man, and a seventy-something woman. Neither the death angel nor her suspected accomplice have shown up anywhere," Edberg told us.

"They're out there. We'll find them," Smoke said.

"I don't get it. She knows I work for the sheriff, that we'd be all over this. Does she look at taking my mother as some sort of coup? Some big achievement, like she's the genius and we're bumbling idiots and will never catch her?"

I stepped in front of him and put my hands on his shoulders to capture his attention. "She wouldn't be the first criminal to think that. But eventually they either slip up or we uncover evidence of their crimes. And we track them down. She may think she's untouchable, but she's not. She did something incredibly stupid taking your mother. Like Smoke said, we will find her."

As Edberg stared into my eyes, his own filled with tears. "Chief ordered me not to look for her on my own, but it's been over four hours since Mom disappeared. I haven't decided what to do."

Smoke moved in beside me, and I dropped my arms. He laid a hand on Edberg's bicep and gave it a little shake. "Bob, you need to listen to Randolph. You can't be objective and might get yourself caught up in some vigilante justice before you knew what happened. If things went south, who would take care of your mother?"

Edberg shrugged. "If I find out where that devil is, I'll call for backup."

That didn't give me the least bit of reassurance. "Bob, you're not the Lone Ranger here. Let the chief make the call. Maybe he'll let you ride along with another deputy. Then he'd be the one to call for backup."

Chief Deputy Randolph found us in the corridor. "Captain Armstrong and I have been working about a hundred miles an hour for the last thirty minutes. We called in sixteen off-duty deputies and are stationing them at points on the state highways and county roads. Half of them will be in unmarked squads and undercover vehicles. We got photos of the suspect and a facial composite of the man you two met outside the apartment building in Emerald Lake."

Randolph gave a nod to Smoke and me, then continued, "Communications sent the photos to every deputy and they're working on getting them posted on our Facebook page, asking the public for information. Plus, they'll be contacting all the cities in the county, see if they'll share the post on their pages. If they've got one."

"How about Sherburne and Meeker?" I said.

"Yeah, forgot to mention they're contacting them, too," Randolph said.

"That's gotta generate responses. The suspect's worked with how many people over the years," Smoke said.

"Keep praying," Edberg said.

"Chief, we need to assemble a list of all the elder care facilities and agencies in the county, get those photos to them, see if any have a current employee who matches up with one of the offender's identities. And what address she's using," Smoke said.

"Yes. I'll see if Dina is available to get on that right away." Dina was a top-notch administrative assistant. But was she available? "Even so, there may not be the right people at those places who can answer our questions tonight."

"There aren't that many facilities county-wide. I've done a little research because Gramps will probably need more help than Mother can provide some day. I think there's seven or eight nursing homes. Ten or so assisted living places. Maybe six home care agencies that provide service here," I said.

"Good to know. Bob, you'll be my partner. We'll be in my unmarked at the intersection of County Road Thirty-seven and County Road Eight in Emerald Lake. We have as good a chance as anyone of catching her."

Edberg sucked in a breath. "Copy." Randolph had included him, after all.

"Sergeant, will you station at Thirty-five and Seven; Detective at Thirty-five and Six?"

"Sure. I'll pick up Gramps' car," I said.

A puzzled look crossed Randolph's face for an instant. "That's right, you're off for three days and would've turned your squad over to Holmes. One last thing, all radio communication will be on channel three. Any bases we didn't cover?" When no one answered, he said, "I'll call Dina and then we'll head to our post, Bob. Good luck, team."

Smoke dropped me off at Gramps' house and I drove away in the old Buick about a minute later. The investigation that turned into a search for Mrs. Edberg took on a surreal feeling. It was closing in on 7:00 p.m. Less than two hours to sunset, when dusk would set in. Corbin/Wiley/Whoever may have planned to use the cover of night for traveling, transporting her victim to a location we needed to find. Randolph hadn't indicated how long he wanted us to keep watch. It likely depended on what transpired before he made another call.

Five hours had passed since Edberg's neighbor spotted the gray Toyota Camry leave his driveway. Every hour since, with no sign of the wicked ones and their captive, was torturous. Randolph, Smoke, and I tried our best to appear cautiously optimistic, but I doubted it gave Edberg an ounce of assurance.

The one bright spot for me was that Edberg hadn't made it to the crime scene at Coyote Bog on Monday. He'd been dispatched to Oak Lea High School instead, when Jaxson Kenner punched Sawyer Harris in the parking lot. Had Edberg personally witnessed the markings on the victims' bodies and thought his mother might face the same fate, he would be in far worse shape than he already was.

I shook the thought from my head and phoned my brother to check in. "Hey, John Carl."

"Corky, what's up?"

"I got assigned a detail and I'm not sure how late I may be working."

"Since I moved back to Oak Lea I've noticed that happens a lot," he said.

"We do our best to control criminal activity so I don't go into overtime, but it still happens. You and Sara have a date tonight?"

"We do—she's at my house. I'm guessing you need us to check on Queenie and Rex again?"

"Please. Let them run around for ten or so minutes, give them fresh food and water. I appreciate it, Brother, and tell Sara 'hi.'"

"Hi, Sara . . . She says 'hey' back. And we'll take care of the pooches."

"Thanks." I phoned Smoke next.

"You're at your post, Corinne?"

"I am. And you?"

"Yep. We got the roads covered on either side of Coyote, anyway. No one can sneak by us."

"I wish they'd try so we could grab them," I said.

"I hear ya. This turn of events with Bob's mom is eating at me. Why didn't we show him the personnel files when we first got them? He could have picked her right then and there. Missus Edberg would still be home and the angel of death would be locked up where she belongs, before she had a chance to take his mother."

"Smoke, you're talking twenty-twenty hindsight again. We got back to the office with the first of the records yesterday, at the end of Bob's shift. Had he been the one to show up when we sorted through them, instead of Weber, we would have taken a different course. If we'd had the slightest clue what was about to happen, Bob would've been the first person to see the photos."

"You're right. My brain must be fried."

"We're all in the same boat—"

"That feels more like a sinking ship," he interrupted.

"We may get a lead from the care facilities and agencies in this county if anyone worked there who fits the deadly chameleon's description."

"But we're a day late and a dollar short."

"Not if we get her current address," I said.

"Hold on to that hope."

"Smoke, back to the bad and the ugly, I've been thinking about the chameleon and her captives, wondering how long she holds them." I flipped open my memo pad. "Looking at the dates the victims went missing, there isn't a common day. The ninth, seventeenth, fourteenth, eleventh, thirteenth, fifteenth. Today is the nineteenth. That's a range of ten days."

"Erley said she had a psychotic break in May. We don't know what day of the month that was. Since the people disappeared different days, she likely abducts them when it's most convenient for her. And then she holds them until the fateful date when she kills, brands, and buries them."

"Smoke . . ." My voice cracked.

"I know. I'm scared, too."

"Maybe you should take a swing up Floyd Myren's driveway. The deputies haven't had any luck so far catching either the caretaker or the owner himself, when they've checked," I said.

"Sure. Wait, did you say the caretaker drives a gray car?"

"Oh, you mean like the one Jasmine Wiley's? No, I think the caretaker's car was silver, and I couldn't tell the make or model from this distance the last time I sat at this intersection."

"It looks damn quiet at the house, but I'll run up there and have a look." He hung up and called back a few minutes later. "No sign of life there, and no sighting of a gray car, or any other vehicle."

The sun set at 8:47 p.m. and darkness closed in around us by 9:15. I'd spoken with Smoke a few times while we watched traffic travel the county roads to the detour and head either west from County Road 6, or east from County Road 7. No one drove around the barriers, braving the rough single lane that was marginally passable. My eyes were continually beckoned back to the house on the hill that overlooked Coyote. I was frustrated deputies hadn't been able to get an answer at the door. Floyd Myren must be among the winter snowbirds that waited until summer to return to Minnesota. Why was he so elusive? When I started my next rotation, I'd run another check on him, send him an email to see if I could locate him.

Radio traffic on channel 3 was light and none of the deputies' stops brought us closer to finding Mrs. Edberg. I phoned her son to see how he was holding up.

"Hi, Sergeant." Edberg's voice was flat.

"Bob, you want to crash in my spare bedroom or den tonight? I'll make sure Detective Dawes is there to protect your reputation."

He made a "ha" sound. "Thanks, but I'd rather wear out the carpets at home."

"That's why I have hardwood floors on the main level. Even after years of my pacing/thinking sessions, they still look pretty good," I said.

"Thanks, though."

I tried not to obsessively check the time, but it had gone into ultra-slow motion. At 9:29, I tried to stifle a yawn. Unsuccessfully. When my mouth opened wide and didn't want to close again, it set off a series of yawns that alerted me I was at a low ebb. Sitting in Gramps' car in the dark, spotting bats swooping in and out from the treed area to my right, it was starting to feel like a surveillance from hell. Traffic had been a minimum over the past hour.

When my phone buzzed, I got startled, and my shoulders shot up a couple of inches.

"Did I wake you?" Smoke said.

"Pretty near. I wish Randolph would tell us how long he wants us out here. Or if he's sending relief."

"I'm the messenger letting you know he's calling it at ten. He didn't want it over the radio, even on channel three. He'll keep deputies on the main roads until midnight. The unspoken message I got from Randolph is he thinks the deadly chameleon has landed somewhere by now. I do, too."

"Yeah. As much as I hate to admit it. Meet you at my house? Rex and Queenie are probably settled in for the night, wondering where the heck we've been since seven this morning. Thank goodness for John Carl," I said.

"We owe that guy dinner at a fine restaurant."

"Good idea," I said.

"See you soon."

I plucked the bottle of water from the cup holder, removed the cap, and poured it down my parched throat. I ate and drank next to nothing on surveillance for two reasons: I couldn't leave my post and even if I could, there never seemed to be a restroom close by. With twenty minutes until I was home, I'd reached the safe zone.

38

The sun rose way too early Sunday morning. Sunday fun day? Not by any stretch of the imagination. I heard noises in the kitchen downstairs. Smoke and the dogs. I rolled on my back and stared at the ceiling for a moment. Unsettling and terrifying things were going on in our world: a serial killer had abducted Mrs. Edberg, and Jaxson Kenner, a fugitive from justice, was hiding from the law. Somewhere out there. Life was off kilter, spinning out of control.

I gazed out the window and thought, *I'm grateful the sun is shining,* dragged myself out of bed, and headed downstairs. Queenie's and Rex's happy whining sounds brightened my spirits more than the sun. I gave each of their heads a quick rub.

Smoke held a cup of coffee in one hand, slipped the other one around my waist, and bent over for a welcomed kiss. "Good morning, sunshine."

"The best way to start the morning. Why don't we have our coffee outside on the deck?"

"Sounds like a plan."

Smoke filled a cup for me and topped off his own. We settled in deck chairs and the dogs went on their customary exploratory run.

"I woke up before first light at five this morning," Smoke said.

"It's hard to rest with all we've got going on, that's for sure."

"I don't know if the victims' families will be available to meet with me this morning, but I'll wait until a more respectable hour to call them. Six is too early for most folks on Sunday."

"No messages from the overnight deputies, that they found the deadly chameleon?" I said.

"No. I'm counting on Dina's research to come up with a new lead, a new address to check."

"My heart goes from aching to pounding fast and furiously, scared half to death by what Missus Edberg is dealing with."

"Both she and Bob are front and center in my thoughts. Everything else has taken a back seat," Smoke said.

"Definitely. Back to the victims' families. Can I be your off-duty ride along today, Smoke?"

He reached over and laid his hand on mine. "Corinne, you need the day off. This week's been brutal. If we get a lead on the offender, I'll let you know a-sap. Meantime, it'd make your mother and your gramps mighty happy to see you in church."

"You're right. I've barely talked to either one this week. Besides, I need spiritual nourishment."

He slid his palm into mine and squeezed. "Since you put it that way, I'll go with you."

My church was in the country, not far from my home, with a picturesque steeple visible from miles away. As a child I thought the top reached the clouds. It was old and quaint with a congregation of dedicated volunteers. I was not a regular attendee, mostly due to my work schedule, and partly due to falling out of habit. Sitting close to Smoke, Mother, and Gramps in the pew, singing the hymns and hearing the pastor's message gave me the reassurance I needed, a reminder that all the bad in this life would not be with us in the next.

It was difficult for Gramps to stand for long, so he and Mother left right after the service. Smoke and I were the last ones in the church and Pastor Hobart greeted us like we were family he hadn't seen for a while. After some minutes catching up, the pastor said, "Your sheriff's office has quite the case after finding those bodies in the Coyote Bog. Trying to figure out who they are."

"Yes. Actually, the medical examiner has been able to identify most of them, thanks to the miracle of DNA testing," I said.

"I'd say so," he said.

Since no one else was around, I told him, "This is something that wasn't released to the public, or even to the families, but the victims were all branded with the image of an angel on their foreheads and crosses on their wrists."

His eyebrows knitted together. "Oh, my."

"We're looking for an angel of death who poses as a caregiver."

Pastor Hobart shook his head. "Why did this angel of death go to the dark side? Corinne, when you came to me about that case you were working on a few years ago—the one where a woman was killed and dismembered—we talked about all the times in our vocations when we know there is a battle waging between good and evil."

"I remember you telling me that you and I fight the same battles, but we use different weapons."

I noticed Smoke's eyes on the bible Pastor Hobart held. Then he lifted his elbow and subtly rested it on his sidearm. "That's a good way to put it, Pastor. I like that," Smoke said.

Smoke contacted members of the Keats, Petty, and Wright families, and gave them tentative times when he'd stop over with "new" information. He was on his way out the door when Chief Deputy Randolph phoned. "Hey, Chief . . . Aww, wouldn't you know. New plan of attack? . . . Progress, anyway. Have you checked in with Bob this morning? . . . Okay. I should be wrapped up with the family notifications by noon. If anything comes up on your end, you have me on speed dial."

Smoke shook his head and disconnected. "Can we catch a break here?"

"What?"

"Dina got the list together of the facilities and agencies. Randolph divided it up for the night deputies. They paid visits to the nursing homes and assisted living places, armed with photos of the deadly chameleon, and met with the RN supervisors. But not a one of them recognized her from the images," he said.

"Man."

"Randolph told them to leave the photos at the homes so the HR folks can have a look tomorrow, see if she ever applied there and wasn't hired. Randolph's also gotten a hold of a few of the home health agencies. Even though it's Sunday, the managers agreed to meet with deputies. He'll contact the rest.

So that's in the works. He also has eight deputies posted at the main roads where people exit Winnebago County, keeping an eye out for the Toyota. Of course, all the deputies on duty are on the lookout," Smoke said.

"A lot going on. What'd he say about Bob?"

"Randolph's keeping Bob with him for the day. It was the best way he could think of to keep Bob safe and involved at the same time."

"Smart. We won't have to worry as much."

"Right. So you're off on a run?" he said.

"A long one. It's been a while since I've done a ten or twelve-miler and I'll feel better after my brain releases a healthy dose of endorphins. It'll help me think more clearly."

"That's what makes you so smart."

"Now you know my secret."

It was 62° with a cloud cover and a gentle cooling breeze from the south. Perfect running weather in my world. I wore a loose-fitting shirt to cover my Smith and Wesson and zipped the freeze plus pepper spray I carried on long runs in the side pocket of my pants, in case a loose dog gave me trouble. I left from my house and turned west at County Road 35, planning to run the first mile in ten minutes, and each subsequent one a minute faster, until I achieved a six-minute mile. Then I'd pull back my speed again.

The farther I ran the better I felt, emotionally and physically, releasing all the stored glycogen in my muscles. I smiled as I passed Smoke's driveway and pondered where we'd live together as man and wife. Neither of us wanted to maintain two households, going back and forth between them. As much as I loved my home and its close proximity to my family, I'd be happy to call Smoke's place mine as well. Home is where the heart is, right?

Mrs. Edberg was foremost in my mind but other thoughts swirled around, jumping from wondering how Bob Edberg was holding up, to Jaxson Kenner and his well-being, to the bog victims I carried photos of, to hoping Smoke's visits with their families were going well, to the angel of death and her accomplice. Where were they holed up?

Praying for Mrs. Edberg's safe return had me running faster than I'd planned. When I reached County Road 7, the five-and-a-half-mile mark, I debated about going another half mile or turning around. As per usual at that intersection, I glanced up at the house on the hill that overlooked Coyote Bog. The sun reflected off something in the picture window, and the drapes opened slightly from the middle then closed again. I did a double take. *Someone was in the house.* Finally.

I pulled out my phone and sent Smoke a text message. *Floyd Myren might be home. Running up there to check. Call when you're clear.*

I jogged through the construction zone, taking care not to step on a rock or into a hole, mindful of a few falls I'd taken over the years. When I reached Myren's driveway, something made me pause. Would it be better to drive up his road? Out in the middle of the country people rarely walked up to a residence, unless they had some sort of trouble. On second thought, I'd identify myself when I knocked on the door so it should be good.

As I neared the edge of Myren's lawn, prickly sensations danced over the skin of my entire body and my senses heightened. Especially my sixth sense. I stopped to assess why. No vehicle in Myren's driveway, but he had a double car garage and was likely parked in there. No one was outside and no audible sounds came from the house. Something was off. Hinky. Raised the hairs on the back of my neck.

I was about to turn tail and run away when someone stepped out from the treed area and grabbed me from behind, above the waist, pinning my arms to my sides. He pulled my body against his, lifting me what felt like two feet off the ground. A giant of a man. I couldn't see him, but my instincts told me who he was. The man Smoke and I saw leaving the Emerald Lake building. The one who had most likely been in Dolly Corbin's apartment. I was too stunned to speak. Every ounce of my energy and focus went into plotting how to escape.

"I watched you." He spoke slowly, like each word took effort. But the meaning behind them filled me with dread. The sickening truth of why the giant was at Floyd Myren's house hit me like a rock. How had I let myself walk into a trap without backup? My one crazy thought was, *If I go missing, at least Smoke knows where I was when I disappeared.*

He held me tightly around my diaphragm and I had trouble catching a full breath. "I'm here to see Floyd Myren," finally spilled out when he loosened his grip a bit.

"Can't."

"Are you his caretaker?" I said.

"No. Mister Myren is gone."

"Still in Florida?"

"No, in Heaven," he said.

Dear Lord, have mercy. It took everything I had to keep my voice level. "Like the others?"

"Mama told me not to say."

Mama. "Is she here?"

"She's gone somewhere," he said.

"But Emma Edberg is here."

"Mama told me not to say."

Mrs. Edberg is here! I was being held captive by an intellectually challenged giant of a man, bullied by his petite, abusive killer of a mother. "That's fine. You don't want to disobey your mother."

"Uh, uh."

"I'm Corky, what's your name?"

"Mama told me not to say."

"Okay. Well, I was just wondering if I could go home now, since I can't visit Floyd after all," I said.

"No. I have to keep anybody who comes here."

He has to keep? Anybody? Are there more people here somewhere besides Mrs. Edberg? "Okay. Where are you going to keep me?"

"In the house." As he walked with me toward the door, I contemplated survival tactics. My right wrist was a couple of inches from my sidearm and my left hand was a few inches below the zipper of the pocket holding the pepper spray. The giant's arms held me above the waist, and he hadn't noticed either the gun or the spray. Or my phone. Thankfully. But if I tried to manipulate either arm to grab one of the weapons, it would alert him, and I'd likely lose all three.

When we got to the side door of the house, he kept his left arm wrapped around me and used his right hand to turn the doorknob. As he pulled it open wide enough to get us through, his grip eased and allowed me to drop to the floor. I scooted a few feet then jumped up, ran past the kitchen through the living room into a hallway, and entered the first door on the right. It was the bathroom.

I shut and locked the door behind me and did a quick assessment of the small room. The sink was straight ahead on the south wall. The window above the mirror was five feet up and maybe twelve inches high by three feet wide. Not big enough for me to scoot through. The bathtub was on the west wall and the toilet on the east wall. The door opened from west to east.

My heart pounded so fiercely against my rib cage it felt like a few ribs would crack. I pulled my phone from its holder and dialed Smoke. It went to voicemail. I whispered I was at Myren's, in trouble, send help, disconnected, and turned the ringer off so the giant wouldn't hear it.

I was dialing 911 when he knocked on the door. "You have to come out," he said.

"I'm using the toilet."

"Come out in five minutes." *Five minutes?*

"Okay."

"Nine-one-one, what's your emergency?" Communication Officer Robin's voice.

I turned on the water to cover the sound of my voice and spoke quietly. "Corky Aleckson. I'm being held by someone I believe is involved with Missus Edberg's abduction at the Floyd Myren home near the intersection of County Thirty-five and Seven. I suspect Missus Edberg is here. I locked myself in the bathroom. Tell deputies to come in quiet. I don't want anything to happen to Missus Edberg if my captor hears them and panics. He's big, close to seven feet, over three hundred pounds. No idea about firearms in the house. I've got my Smith and Wesson and pepper spray."

Robin's voice quivered when she said, "We have the address and my partner is dispatching all available. Closest is six to eight minutes out. Glad you're armed."

Damn. Six to eight minutes? "Tell them to hurry."

"Stay on the line."

"I will but my phone will be in its holder on my hip." I replaced the phone then reached up and opened the window so the breeze would help carry the freeze pepper spray away from me if I used it. In case the giant broke through the door, I stepped onto the side of the bathtub, near the door, pulled the pepper spray from my pocket with my finger on the trigger.

He banged on the door again. It hadn't been five minutes. "I heard talking."

I was inspired to say, "I'm praying."

"To God?"

"Yes, to God."

"Oh. Come out, okay?" he said.

"I will when I finish praying."

"Okay. Five more minutes. I have to check something."

Was he actually watching a clock, or was the five-minute warning something his "Mama" had used on him over the years? Deputies were still minutes away and I hoped whatever the giant was checking on took at least that long. I leaned over, my ear to the door. I heard the giant talking and whimpering sounds from a woman. *Mrs. Edberg*? Was he hurting her? The hands on my watch weren't moving, it seemed. How could a minute take so long to pass?

39

Heavy footsteps came my way again and I drew the Smith and Wesson from its holster. Thank God he'd left the suffering woman. A muffled voice spoke from my phone, but I didn't dare put down either weapon. I prayed it was Robin telling me deputies were arriving.

"You have to come out now," the giant said.

"Rufus, who are you talking to? Do you have our patient in there?" *Rufus. A woman's angry voice. Was that his mother? Dear Lord, the angel of death was here? Who was she pretending to be today?*

"No, Mama. I think it's a cop. I seen her before." He remembered me from the apartment. Had he also seen me at the Coyote Bog crime scene? Probably.

"*What?* Get her out of there this *instant*." Her growling voice matched her demented personality. The one she'd hidden from the world. But her reign was about to end.

Where is my backup? My options were diminishing. Unless the death angel had a weapon and refused to drop it, I couldn't shoot her. The giant on the other hand was a different story. His whole body was a weapon. If I blasted them both with pepper spray, I'd get a measure of it myself. More importantly, if the whimpering woman I believed was Mrs. Edberg was close enough to catch a dose of the debilitating spray, it could prove dangerous. She already suffered from compromised health.

Rufus the giant pounded on the door. "Mama says to come out."

Me opening the door would not happen. I heard movement on the other side and was both prepared and unprepared for what might transpire. I counted on fast thinking and training scenarios to carry me through. A loud, blunt force cracking sounded, and the door burst open. The giant stumbled in, unbalanced, as the door hit the east wall. I aimed the spray bottle at his face, released the trigger, then jumped past him through the doorway.

I heard him cry out in pain as I peered into the stunned face of the angel of death herself. My split-second impression was she looked like all her personas rolled into one. I didn't know where her "patient" was but no longer worried about taking any back spray myself. I shot her with a dose of pepper and backed away as she gasped and coughed and cried. Water ran in the bathroom and I declined advising Rufus that washing his face would only intensify the effects of the spray.

Mother and son howled and cursed with defensible reason. I'd taken a *half* dose of it in training. My eyes and nose had been on painful fire and didn't stop dripping for hours. I slipped the spray in my pocket and kept my gun in a low-ready position as I searched for Mrs. Edberg. I couldn't hear any sounds from her over the two of them wailing. There were three other doors in the hallway. Two on the opposite side from the bathroom and one on the end.

No one in the first or second rooms, but when I opened the door on the end, I saw the person who made the past minutes from hell worth every second. Mrs. Edberg was lying on a twin-size bed facing the door. Her eyes were wide open, and she smiled when she saw me. I didn't know if she recognized me, so I identified myself and rushed in to assist her. Her wrists were secured with vinyl-coated clothesline, tied to the headboard's leg posts.

My disgust for her captors went through the roof. I didn't have anything to cut the line with, nor did I have time to untie it. *Damn.* I laid my hand on hers for reassurance. "I'll keep you safe, Missus Edberg, and our deputies are on the way to rescue you."

"My son Robert, he's a deputy."

"You'll see him very soon."

The giant's slobbering noises got closer. I ran to the door, shut and locked it. Not that it would stop him, but it would slow him down. If he broke in, I'd use deadly force. Justifiable, without argument. I feared for Mrs. Edberg's life and for my own. *Where were the deputies?*

The giant didn't bother to knock on the door or shout out a warning. He pushed through it like it was a piece of cardboard. His eyes were red, watering, and kept squeezing shut. Slobber dripped from his nose and mouth. His vision was impaired so a moving target would pose a challenge. I trained my Smith and Wesson on him.

"Winnebago County Sheriff's Office. I have a gun aimed at you. Do not take another step forward. Stop or I will shoot!"

He stopped, thank God.

Mrs. Edberg started to cry.

"Get her," the vile one spit out behind him.

He didn't move. "Mama, she's gonna shoot me."

"You'll be fine," she retorted.

"Rufus, you will *not* be fine. If I shoot you, you will die. I don't believe you want to die. Do *not* listen to your mother. She does bad things to people."

"She sends them to Heaven."

"Rufus, let the people in our office take care of you so your mother can never make you do what you don't want to again."

I heard deputies storming in, probably from both the side and front entrances. The angel of death screeched. Three deputies rushed into the bedroom with their weapons drawn. One ordered Rufus to turn around. He complied, without further struggle. Given Rufus's size, a deputy interlocked two sets of handcuffs to serve as a single set and locked them on his wrists behind his back. The deputies and I exchanged nods as they escorted Rufus out of the room.

"I'll be right back, Missus Edberg." I patted her hand and followed the group through the door. The angel of death had her hands cuffed behind her back. She lifted her shoulder, trying to catch some of the snotty mucus that ran from her nose. A deputy was guiding her out. Seeing her in distress filled me with a large measure of pleasure. But it was nothing compared to the joy and enormous relief I felt knowing Mrs. Edberg was safe, and the killing spree of her captors had come to an abrupt, and final, end. I holstered my Smith and Wesson. The angel of death and her son were in custody, on their way, in separate squad cars, to the Winnebago County Jail.

"Deputy Holman, I need your help," I said.

He followed me to the bed where Mrs. Edberg was held captive. I snapped a photo of her as evidence then pointed at the clothesline on her wrists. Holman drew the knife from his belt and cut the bindings. The line left some marks but hadn't cut into her paper-thin skin. We worked together and carefully assisted Mrs. Edberg to an upright position on the edge of the bed.

"Where's Robert?" she said, like none of the traumatic events had impacted her. A small blessing of the dementia's effect.

"Robert's on his way and should be here any minute," Holman said. He caught my attention, half-smiled, and nodded. "Good work, Sergeant, all the way around."

"Thanks. Right place, right time."

"Where's Robert?" Mrs. Edberg said again.

"He'll be here any minute," Holman said.

Thankfully, Bob Edberg ran in seconds later and Chief Deputy Randolph trailed close behind. Edberg squeezed my shoulder then sat down next to his mother and gently wrapped his arms around her. Tears welled in my eyes but didn't spill out until I saw Smoke in the doorway and went to meet him. He drew me close and held on tightly. Neither of us had words.

"Ambulance is here," Holman said.

I eased away from Smoke and told them, "Missus Edberg's in there." Smoke and I stepped aside to allow the team access.

Randolph joined us in the living room and called Holman over. "I have Detective Harrison writing a warrant to search the property, but I want you to do an initial check of the house, garage, barn, make sure there aren't any other people—or bodies—in plain sight around here." I cringed at the thought. "We'll dig in deeper when the major crimes guys get here, and we have the signed warrant." Harrison was the backup detective on weekend call.

Edberg followed the paramedics who wheeled his mother out of the bedroom. He stopped and caught me off guard when he threw his arms around me. I was speechless when he said, "I love you. Forever." I responded with an extra squeeze.

Randolph and Smoke gave him half-hugs and uttered words of reassurance, then Edberg left to accompany his mother on the ride to the hospital.

"The last twenty-plus hours have been hell on earth for Bob. I don't know what he would've done if anything worse had happened to his mother. If you hadn't found her," Randolph said.

"All I can say is I believe I was sent here for a reason."

Smoke sucked air into his nostrils then exhaled. I knew he struggled with what I'd gone through. "When Communications raised me on the radio, I was wrapping up with Claire Bolton, Oscar Wright's daughter, in Harold Lake. I couldn't get here fast enough."

Randolph concentrated his eyes on me. "How are doing, Sergeant? Injured in any way? That brute looked downright intimidating, even to a big guy like me."

"I'll be fine. Rufus didn't hurt me. If it wasn't for his mother telling him what to do, I don't think he'd swat a pesky fly. It took about a minute for me to realize that her manipulations controlled him. Ruined his life," I said.

"Tell us what happened. Communications caught part of it over your phone and relayed it to our mobile data terminals," Randolph said.

"Everything, from the beginning. I'll put it in my report," Smoke added.

I walked them through the ordeal, step by step. I had trouble processing the reality that from the time Rufus grabbed me to the time deputies arrived spanned about twelve minutes. Abject fear and heightened senses made time move at a snail's pace.

"From what Rufus said about Floyd Myren being in Heaven, we need to find out if he's the seventh victim. The one who hasn't been identified," Randolph said.

"I have a strong feeling it'll turn out he is. One of the sad parts in all this is that Mister Myren was never reported missing," I said.

"From what we learned, he survived his wife, daughter, and brother. After his brother died a few years ago, apparently no one kept in touch with him," Smoke said.

"Except for the one who took over his house and his life. A typical abuser makes that happen. We've mostly seen that with couples. They get married and within a year or two one of them has managed to estrange the other from their own family. The abuser keeps the spouse all to himself. Or herself. For complete control," I said.

"You got that right," Smoke said.

"The neighbor told me Myren was in Florida, from what she heard. I wonder who put that information out there?" My voice dripped with sarcasm knowing it was his "caretaker."

"We'll follow up on that. And how the death angel found him, victimized him, took over his home," Randolph said.

"It's possible he needed help so he could stay in his home. And he called the wrong agency," I said.

"Could be," Randolph said. "Sergeant, all I can say is thank you for what you did here, finding Bob's mom, holding the offenders at bay till we got here."

It took me a moment to answer. “I learned an important lesson in all this: I will forever carry my pepper spray when I go running.”

Smoke put his arm on my shoulder. “Added protection and life-saving, as it turned out.” He gave me a firm squeeze.

Deputy Holman returned. “There are two vehicles in the garage. The gray Toyota Camry and an old, navy Dodge Caravan. The Caravan is registered to Floyd Myren, the Toyota to Rufus Wilkins,” Holman said. *Wilkins.* I looked inside both. There’s a modified, extended-length diving board that folds in half lying in the van that you’ll want to check out. Otherwise nothing else in plain view in either vehicle. Very clean.”

“When Harrison has the signed warrant in hand, you can call for tows and we’ll process them in our evidence garage,” Randolph said.

“Two things to check out on the garage shelves: barbell weights and a roll of clothesline,” Holman said. He’d read the reports.

“That fits,” Smoke said.

“No sign that anyone has been in the barn in years. No lock on the door and when I opened the door, it was so cobwebby I had to fight my way in, looked around. The dust was thick, otherwise it was clean. No equipment, machinery, nothing. And there is no basement. It’s slab on grade,” Holman said.

“Cuts down on what to search, places to hide evidence. Chief, we also need warrants to search the two apartments,” Smoke said.

Randolph tapped his forehead. “I can’t believe I forgot to add them. I’ll call Harrison.” He was able to catch him at the office, made the request, and gave him the addresses for the warrants.

"I'd like to find out where the angel of death stores all her costumes," Smoke said.

"That makes all of us. I asked Harrison to work with our crime scene team to process the property, gather the evidence. Elton, you have any loose ends to tie up with the victims' families?" Randolph said.

Smoke nodded. "One last family to visit. I let them know something came up and I'd get back to them. They had nothing planned and seemed fine with that," he said.

"Good. I want you to interview the angel of death and her son later today, after the pepper spray has dissipated. And when we have some evidence to throw in their faces. I'm counting on you to find out her real name so we can quit calling her the angel of death, or deadly chameleon," Randolph said.

"Will do. I'm thinking her son will be our best bet to give up that information."

I planned to be on the other side of the interview room glass, watching and taking notes.

The on-call major crimes deputies arrived and as soon as they got the go ahead, would process the property and gather evidence. Randolph brought them up to speed then I led them to the bedroom at the end of the hallway and pointed at the clothesline. "You'll find clothesline on the bed that the bad guys tied Missus Edberg up with. I think it'll match the line used on the bodies recovered from Coyote Bog. Holman spotted a roll of it in the garage," I told them. They didn't need a warrant to collect it.

Randolph took a phone call. He disconnected and said, "Good news. Harrison got all three warrants written and Judge Adams signed them. He'll be on his way out here when he finishes something."

"Adams always comes through for us in a timely manner. So we can peruse the closets?" Smoke said.

Randolph nodded. "Have at it."

Smoke handed me a pair of protective gloves and the two of us entered the room the death angel likely occupied. The master bedroom. It was ethereally surreal, with creepy overtones. White walls, white furniture, white blinds, white sheer curtains, white bedspread, white satin throw pillows, large white rugs. Even the woodwork had been whitewashed. "Does she pretend she's in Heaven when she's in here?" Smoke said.

"If so, she's grossly understating what Heaven's like."

Smoke raised his eyebrows. "Oh?"

I smiled. "From what I hear. Maybe it's more to assure herself she's pure, what she's doing is good."

"You think?"

"I'm not a psychologist. Whatever the reason, this room gives me major heebie-jeebies. When I was looking for Missus Edberg, I glanced in here and mostly noticed that she wasn't in the bed and the spread was white," I said.

"I feel some weird vibes myself."

"Missus Edberg was in the other room, but I wonder if this is where they bring their victims to end their lives. Eew."

"I'll ask her that very question when we have our Come-to-Jesus meeting this afternoon." Smoke took out his phone, snapped a photo of the room, and opened the bifold doors of the twelve-foot-wide closet.

"Wow," I said.

Smoke shook his head. "This is too easy."

40

Randolph joined us in the bedroom. He made a "wheeooow" whistle sound that started at a middle C and dropped an octave, one note at a time, as he visually scanned the room. "I've never seen anything like this."

"No," Smoke said.

"What have you got in there?" Randolph said.

Smoke pointed. "See for yourself."

"I'll be. Unbelievably incriminating evidence."

"Yep."

Smoke and I had discussed how the angel of death might keep her characters straight. She had sections of clothes for each of her personas with hanging cloth organizers for accessories such as wigs, body shapers, purses, glasses. And a name and photo of herself in each section. Melody Reed, Dolly Corbin, Jasmine Wiley. Her current angel of death identities.

Melody, age 61, was a size 16, thanks to a buxom, padded body form. She wore frumpy-looking knit pants, blouses, and cardigan sweaters, and a short, curly gray-haired wig.

Dolly, 58, wore size 12 and dressed in coordinating scrubs, like a light blue top with navy blue bottoms. She had a long-haired gray wig pulled into a bun.

Jasmine, 43, size 8, wore new-looking scrubs in a variety of colors. As Bob had described her, she was attractive and slender with green eyes and a blonde-haired wig worn in a high ponytail.

A fourth section of clothes was unmarked. That's what the real angel of death presumably wore. Jeans, tee-shirts, sweatshirts, a few pairs of dress pants and blouses. No picture of her, of course. But we didn't need one. We'd seen her in the flesh. She looked most like Jasmine Wiley, but with shoulder-length medium brown hair and blue eyes.

"She poses with innocent, pleasant looks in her pictures. But I can tell you, when she stared me in the face those few seconds, she was hateful, showed her wicked side," I said.

"Her true identity," Smoke said.

We were silent for a bit then Smoke removed a file box from the top section of a hanging organizer.

"More treasures?" I said.

He opened it and flipped through the cards. "Rhoda Barnes, Jasmine Kerry, Krystal Wiley, and another one we haven't run across yet. There's a description for each."

"Rhoda no longer worked at either of the two care facilities. I guess the death angel retired her for now," I said.

"Geez. Had she used others in the past? Planned to use them in the future?" Randolph said.

Smoke stepped back and shot a photo of the inside of the closet. "Major Crimes will be doing a lot of tagging and bagging."

"I'll recruit more troops to help," Randolph said.

"There aren't that many outfits here. Might be more in her apartments," I said.

"Could be. Chief, after I make that notification, how about I report back here?" Smoke said.

Randolph nodded. "An hour or two would be a big help."

I went over to a nine-drawer dresser and pulled open the top left one. It was filled with a variety of jewelry pieces laying in dividers. "Missus Edberg told Bob she was missing jewelry. The death angel could've stolen from her and others she worked for, too."

"To sell, or keep as trophies?" Randolph said.

Smoke and Randolph moved in beside me. When I opened the middle drawer, it was like unwrapping a long-awaited Christmas present. Boxes of cross pendants, identical to those found at the scene—one recovered in the spoils of the bog and another wrapped around a victim's hand—were lined up in rows on the bottom.

"This just keeps getting better," Smoke said and snapped photos of the contents in both open drawers.

As he replaced his phone in its holder, an unexpected chill ran through me and sent my body into shivers.

"Detective, the Sergeant here should get home, into some dry clothes. Harrison will be here shortly to take over," Randolph said.

It was my first awareness that my clothes were wet with sweat. From the run and following trauma. "Oh. I guess. I thought it was the frigid atmosphere in this place that brought on my chills." I rubbed my arms to warm up.

"Time to take off, Sergeant. All the evidence will be photographed and well-documented for our viewing displeasure," Smoke said.

"Okay."

Smoke put his hand on my elbow and guided me out the door to his vehicle. When I climbed in, I started to shake enough to make my teeth chatter. "I didn't see this coming," I managed, despite my jaw bouncing up and down.

He laid his hand on my arm. "I guess I should have. A delayed response after your adrenaline dump. Sorry. We got too caught up in what we'd uncovered in there."

He started the engine and turned the heat on full blast to warm me up. I would have protested, but it felt good. Poor Smoke had broken out in a sweat himself by the time we pulled into my driveway. "I'll attend to the dogs and you hop in the shower," he said.

The shakes had eased. I soaped up, warm water washing over me. It cleansed my body and helped lighten my spirits.

I found Smoke with the dogs in the backyard. "It's close to lunchtime, you want me to pick something up for you?" he asked.

"No. Thanks. If I get hungry later, there's peanut butter in the cupboard. Smoke, I need to be there when you interview mother and son. From the viewing room."

"Think you'll be up to it?"

"Definitely. I need to hear what she has to say about her victims, her false identities, her extensive planning. I'm more than ready for that. I also want to hear from Rufus. Her pawn," I said.

"The easier one to crack."

"You know how I've felt drawn to Myren's house since we recovered the victims from the bog? Something ate at me about it, but I didn't suspect that pair was living there. Aside from the time I saw her leaving the driveway and the curtains moving today, no one in the department has spotted lights or activity around there."

"You thought she was driving a silver, not a gray, car," Smoke said.

"I did. I think the lighting made it appear silver instead of gray."

"They've been exceptionally cunning. She made sure of that. Truth be told, if I'd met her on the street and she was wearing jeans with her hair in a ponytail and a ball cap on, I might not have recognized her from the photos."

"In what seems to be the soccer mom uniform, she'd blend in with scores of others who dress like that," I said.

"I need to shove off. You'll be okay here alone?"

"I'm not alone."

Smoke nodded at the dogs and smiled.

I dropped onto a deck chair and both Queenie and Rex took that as their cue to lay down at my feet. My loyal friends and protectors. "It's been a really big day, guys. You know that night we sat over by Coyote Bog in the GTO and I went chasing after the car, but lost it? Turns out she is a depraved serial killer. We caught her and she'll spend the rest of her days in prison." Queenie whined and Rex let out a single bark, convincing me they understood what I was talking about.

I leaned my head against the back support and closed my eyes. When my phone buzzed in my jeans pocket, I glanced at the time, surprised that I'd fallen asleep. For over an hour, besides. I pushed the talk button. "Hi, Mom."

"Corinne, it's all over the news. They arrested two people in connection with the bodies that were found in Coyote Bog. Deputies have been at their house for hours. Channel five had footage of the house with the Winnebago County Mobile Crime Unit and squad cars in the yard. And the house has yellow crime scene tape around it."

Randolph must have released a statement.

"As it turns out, I was there when they were arrested," I said.

"How come? It's your day off."

I gave her an overview without expounding on the details.

"Corinne Mae Aleckson, I can hear you're whitewashing what happened at that house." *Whitewashing*. The death angel's room came to mind in living no-color white.

"I'll tell you more about it later. I'm sitting in on the interviews, so I better get rolling."

"You have no idea how much I worry about you," Mother said.

Yes, I do and that's why I spare you the ugly parts whenever possible. "Mom, I appreciate your concern for my safety, but you need to stop stressing yourself out or you'll have me worrying about your health."

"You'll always be my little girl."

"Who grew up to be a cop. They even trust me with weapons and everything."

"Corinne—"

"Sorry for being snotty. I'll catch you later. Love you, Mom."

"I love you, too."

I hung up and shook my head at the irony that my mother and I stressed each other out more than anyone else in our lives. For opposite reasons. My job had her on the edge of her seat every day I was on duty. In turn, her anxiety made me fret about critical incidents that happened on the job. If she found out about them, she freaked out. That kept me from baring my soul to her.

At times I wanted to revert to the little girl that cried in her arms when something bad happened. Like when I'd been beaten down by something on the job. I knew she was there for me and wanted to be there more, but she couldn't deal with bad and ugly. She needed happily ever after endings.

The funny thing was, I wanted a version of that myself. Flushing out bad guys who victimized others, and throwing them in jail, was the closest those of us in the criminal justice world got to happily ever after. Professionally speaking.

On a personal level, I clung to a more optimistic outlook.

Reminding me of Detective Elton Dawes. I sent him a text. *ETA for interviews?* A minute later he responded with, *2:30.* Good. *See you there.* He sent me a thumbs-up emoji. I was glad he hadn't changed his mind because I needed to be there. To scrutinize the offenders' words and gestures and appearances. After the brief encounter Smoke and I had with Rufus outside the Emerald Lake apartment, I thought I'd be able to pick him out of a photo lineup, but I couldn't swear to it.

Then when Rufus barged into the bathroom, I saw a mammoth-sized man with no discernible facial features, bent on capturing me, before I doused him with pepper spray. When he pushed his way into the bedroom, his face was contorted and red and full of slobber.

He was likely mentally challenged and had been manipulated and brainwashed by his mother. I sympathized with the guy to a point.

The angel of death was a different story. Her varied images in the photos were burned into my brain. But when I stood face to face with her, it was like the world got brighter for those seconds. I had mental clarity and the weapons to immobilize her. Take her down. If I were an artist I'd sit down and draw a spitting image of what she looked like. The bleak expression on her face when she saw the glowering look on mine was priceless.

It was still an hour before the scheduled interviews, and I was at a momentary loss of what to do to fill the time. I wanted to help collect evidence at Floyd Myren's house but couldn't. Queenie and Rex were still at my side, making sure I was okay, sensing something was amiss. When had I slept during the day? They stood when I did and followed me inside. I looked for something quick and easy for lunch and thought of the peanut butter. I figured that, topped with a banana on bread, would give me both protein and potassium. Along with a tall glass of milk for calcium.

At 2:20, I pulled my GTO into a parking spot on the street outside the sheriff's office. I'd brought my portable radio with and on my way in heard Smoke tell Communications he was "Ten-nineteen." At the office. When I found him in his cubicle jotting notes on a memo pad, he looked up and smiled.

"All set?" I said.

"As ready as I'll ever be. I'll start with easy then move to difficult. How are you feeling?"

"Better than I figured I would. The incident was traumatic. I was sweating bullets for a while. But the outcome was beyond rewarding."

"The guys were talking about you. After what you did—having the wherewithal to go up against that behemoth and his evil mother—the respect they have for you is off the charts," Smoke said.

The compliment and the description made me smile. “Behemoth? That’s kind of a funny, archaic word.”

Smoke shrugged. “You think? That’s what came to my mind when I saw him. They’re bringing Rufus over from the jail and two deputies will be posted outside the room in case he turns disorderly.”

“How did the bookings go?”

“Rufus was cooperative. The mother not so much. Refused to give her name and date of birth. Hopefully, her son will fill in the blanks before I talk to her.”

41

Two corrections officers escorted Rufus, hands cuffed behind his back, to the sheriff's office conference room where Smoke met them. The deputies were on standby and I was in the adjoining room, ready to take notes. Smoke introduced himself to Rufus and said, "How about we take off those handcuffs? I'm counting on you to be nice and cooperative, so I don't have to call for help. We both know how much pepper spray hurts."

Rufus sniffed. "Uh huh. I'll be good."

Smoke nodded at the corrections officers. One unlocked the cuffs and freed Rufus's hands, then the two of them left. Rufus rubbed his wrists.

"Have a seat, young man," Smoke said.

They sat down with the table between them. Smoke had his back to me, and I had a clear view of Rufus's face.

Smoke turned on the recording equipment. "I'll be videotaping our conversation. I'll ask you questions, but first I need to read you the Miranda Warning." He pulled out the card and read, "You have the right to remain silent. Anything you say can and will be used against you in a court of law. You have the right to an attorney. If you cannot afford an attorney, one will be provided for you. Do you understand the rights I have just read to you?" He spoke slowly, allowing Rufus to absorb the words and their meanings.

Rufus nodded. "Uh huh."

Smoke looked at him. "Please answer with 'yes' instead."

"Yes."

"With these rights in mind, do you wish to speak to me?"

Rufus looked perplexed for a second. "I seen cops on shows saying words like that when they arrest people."

"They do things a little different on TV and in the movies. Rufus, I want to make sure you understand your rights. Would you like me to read them again?" Smoke said.

"Uh uh. You're a cop so I should talk to you, even if Mama says not to."

"If you understand your rights and agree to speak to me, please answer 'yes.'"

"Yes."

"Can you give me your full name?"

"Rufus Wilkins."

"No middle name?"

"Uh uh. Just Rufus Wilkins."

"Your date of birth?"

He recited it, and I calculated he was twenty-two years old.

"And your mother's name?"

"Jasmine Wilkins." *Jasmine.*

"Does she have a middle name?"

"Ann."

"And her date of birth?"

When he said it, I was surprised to hear she was only thirty-nine years old. Seven years older than me with a twenty-two-year old son. Seventeen when he was born.

"Rufus, on Monday, May fourteenth we recovered seven bodies from the bog just south of the home where you were living. The home belonging to Floyd Myren. Do you know Mister Myren?"

"Uh huh."

"How do you know Mister Myren?"

"Mama was friends with him for a long time. She helped him when his daughter was sick. Then she died," Rufus said.

"When was that?"

"Eight years ago. I was fourteen." Before the elderly persons—that we know about—started disappearing.

"Go on."

"We've been mostly staying at his house a few years now, helping him, ′cause he was getting old and losing his mind."

"Mister Myren is no longer living?"

He shook his head. "Mama sent him to Heaven."

"How did she do that?"

"Mama put a pillow over his face because it was time for him to go to Heaven." My stomach muscles tightened.

"When was that?"

"Umm. I think two years ago." He nodded. "Uh huh, two years. In May, too. Mama finds really sick people in May. They need to go to Heaven on May twenty-sixth."

"Why is that?"

"Because my grandpa made her send his mama to Heaven on May twenty-sixth."

"Your great-grandma, your mother's grandma?" Smoke said.

"Uh huh."

"What was your great-grandma's name?"

"Rhoda Wilkins." *Rhoda.*

"And your grandpa's name?"

"Rufus."

"Same as yours. How long ago was that, that your grandma went to Heaven?"

"Nine years, when I was thirteen."

"Where did your great-grandma Rhoda live?"

"In Iowa, where we came from."

"The name of the town?"

"Des Moines."

"How long have you been in Minnesota?"

"Since right after Grandma Rhoda died."

"When did you move to Winnebago County?"

"Umm, four years ago."

"Tell me where else you lived, and when you were there."

He frowned then looked at his fingers and moved them like he was counting. "Um, Minneapolis, first. Dassel, we moved there eight years ago. Elk River, five years ago. Oak Lea and Emerald Lake, um, four years ago."

"Both places at the same time?"

"Uh huh. And at Mister Myren's, too. Mama likes to pretend she's different people and live different places."

"How can she afford to have more than one apartment, and buy all of her outfits?" Smoke said.

"My grandma left her a lot of money in a safe deposit thing. It was a secret from my grandpa."

"When did your grandma die?"

"A long time ago. Before my great-grandma did." Jasmine had escape money when she needed it.

"Do you have a father?"

"Uh uh."

"Getting back to Mister Myren. After he died, how did your mother send him to Heaven?"

"First she had to put an angel here." Rufus touched his forehead. "And crosses here and here." He touched one wrist then the other.

"How did she put the angel and crosses there?"

"Mama has iron things. She put them on a burner so they got hot, and then she put them on Mister Myren. It smelled icky and I can't be there when she does that."

"And then what?"

"She wrapped a necklace around his hand. Then she made me bury him."

"In the bog?"

Rufus pursed his lips. "Uh huh. I put him on a slide and I slided him into the water."

"Is that what happened with the other six people in Coyote Bog?"

"Uh huh, mostly. The light ones I could throw in."

"Were there other people, besides the seven we found in the bog, that she sent to Heaven, too?"

"Uh uh."

"Did Mama say why she buried them in a bog?"

"For their heavenly journey."

"How did Mama know about the bog?"

"Mister Myren talked about it. He said bogs keep things almost like new ′cause his grandpa kept some food in it in the hot summer to keep it good."

"I see. Well, Rufus, we'll wrap this up for today. You've been very helpful, and I appreciate you answering all my questions. Thank you."

"That's okay."

I met Smoke in the hallway after the corrections officers escorted Rufus back to the jail. The two deputies left to grab beverages from a vending machine. "Wow," I said.

He raised his eyebrows and stretched his lips out to the sides of his cheeks. "Rufus identified the event that Special Agent Erley said caused Jasmine Wilkins' psychotic break, it seems."

"A horrible thing to make your daughter do. Her father controlled her life, and then she controlled her son's," I said.

"Both of them had it rough. And for Rufus Wilkins, he knows right from wrong and was forced to do wrong."

"And hated it. Only fifteen, just a kid when he had to bury the first body in the bog. What a cruel thing for an already challenged teen."

"No question. I'll have Communications do a search on Rufus Wilkins and Jasmine Ann Wilkins. See what turns up. We collected photos of Floyd Myren from his house and will get them to the M.E.'s office tomorrow, see if they match up with the seventh victim. Corrections is bringing Jasmine over after Rufus is back in his cell. They were told it's imperative the two never cross paths, as long as they're here," Smoke said.

"I'll wait in the viewing room. I don't want to be in the corridor when the angel of death gets here."

"You don't have to stay."

"Yes, I do."

Jasmine Wilkins, the angel of death, was brought to the interview room. She stared straight ahead, standing stock still as the corrections officer removed her handcuffs. After he left, Smoke instructed Wilkins to sit down. She sat and continued to stare ahead, seemingly at nothing.

"Jasmine Ann Wilkins," Smoke said.

A slight flicker in her eyes and blink of her eyelids.

Smoke told her he'd be recording their conversation and read the Miranda Warning. He asked if she understood and if she'd talk to him. She didn't acknowledge him in any way.

"I won't ask you any questions, so you won't have to provide answers." Smoke opened his notepad. "We exhumed all the bodies you had your son bury in Coyote Bog. We've been in contact with the victims' families in three counties, except for Floyd Myren's. He's the one who still had a crucifix wrapped around his hand. The others lost theirs in the bog."

Wilkins appeared deaf and blind. It was unnerving. Smoke went on to list each victim's name and age and the locations they were at when they went missing. Slowly, drawing out each one's information. But it didn't get a rise out of Wilkins.

"We've traced the employers and residences you've had, and the disguises you've used over the last seven years. I gotta say, abducting a deputy's mother was mighty stupid of you, as ingenious as you must've thought it was. Outwitting the sheriff's office. I'm sure you figured you'd get away with it, like you had in the past. It's amazing, isn't it, how things turn out? There may not be true justice this side of Heaven, but we do our best to get as close as we can."

Wilkins looked like a lifeless mannequin, not even blinking.

"You won't have to say a word. Because we have enough evidence and firsthand testimony of your deeds to ensure you will never experience another day of freedom in your life. And I gotta say, all those people whose lives you ended, their families are going to be mighty grateful to hear that. They've been waiting a long time to find out what happened to their loved ones. And now they know. Knowing you can never harm another human being is frosting on their cakes."

Wilkins did not appear to register a single word Smoke said. I sent him a text. *I think she's catatonic. Meet me in the corridor.*

"Jasmine, stay put. I'll be back in a few minutes," Smoke said.

When he met me, I raised my eyebrows and mouthed, "Stay put? That was almost funny."

He shrugged and signaled for one of the deputies to go into the adjoining room to watch Wilkins through the glass, and the other to remain outside the interview room door. Then he followed me down the corridor and around the corner, out of earshot.

"She's not faking it?" he said.

"It looks real to me, but I'm not a doctor. Even if she snaps out of it, she needs to be seen by one who is. Escorted by two deputies. Her completely blank look freaked me out. I flashed back to that case a few years ago, when I was in the interview room with Alvie Eisner and she stopped talking, lost consciousness, and went into a seizure." Alvie Eisner had also killed a number of people for what she thought was a valid reason.

"Turns out, she did have a medical condition. A serious one," Smoke said.

I nodded. "On the other hand, Wilkins may be trying to establish incompetency."

"Could be. Let's get her back to the jail. I'll have Corrections move her to a holding cell by booking, put her on a fifteen-minute watch until we can get her in for a checkup tomorrow."

"Good deal. I'm going to take off and I'll see you later," I said.

Smoke nodded with a smile.

It was a relief to be home again, trying to unwind. Bob Edberg phoned to say his mother was a little dehydrated, but otherwise doing well. They were keeping her overnight for observation. "We can never repay you for what you did."

"Bob, I have been paid in full, and then some. I believe I was sent there. The power of prayer, huh? Anyway, I wasn't hurt. The bad guys are in jail. And more importantly, your mother's safe and sound."

"No argument there. Now that I've got her back, I'm struggling with what to do about her care. It's going to be hard to get over this, to trust caregivers again."

"Do your own background investigations, make sure they check out a-okay."

"Yeah. Well, I better get back to her room. I'll catch you later."

Even though the chances were probably one in a million Bob would get a bad caregiver, if I were in his place, I'd be leery, too. He'd had the scare of his life.

A number of text messages had come in from deputies, checking to see how I was holding up. I responded to each, assured them I was doing well. That was the truth and it surprised me. Critical incidents usually knocked the wind out of my sails for some time. Trying to analyze the difference, I thought maybe it was because I'd been under the threat of danger for a short time. But I'd been in similar circumstances before, so it wasn't the time span. It came down to the overriding joy I felt that Mrs. Edberg was safe, and the angel of death was locked up.

My phone rang again, and when I saw Sheriff Kenner's name on the display, the first thing that came to mind was I hadn't thought about Jaxson since I'd spotted the moving curtains at Floyd Myren's house. "Hello, Sheriff."

"Sergeant, the chief deputy filled me in on what happened today. All I can say is you did the department proud."

"Thank you. It's a good feeling when things turn out the way they should. How are you and April?" I said.

He paused then said, "Not the best, but we're hanging in there."

"Good. Thanks for the call, Mike."

We disconnected and I started to pace and woke the sleeping dogs. Where was Jaxson Kenner? He'd been on the run for days, and probably without a car the last three. A guy who every law enforcement agency in the state had a description and photo of. Maybe he had slipped into Canada somehow.

Acknowledging my restlessness made me realize I wasn't totally fine. I headed for the back door and the dogs followed. The great outdoors provided me a longer, broader walking area. We jogged around the backyard a while, until Smoke phoned me. "Still writing reports?" I said.

"No, I'll finish them tomorrow. I thought I'd pick something up for supper. How about we meet at my house at six? We'll toast with a brew, have a bite, and relax. I need to spend a night at home."

"Sure. Am I included in the overnight part?"

"Every time," he said.

My heart felt lighter.

42

I was packed and ready to go by 5:30. “Hey guys, let’s swing over by Coyote Bog, see if there’s still any action at Floyd Myren’s place.”

We were in the car and off in no time. When we got to Coyote, it hit me: what was the point of either driving around the barricade, or taking the detour to get to Myren’s? I’d get the search details in the next day or two. I was curious, but needed to decompress, calm my soul and mind, not add anxious thoughts.

Seven days spent trying to process the atrocities the deadly chameleon had committed. Seven days intently working to identify the victims, meeting with families and law enforcement in other counties. Seven days trying to track down the angel of death. Seven days worrying about Jaxson Kenner and his family. And grieving over Sawyer Harris.

I pulled the GTO up to the barricades and stared at the bog, pondering what led the pagans to believe they were sacred places. What made Jasmine Wilkins perpetuate that belief, branding Christian symbols on her victims? And then force her son to dispose of their bodies? I reached in the glove box, withdrew the pictures of the six victims we had identified, and looked at them one by one. I'd add Floyd Myren's as soon as I got it.

I tried to blink away tears in my eyes, but they spilled out and rolled down my cheeks. "I'm so sorry she took your lives, but she can't victimize anyone else the way she did all of you. Rest in peace, knowing that."

Smoke waited for us as we arrived at his house. When he wrapped his arms around me, I could have stayed there for the rest of my life. I tightened my hold. "Feeling emotional?" he said.

"You read me like a book. We've had so many ups and downs this last week, I'm realizing I've been on an emotional rollercoaster right along with them. It'll be good when things settle down a bit."

"You got that right."

"We'll all be relieved when the families have their loved ones back. And they can bury them where they choose," I said.

"One of the reasons we do what we do."

"I'm jumping ahead here, but I wonder what their trials are going to be like."

"After the interviews today, you gotta wonder." He took a step back, reached for my hands, and kissed each one. "Ready for that toast?"

"Sure. What'd you find for supper? Something sure smells good in here."

"Broasted chicken, Jo Jo potatoes, and coleslaw from Charlie's Grocery Store."

"Yum."

Smoke gave me a peck on the lips then walked to the refrigerator, pulled out two Heinekens, used a bottle opener to pop off the tops, and handed one to me. We clicked the necks of them together. "Here's to you, my brave and beautiful Corinne."

"And here's to you, my seasoned, smart, and sexy Elton Dawes."

The sip of cold beer tasted fine. We celebrated the end of the angel of death's reign of terror, closure for waiting families, and our love. After a few more sips, we opened the food containers and filled our plates. After settling at the table and saying a prayer, we dug in.

"Who needs to cook when Charlie's does it better?" I said, between bites.

"You have a point."

We ate in silence, dividing our attention between the food and looks that expressed how we felt.

Rex barked and ran to the front door, alerting us someone was outside. "What the heck?" Smoke got up and headed into the living room. I followed, both curious and wary of unexpected company. Smoke checked the peep hole. "Well, I'll be." He opened the door, pulled Jaxson Kenner in the house, and into a bear hug.

I was stunned, unable to move for a moment. Finally, I slid in between them and laid my arm across Jaxson's back, along his waist. He wore glasses with black frames that covered half his face, and smelled of both fresh air and wood smoke, an unusual combination.

"I can't deal with hiding out anymore. I'm turning myself in," he said.

"The right thing to do," Smoke said.

"There are some scary people out there. At least in jail, there are corrections officers to help if you need it," I said.

"You met up with unsavory characters?" Smoke said.

"That's one way to put it."

"Is that what made you change your mind, brought you here?" I said.

"Reason is, I saw you two in the Sherburne refuge. I shoulda turned myself in then but couldn't."

"Where were you?" Smoke said.

"Up in a tree, between the Oak Savanna Trail and my car. I was about to leave when you got out of that old car, looked around, and then drove in near where I hid my car. I stopped and climbed up the tree as fast as I could," Jaxson said.

"Wait. We called in the K-9 Unit and Boomer indicated you'd left the park," Smoke said.

"I did, right after I heard they were coming. You two were talking with the Sherburne deputies and I snuck through the trees barely making a sound to the road, and then ran like the wind."

"I guess," Smoke said.

"What you said in the refuge started sinking in yesterday," Jaxson said.

"What was that?"

"You called out like you knew I was there. You said, 'Where are you, Jaxson? Turn yourself in so we can help you.'"

"I guess I did say that. Jax, where's your backpack and your mother's gun?" Smoke said.

Jaxson's eyebrows shot up. "You know about the gun?"

"Where is it?"

"In my backpack, on your step."

Smoke retrieved it, opened the pack, and looked inside. He set it down while he reached in his pocket, found a glove, and pulled it on. When he had the gun in hand, he slipped it in his pocket. "I'll return it to your folks. Anything else in the backpack I should be concerned about?"

Jaxson shook his head.

"How did you get here without being spotted?"

"I hitched a ride. I've been doing that since I left the car behind. I hope you'll bring me to see my parents before you take me to the jail," Jaxson said.

Smoke nodded. "I can do that. But before we go, if you're hungry, we got plenty of food here."

"Umm, I guess I could eat a little."

He ate a lot, like it was his last meal. In fact, it probably was, before a long incarceration.

Smoke told me to, "Hold down the fort," and left with Jaxson. I was more than content to do just that. After being on emotional overload most of the day, had I been part of Jaxson's brief homecoming at the Kenners, it might push me over the edge.

I cleaned up the kitchen and changed into pajamas, assuring myself 7:30 was not too early to get ready for bed. Smoke had a stadium blanket on his couch. I pulled it over my body and stretched out on the couch with a view of the lake out the glass double doors, a short distance from the house. The dogs settled on the floor beside me. I mentally worked through the events of the day. Descriptive words popped into my head. Unpredictable. Inconceivable. Terrifying. Rewarding. Mind-boggling. Unreal.

Rufus Wilkins had willingly spilled out all the information Smoke requested. His mother appeared to be in a catatonic state. Was it real, or was she faking it? Either way, it was a freaky thing to behold. And may have an impact on how they proceeded in the case against her.

On top of flushing out the Wilkinses and finding Mrs. Edberg, Jaxson Kenner had appeared out of the blue. I pinched my arm. Yep, I was conscious and fully aware. I thought about Floyd Myren. The poor guy had been victimized for a long time—even after his death—by the angel of death. That, and the fact that he'd been dead for two years and no one had noticed, made me tear up.

When Smoke returned, I realized I'd dozed off. He took off his gun belt and hung it on a coat rack hook. I sat up and he laid down with his head on my lap. "I'm on call until seven tomorrow morning and I'd greatly appreciate no major incidents tonight."

I combed through his hair with my fingers. "How did Jaxson know where you lived, Smoke?"

"He's been here before, with his dad."

"Ah, so how'd it go at the Kenners?"

"Better than I'd anticipated. Mike and April were ecstatic to see Jaxson. Both sad and glad he's ready to face the consequences. And I think actually relieved he'll be in jail, so they'll know where he is and Corrections can keep an eye on him."

"I think I'd feel the same way."

"Mmm." A second later, his breathing deepened. He was fast asleep.

We were having coffee on Smoke's deck Monday morning when Chief Deputy Randolph sent him a text. *I watched the interviews and read your reports. We're taking Jasmine Wilkins to the clinic. Catatonic?*

Smoke texted back, *Maybe. I'll be in later. Holler if you need me.*

Will do.

"I gotta say, Randolph's done a good job in Kenner's absence," Smoke said.

"What do you think will happen, will Kenner come back?"

"The jury's still out on that one. Hard to believe it's only been a week since Jaxson delivered that fatal blow."

"And Highway opened up the bog bodies investigation," I said.

"What are you doing today?"

"I don't know, decompress a little, maybe visit Gramps."

"Sounds like a plan," he said.

"Smoke, switching gears, we've had discussions on where we might live when we get married and I want you to know I'd be happy living here. I love your house and it's closer to the lake than mine is. We both love being on the water. It's peaceful. Quiet."

He reached for my hand, drew me out of my chair, and pulled me onto his lap. I set my coffee on the end table. "Have I showed you lately how much I love you?"

"Umm, define 'showed me.'"

"I'll demonstrate instead." His lips closed over mine with fervor, the intensity of his kisses growing with each passing second until I was weak with longing. Every inch of my body tingled in response, and my pulses drummed staccato beats.

We were on our feet, out of the living room, and on his bed seconds later where his demonstration left no doubt about how much he loved me.

I was lounging on Smoke's couch when he arrived home midafternoon. I'd been content to unwind and hide from the world. He loosened his tie, pulled it off, and dropped it on the coffee table. He plopped down next to me and gave me a kiss. "You are a sight for sore eyes, Corinne."

"Ditto, Elton. Any updates on the death angel's condition?"

"They did a psychiatric evaluation on her and diagnosed her with catatonia. There's a list of twelve symptoms, and a person needs to display three for the diagnosis. She shows at least four and I wrote them down." He pulled out his memo pad. "The two most common are mutism, or not speaking, and stupor, or decreased response to stimuli, including when people are talking to her. Catalepsy is a trance-like state, and wavy flexibility is when a person doesn't respond to commands and has a rigid posture."

"Wavy flexibility? That's a different way to describe it. Those symptoms certainly match what we observed," I said.

"They do. Catatonia is a form of depression and one of the treatments is with antidepressants. They tried giving her oral meds and got nowhere, so they're getting a judge to sign an order to get her into the Minnesota Security Hospital in St. Peter where they can give the drugs through IVs." A psychiatric facility for the extremely ill and dangerous.

"Sounds like that's where she belongs."

"She might snap out of it in a few days. We'll see," Smoke said.

"Does Rufus know? How is he doing, anyway?"

"Seems to be fine, doesn't know about his mother. They're keeping a tight lid on that."

"Speaking of a tight lid, I've had a number of media people try to get a hold of me today. Looking for comments I don't want to give," I said.

"You don't have to. That's one of the chief deputy's jobs. Public relations and statements to the media. In fact, Randolph set up a conference with them at four o'clock today, to assure the world those responsible are incarcerated."

"Good."

43

The medical staff at the hospital had Jasmine Wilkins on intravenous nutritional supplements, along with medication, and were closely monitoring her. Her level of catatonia carried a high risk of sudden death, most often due to pulmonary embolism. Without knowing her medical history, or having the opportunity to question her, doctors didn't know if an underlying cause such as depression, schizophrenia, or some other illness brought the condition on.

Smoke met with Rufus to tell him his mother was sick and in the hospital. Rufus's only response was, "Okay." At his first appearance in court, the judge appointed a public defender for him. Given Rufus's situation as a victim of his mother's control and abuse, the county attorney would not seek a life sentence.

The medical examiner positively identified Floyd Myren's remains from his dental records. The sheriff's office executed a search warrant at his home and property, looking for personal records, hoping to find a relative's name. No known family, but they located his attorney's contact information.

Smoke and I met with Attorney Craig Bentley. He was shocked and saddened over how Myren's life had ended. "Floyd led a quiet life, didn't have any kind of social life that I could gather from him. After his wife died, he met with me to prepare his will. It was difficult for him, wondering what would happen to his daughter if he predeceased her. He wanted to make sure she was taken care of.

"It broke his heart when his daughter died, but he was a little relieved, too, knowing she wouldn't have to go to a care center where she'd be with strangers. He determined how his money and assets would be disbursed upon his death. I have power-of-attorney to divide his estate accordingly," Bentley said.

"Did he happen to say if he wanted to be cremated or buried? Any kind of service?" Smoke said.

"Yes, he has a plot by his wife and daughter. His brother and parents are next to theirs. Floyd didn't want a formal service. Just a graveside committal," Bentley said.

"What about his possessions?" Smoke said.

"He had no one to leave them to and told me to auction it off, including his house and acres. He named the auction company he wanted me to use. I have the combination to his safe where he kept personal documents and other treasures. He wanted me to check with the historical society, see if they want any of the old photos he has of his farm from back when. If not, I'm supposed to dispose of them. He prepaid his funeral expenses. All of his wishes are documented and notarized."

"It seems so lonesome to make those decisions, knowing he had no one special to leave his things to," I said.

"I agree, and it happens more often than you'd like to think," Bentley said. "I'm looking into the legalities of the VA and Social Security making deposits into his bank account two years past his death. Most of it was sent through automatic payments, likely set up by Jasmine Wilkins, but will probably need to be paid back. It might be more complicated than it's worth for them."

Word spread among the county employees, especially in the sheriff's office and highway department. Over sixty of us gathered at the cemetery that adjoined a country church, a mile down the road from Floyd Myren's house, to pay our respects at his second burial. None of us had known him, but we all cared. With all he'd dealt with in his last years, it was sad to think the two people close to him at the end were the angel of death and her son. The one consolation I had was he wasn't alone. A messed-up thought, given who the people were and what they'd done to him.

Smoke slid his hand into mine, consoling me. The pastor shared words of comfort then closed in prayer. I heard a lot of sniffling among the troops. The highway guys and many of the deputies had been involved in recovering the bodies buried in Coyote Bog and were moved by the brief service.

When the prayer ended, some shook hands or exchanged hugs, and others quietly slipped away. My closest friends and I migrated together by our vehicles in the parking lot. Smoke, Vince Weber, Amanda Zubinski, Brian Carlson, Todd Mason. Each one had red eyes, either from holding back tears or from letting them fall.

"Huh. Well, I didn't think it'd hit me like this, not even knowing the guy," Weber said.

Zubinski stuck a finger in his ribs. "You've wanted to know who he was ever since you helped pull him out of the bog."

Weber shrugged. “Yeah.”

“All I can say is identifying Mister Myren and burying him with his family was a good way to close the books on this case,” Mason said.

“That’s for dang sure,” Carlson added.

“I have to add, in all my years here, this was one of the toughest investigations. But in the end, the good guys took down the bad guys,” Smoke said.

“It’s what we work for, and it surely does our hearts and souls good when justice prevails,” I said.

I lifted my hands and smiled. The others followed suit and we exchanged high fives all around.

Winnebago County Mysteries

Murder in Winnebago County follows an unlikely serial killer plaguing a rural Minnesota county. The clever murderer leaves a growing chain of apparent suicides among criminal justice professionals. As her intuition helps her draw the cases together, Winnebago County Sergeant Corinne Aleckson enlists help from Detective Elton Dawes. What Aleckson doesn't know is that the killer is keeping a close watch on her. Will she be the next target?

Buried in Wolf Lake When a family's golden retriever brings home the dismembered leg of a young woman, the Winnebago County Sheriff's Department launches an investigation unlike any other. Who does the leg belong to, and where is the rest of her body? Sergeant Corinne Aleckson and Detective Elton Dawes soon discover they are up against an unidentified psychopath who targets women with specific physical features. Are there other victims, and will they learn the killer's identity in time to prevent another brutal murder?

An Altar by the River A man phones the Winnebago County Sheriff's Department, frantically reporting his brother is armed with a large dagger and on his way to the county to sacrifice himself. Sergeant Corinne Aleckson takes the call, learning the alarming reasons behind the young man's death wish. When the department investigates, they plunge into the alleged criminal activities of a hidden cult and the disturbing cover-up of an old closed-case shooting death. The cult members have everything to lose and will do whatever it takes to prevent the truth coming to light. But will they find an altar by the river in time to save the young man's life?

The Noding Field Mystery When a man's naked body is found staked out in a farmer's soybean field, Sergeant Corinne Aleckson and Detective Elton Dawes are called to the scene. The cause of death is not apparent, and the significance of why he was placed there is a mystery. As Aleckson, Dawes, and the rest of their Winnebago Sheriff's Department team gather evidence, and look for suspects and motive, they hit one dead end after another. Then an old nemesis escapes from jail and plays in the shocking end.

A Death in Lionel's Woods When a woman's emaciated body is found in a hunter's woods Sergeant Corinne Aleckson is coaxed back into the field to assist Detective Smoke Dawes on the case. It seems the only hope for identifying the woman lies in a photo that was buried with bags of money under her body. Aleckson and Dawes plunge into the investigation that takes them into the world of human smugglers and traffickers, unexpectedly close to home. All the while, they are working to uncover the identity of someone who is leaving Corky anonymous messages and pulling pranks at her house. An unpredictable roller coaster ride to the electrifying end.

Secret in Whitetail Lake The discovery of an old Dodge Charger on the bottom of a Winnebago County lake turns into a homicide investigation when human remains are found in the car. To make matters worse, Sheriff Twardy disappears that same day, leaving everyone to wonder where he went. Sergeant Corinne Aleckson and Detective Elton Dawes probe into both mysteries, searching for answers. Little do they know they're being closely watched by the keeper of the Secret in Whitetail Lake.

Firesetter in Blackwood Township Barns are burning in Blackwood Township, and the Winnebago County Sheriff's Office realizes they have a firesetter to flush out. The investigation ramps up when a body is found in one of the barns. Meanwhile, deputies are getting disturbing deliveries. Why are they being targeted? It leaves Sergeant Corinne Aleckson and Detective Elton Dawes to wonder, what is the firesetter's message and motive?